SAND

# MERLIN RADICAL FICTION

edited by
## John Lucas

*Out of Work* by John Law (Margaret Harkness) (1888)
*Sandwichman* by Walter Brierley (1937)
*The Story of a Modern Woman*
by Ella Hepworth Dixon (1894)
*The Wild Goose Chase* Rex Warner (1937)

# SANDWICHMAN
by
# WALTER BRIERLEY

Introduction by
Philip Gorski

# LONDON
# MERLIN PRESS

Published in 1990
by the Merlin Press Ltd.
10 Malden Road
London NW5 3HR
First published in 1937
by Methuen
Introduction © 1990 by Philip Gorski
Printed in Denmark by
Nørhaven A/S, Viborg
ISBN 0 85036 391 8

# GENERAL INTRODUCTION

The aim of *Merlin Radical Fiction* is soon stated. It is to make available for present-day readers a number of once well-known novels which have been languishing out of print, if not out of mind. Not all novels that were famous in their day deserve or need resurrecting; the ones we have chosen to re-print are important, not merely because they were once celebrated, but because they have qualities that make them durable works of fiction. We certainly do not intend to re-print novels that can be called radical only because of their "message". We understand radicalism in a more rewarding way, one that includes the means of telling as much as what is told. For example, Rex Warner's *The Wild Goose Chase* is a wonderfully inventive political and social allegory, entirely different in conception from the social realism of Walter Brierley's *Sandwichman*. Yet Brierley's method works. It is admirably suited to the grim, moving story he has to tell. Different as they are from each other, Margaret Harkness's (John Law's) *Out of Work* and Ella Hepworth Dixon's *The Story of a Modern Woman* are adroit and compelling works of fiction in their own right.

It is part of our ambition for the series to range as widely as possible, over time, style, authors. Later re-prints will be of fiction of the 1790s, at one extreme, and of the 1950s, at the other. We also hope to include novels from North America and, in translation, novels from Europe. Each book will be introduced by a writer who is an authority on the novel and its author, and the introductions will blend biographical and critical matter.

It is our hope that in the coming years the Radical Fiction Series will enable new generations of readers

"To confer with who are gone.
And the dead living into counsel call."

John Lucas

# INTRODUCTION

by

## PHILIP GORSKI

In Chapter 10 of *The Uses of Literacy*, as Richard
Hoggart discusses the predicament of the working-class
'scholarship boy', he makes the following observations;

> He has to be more and more alone, if he is to 'get on'.
> He will have, probably unconsciously, to oppose the
> ethos of the hearth, the intense gregariousness of the
> working class family group. Since everything centres
> upon the living room, there is unlikely to be a room of
> his own; the bedrooms are cold and unhospitable and to
> warm them or the front room, if there is one, would not
> only be expensive, but would require an imaginative
> leap—out of the tradition—which most families are not
> capable of making. There is a corner of the living room
> table. On the other side Mother is ironing, the wireless is
> on, someone is singing a snatch of a song or Father says
> intermittently whatever comes into his head. The boy
> has to cut himself off mentally so as to do his homework
> as best he can. . . This description simplifies and
> overstresses the break: in each individual case there will
> be many qualifications. But in presenting the isolation in
> its most emphatic form the description epitomises what
> is very frequently found. For such a boy is between two
> worlds, the worlds of school and home; and they meet at
> few points.[1]

Hoggart is writing in the Nineteen-Fifties, and is
considering the post-war phenomenom of working-class
boys taking up scholarships to study at Grammar
School. *Sandwichman* was published in 1937, and deals
with a young Derbyshire miner studying day release for
entrance to a thinly disguised Nottingham University
College. Despite differences of circumstance and
approach, both writers are concerned with a common

problem, that of working class individuals who move out of their own class by way of the educational system. It is an experience shared, in changing ways, by many people in each new generation, and whereas Hoggart *describes* that attempted transition, Brierley *dramatises* it, in novel form, thus achieving greater power and complexity. In *Sandwichman*—in which the consequences of Arthur Gardner's attempts to 'better himself' are traced throughout related areas of his life (his family, work and courtship)—events are recorded with a calmness and control that result in a fiction of sustained intensity, one which offers eloquent testimony to a continuing experience in our divided society. As such, the novel deserves to be re-published after more than fifty years of neglect.

Walter Brierley was born on 25th June 1900 in Waingroves, Derbyshire. His father was an engine winder at Denby Hall pit. Brierley left school at the age of 13 to start work at Waingroves Pit, although there had been a possibility of his entering Heanor Grammar School. It seems however, that his headmistress did little to encourage this, it being rare for a pupil to be allowed an attempt at the entrance exam.

Brierley, though, never fully reconciled himself to life as a miner, and his continued efforts at self-education (by way of local classes in French, English and Maths) created in him a sense that 'there was something better in life than the pit'.[2] This belief ultimately led Brierley to apply for a place on the Miners Welfare Scholarship for a non-vocational course at Nottingham University College. Between 1927 and 1931 he studied two days per week at the college, working the other days at the pit. However, out of the four subjects, History, English, Latin and Logic, he first failed Logic and then Latin, consequently failing to secure a full-time place. He returned to the pit but was made redundant shortly afterwards, despite the supposed guarantee covering his job. He was then out of work until 1935. This lengthy period of unemployment provided the material for *Means Test Man* (1935) his best known work. However, it was his previous involvement with higher education that formed the basis for *Sandwichman*.

During his unemployment Brierley continued to write, and achieved some small but increasing successes, in particular an essay dealing with unemployment published in the *Listener* in August 1933. This article 'Frustration and Bitterness'—A Colliery Banksman' led to other articles in the *Spectator* and the *London Mercury*. Most importantly for Brierley, his article was read by John Hampson[2] (author of *Saturday Night at the Greyhound* and *O, Providence*) who subsequently wrote to him and also introduced him to Walter Allen (later to become an influential literary critic). Hampson and Allen were 'full of admiration' for Brierley's work, passing it on to figures such as E.M. Forster and the Woolfs, and they played a major role in his development and consequent publication. Two examples: they advised Brierley against making Arthur Gardner illegitimate (he eventually made him a step-son) and they suggested the title *Means Test Man*. It was in fact with that novel that Brierley achieved his first and greatest success. The book won rapid fame, partly because of its topicality, and partly because of its apolitical stance, something which made it popular with the majority of critics (although not with the *Daily Worker*'s reviewer, who regretted that it did not reflect 'the fighting spirit of the unemployed').

Brierley's next published novel was *Sandwichman*, and it was followed by *Dalby Green* in 1939 and *Danny* in 1940. The sensation caused by *Means Test Man* was not repeated, and Brierley's brief period of fame came to a close. By now he had found employment as a child welfare officer, a job he kept until retirement in 1965.

He continued to write but nothing more was published.[3] He died in 1972, writing that year in an auto- biographical fragment, 'I am as old as the century and living, as they say, on borrowed time'.

In *Sandwichman* Arthur Gardner is studying part-time for entrance to 'Trentingham University College'. The introspection and even self-centredness that this re- quires from Arthur creates a rift between him and his family (especially his step-father), his workmates, and the woman he is to marry—Nancy. The resulting tension in turn affects Arthur's studies, and culminates in a fight between him and his step-father on the night before an exam, which seriously affects his performance. Arthur is sacked from his job after being blamed for a pit accident, supposedly caused by his habit of revising from a notebook during quiet intervals at work. (The real cause was his lapse of attention after being jeered by workmates—'Go on, you bloody college swank; thinks tha'rt iverybody cos tha goos ta—') Meanwhile, Nancy's increasing frustration with Arthur's educa- tional ambitions leads her into a brief relationship with another youth. She becomes pregnant, and she and Arthur separate.

For all his qualifications, and despite a course at a national unemployment centre, the only job Arthur can find is a humiliating day as a sandwich-board man. Ultimately, he fails the means test. His failures, and the months of family strife, have taken their toll on his mother, who dies shortly after the visit of the means test investigator. Arthur consequently leaves home and goes off to tramp the streets.

It is clearly a grim tale, if not a tragic one. This has much to do with Brierley's prose style, which has an austerity and straight-forwardness perfectly suited to the subject. Brierley's naturalism is of a subtle kind that meticulously re-creates the details of pit-town life whilst investing the overall scene with a sombre intensity. A good example of this is to be found in the opening pages, as Arthur descends the hills from work, down into Pirley;

> Arthur dabbled his hands in the water, breaking the glass-smooth surface and distorting his own and the tree's reflection. As he rose again, clapping his hands together and making drops of water fly in all directions, a cloud-shadow rode over the valley, thickening the light in the waters, wiping the gloss from the slanting meadows. He crossed the bridge and climbed steadily for half a mile, his head and trunk forward, arms hanging as if incapable of use. On the rim of the valley he paused and turned to face the strong stream of wind which had dipped into the bottoms and now rushed, humming, up the dull slope. A mile away to the south-west a stubby chimney and thin steel headgear rose above the engine-houses, workshops, screens of the mine which had kept him hidden eight hours from this fresh spring day. But he had not turned for the express purpose of gazing at the squat huddle of dingy buildings: he was peering far beyond, into the very heart of the wind, marking the labouring heaviness of the sky lifting itself from beyond the rim of the world. A suggestion of disappointment moved his brows, then he drew in his gaze to the mine. A smile, cynical, confident, lightened the strong line of his mouth as he watched a sudden billowing of thick smoke flow from the top of the chimney and begin to ride towards him on the wind. He turned and walked away over the high, flat land; the wind, roaring through the trees, humming through the hedges, helped him as he grasped the corners of his coat and extending his arms, formed a kind of sail.
>
> On his right now, ploughland and meadow sloped into the sky, except where the long black mass of Devil's Wood fringed it. To the left, a mile away, Pirley squatted about its three tallest buildings—the Town Hall, the Waterworks tower and the Co-operative Society's office buildings. Behind Pirley, far back, the dim lines of Steep tors cut a dark patch into the afternoon haze.

One of the very few critical essays that deals with Brierley's work is Carol Snee's *Working Class Literature or Proletarian Writing*.[4] It has some harsh things to say about Brierley, not least his prose style, which she calls 'self-consciously literary' and 'lifeless and static'. Such views seem to me to be the result of an inattentive reading, especially in the light of the above, representative passage, with its foreboding realism. Brierley's style is deceptively simple and repays close attention. As Walter Allen says in a letter, discussing with Brierley the manuscript of what was to become *Sandwichman*;

> I do believe the sandwichboard and means test parts to be unsurpassable—I don't think I exaggerate—in their directness and simplicity. I don't think much more work is needed to bring the rest of the book up to that standard
>
> (April 22nd, 1934)

This can be illustrated by quoting from the scene in which the means test man visits Arthur at home;

> The man was writing. Arthur looked at the question to follow and his heart almost stood still.
> 'Where do your step-father and step-brothers work?'
> 'Check number'. 'Pays to home'. 'Wages'. Arthur was reading the questions, shuddering into bewilderment; his legs seemed thin lines of pain, the back of his neck hurt him, and a heavy weight hung to each eyeball. He got no sense from the man's question and murmured, 'Pardon'.
> 'I said, "Where do they work?"'
> 'Oh—sorry. Shenton Colliery, all three of them'.
> Mrs. Shirley sat down again; her arms rested on the chair arms, her hand gripped the wood, she was pulling strength into herself. Arthur glanced at her, saw a greyness in her face, closed eyes. He tore his gaze from her and swept it to the sofa, but saw only the legs of his step-father hanging below the stretched sheets of newspaper. The man had not moved during the questioning; the two pages had occupied him the whole of the time.

The Means Test man had done writing and he glanced
at the newspaper before he asked the next question. He
was a mild sort of man, not quite strong enough for the
job; the invisibility and silence of whatever was behind
the newspaper upset him. Still, he'd his job to do, his
money to earn, his wife and children to keep. He was
gaining courage in the way a weak man does. This was
just a 'case' in hundreds. But the man might have shown
himself; he did not even say good-morning, had not
spoken once. Oh, he must get on.

'Could I have their check numbers and the wages they
earn?'

The dry dashing of paper sounded. Mr. Shirley was on
his feet.

'Put that bloody pen up an' gerrout.' The investigator
jerked his head sideways. 'Tha can look. Come on, get
off that chair'. The man did not move; he could not quite
grasp the circumstance. (p253–4)

This is a brilliant piece of dramatic writing. The
tense atmosphere, the silent, threatening presence of the
stepfather, the dislocation of Arthur's concentration
(gazing vacantly at his step-father's legs) the mother's
despair and the investigator's discomfort—all are
captured with great economy. To describe this as
'lifeless and static' is ridiculous.

Carol Snee's remarks are made as part of an attempt
to theorise and evaluate differences in working class
fiction. She devises two categories; 'Working Class
Literature' and 'Proletarian Writing', the latter of
which she prizes more highly since it covers works
which have 'a greater awareness of class as a primary
determinant'. Of the writers she examines, only Lewis
Jones, the Welsh miner, fits her criteria. Brierley's
work, however, is mere 'working-class literature', since
he

... takes upon himself the mantle of creative writer, and
stops really looking at his experience of the world and
what that might mean. With no conscious ideological

stance, and without the litmus paper of his own experience, his novels become an uncritical assimilation of liberal ideology, and his working-class origins of no relevance.

Snee is presumably attempting to replace traditional academic assumptions about what constitutes 'Great Literature' with an alternative, 'marxist' model that can judge working-class fiction by more appropriate standards. Unfortunately, the result is to replace one form of dogmatism by another which, if ever widely applied by critics, would quickly relegate large amounts of valuable fiction to a second-class status.

To say that Brierley 'lost the litmus paper of his own experience' appears to me to be nonsensical, since as we have seen, *Sandwichman* developed directly out of his own experiences of unemployment and higher education. And to bewail his lack of a 'conscious ideological stance' is to reproduce the attitudes of so many orthodox critics who, when faced with working-class fiction, judge it according to their own often inappropriate concerns rather than those of the author. That is, they judge it according to a normative standard of what is valuable in literature, rather than by the specific qualities of each particular work. Brierley deliberately set out to be as naturalistic and unpolitical as he could, in the belief that this would give his observations greater effect. As Walter Allen remarks in a letter to Brierley;

> The important thing is that in the main the book seems to me to be the best unemployment novel I've read. By that I mean that its attitude is right. Most authors of such books break out into passionate and hysterical attacks upon the capitalist system—or let their heroes do so. That's too easy. And you don't do it. There's no need to. The indictment is in the account of Ahab [Arthur] itself.

(April 22, 1934)

Allen continues, in a further letter;

It is comparable to Wilfred Owen's war poetry, when he says in the preface 'The poetry is in the pity'—and the pity is unstated.

Sept 11th, 1934

Another contemporary of Brierley's who could grasp what was important about *Sandwichman* was the anonymous reviewer in the *Times Literary Supplement* in 1937. 'Once again, without emotion, without propaganda, with a calm that succeeds where sound and fury would have been futile, Mr Brierley has given us a picture of contemporary life almost unbearable in its truth.'

Brierley's quiet, self-effacing prose allows a genuinely radical message to emerge. Stated crudely, it is that class society wastes individual potential. However, the subject matter of *Sandwichman* (the working classes) and its 'apolitical' approach has made it unpopular both with the guardians of the Great Tradition on the one hand and mechanical marxism on the other.

How, then, can we most accurately evaluate *Sandwichman*? As I indicated at the beginning of this introduction, the novel is perhaps best seen as a study in the effects that a desire for education, or 'culture', may have upon a working-class individual. In Arthur's case his ambition to 'get on' and educate himself in the traditional academic disciplines is largely unquestioning. He accepts the orthodox definition of self-improvement that such academic ladder-climbing implies. Brierley's attitude, however, is more complex, since what he shows us is that Arthur's ambitions end in disaster. No simple explanation is given for this; Arthur is not simply mistaken in wanting to educate himself in such a way, neither is he at base academically 'inadequate'; nor can the unsympathetic, even hostile attitude of friends, relatives and workmates towards his studies be identified as the causes of his failure. Rather, it is a combination of the varying degrees of truth contained in these statements, allied with the exhausting burden of mine work, that makes academic ambition so unusual (even strange) and so costly. Arthur's attempted 'imaginative leap out of the tradition' can never be smoothly achieved; the two worlds of work and culture have long been too polarised. Brierley's achievement is to reveal the working of this polarity and its effects through the action of his novel. Here for example, Arthur is attempting to revise;

> The gangers came and went, the empties and loaded trams rushed in and out of the light circle of Arthur's lamp. By snap-time at eleven o'clock, he was waiting for coal, and he sat in a manhole for short periods. Each time he rested, he fetched a small note-book from the inside pocket of his coat, and bent over its pages, holding his lamp on one knee. He mumbled the lists of Latin verbs, turned over, examined different grammatical constructions, turned over, and with a small pencil from his waistcoat pocket, attempted a translation of a passage he had written the previous day. All this was done in spasms; when the ganger came by he left it, when the deputy or the under-manager passed, he was busy over something if not actually working at the trams. In other intervals, he wrote logical symbols on a smooth piece of rock in the manhole side, and mumbled, as he looked at them.
>
> 'SaP SiP SeP SoP'
>
> He recited aloud poems and chunks from Shakespeare and Chaucer, all within the limits of the Inter Arts syllabus. The ganger heard him sometimes
>
> 'Wot the 'ell are yer mumblin' and grumblin' about Gardner? Learnin a piece for t'chapel anniversary?'

Arthur's position is impossible. Even absurd. The attempt to combine—however surreptitiously—the worlds of work and education simply results in the sack and academic failure. Labour is monotonous and exploitative, education is formalised and elitist. The separation impoverishes both worlds, as can be seen in the contrast that Trentingham presents;

> Arthur turned with others into the Latin lecture-room,
> and there was a scramble for the back row of chairs. He
> never dashed about; he felt faintly out of it among these
> young, soft-skinned youths and maidens who always
> seemed to be laughing and playing. Yet they came to
> lectures with easy, intelligent discussion and plainly
> pertinent difficulties to be solved. He had watched some
> of them in the library and he liked them better there,
> their young faces composed and alone, beautiful they all
> were in study. There was pain in his studying, always
> something waiting on the fringes of his mind to disturb
> him. Most of these would move easily through Inter,
> through Finals. He was hacking his way, every step, but
> he neither felt nor saw anything heroic in it; he was
> moving towards his satisfaction. . . But he would be glad
> when all the examinations he had to take were over, and
> he could take off the blinkers which forced his attention
> to set things.

It is an ambiguous passage. Arthur is aware that he is
'hacking' and that he is wearing 'blinkers', and yet
these doubts achieve no more forceful articulation;
'there was pain in his studying, always something
waiting on the fringes of his mind to disturb him'. But
when one of the students begins to enthuse about pit-
work, Arthur's reaction is significant;

> David Neil was in the refectory when he walked to the
> usual table. Bob Peel was there and other adult students.
> 'Stripped to the waist, your muscles not hampered by
> clothes, sweat pouring out of you—fit—you feel fit. It's
> a real feeling, you know that you exist—you're vivid,
> alive.'
> Bob's lips were moving quickly, they were moist; his
> hand beat the table emphatically. Neil's lip was curling.
> 'Why, Bob, you make me ill. You can have the bloody
> pit. I know what they can do with it if I've got a chance
> to get away. What do you say Gardner? Here, I've got
> you a coffee.'

    'Same here', Arthur said, 'I shouldn't be working as
hard as I am if I didn't. Bob's gone all Lawrence. That's
about it.'

Arthur is alert to the nonsense that can be talked about
pit-life but less questioning—although still uneasy—
about the life he is trying for. He has developed within a
society that pays lip service to a narrow conception of
'self-improvement' but which hinders its achievement.
*Sandwichman* is thus—in this respect—a more realistic
work than Lawrence's *Sons and Lovers*. Brierley was
clearly familiar with Lawrence's novel, and in some
ways the plots are similar; a young man in a mining
family, trying to 'get on', at odds with the father, leaves
home after the mother's death. However, the particular
ways in which *Sandwichman* differs from *Sons and Lovers*
give it the appearance—whether intended by Brierley or
not—of being, among other things, a reply to Lawrence's
novel. Arthur works during most of the period when he
is studying, he fails academically, his mother's death
coincides with the means-test, Arthur misses her death
because he must sign on, and when he leaves home it is
to walk the streets, rather than to head for the lights of
Nottingham, as did Paul Morel. The final paragraphs
of each novel make an intriguing contrast.

    He got off the car. In the country all was dead still.
Little stars shone high up; little stars spread far away in
the flood waters, a firmament below. Everywhere the
vastness and terror of the immense night which is
roused and stirred for a brief while by the day, but which
returns, and will remain at last eternal, holding
everything in its silence and its living gloom. There was
no Time, only Space. Who could say his mother had
lived and did not live? She had been in one place, and
was in another; that was all. And his soul could not leave
her, wherever she was. . .
    'Mother!' he whispered—'mother!'
    She was the only thing that held him up, himself,

amid all this. And she was gone, intermingled herself. He wanted her to touch him, have him alongside with her.

But no, he would not give in. Turning sharply, he walked towards the city's gold phosphorescence. His fists were shut, his mouth set fast. He would not take that direction, to the darkness, to follow her. He walked towards the faintly humming, glowing town, quickly.

From *Sons and Lovers*

(Arthur and the tramp) walked on towards Derby, through Milford, Duffield, Allestree, Darley. These places were just 'the road' to the tramp; to Arthur they were battlefields where he had fought for the sake of Wingrove's position in the football and cricket leagues, where the girls had tried to 'click' with him after the matches, where he had learned how beer tasted. The lamps by the roadside grew in brilliance and power until they became kingdoms of light on their own. The wind's voice was rising as if sounding the alarm for the world to hurry to shelter from the millions of white flakes riding behind. Already in Nottingham the air was busy with them; people passing from cars into the theatre bent heads sideways to the cold driving. Already in Wingrove the ledges of bedroom windows were white and smooth. Now, as Arthur and his hobbling companion turned in at the gateway of the Derby Institution, the white snow-lines reached forward and marked them.

From *Sandwichman*

What emerges from such a comparison is that two novelists, with shared origins, discussing similar problems, have reached conclusions with widely differing implications. This may have much to do with Brierley's life *as* a miner, something that Lawrence never experienced. Whatever the case, it is clear from the two endings that whereas Lawrence believed in individual transcendance, Brierley knew differently. The former was an idealist, the latter a realist—which is why he made *Sandwichman* a tragedy.

## NOTES

This essay is dedicated to Nicola Grace with gratitude for advice and encouragement.

1. Richard Hoggart, *The Uses Of Literacy*, Chatto and Windus, London 1957.

2. Much of the information for this brief biography came from the collection of letters and manuscripts held at the Local Studies Library in Derby. In particular, the letters from Walter Allen and John Hampson throw a fascinating light upon Brierley's development as a novelist.

   I would also like to acknowledge the research done into Brierley's life by Andy Croft, which is contained in his introductory essay for *Means Test Man*, Spokesman, 1983.

3. The Derby Library collection contains much interesting, unpublished material, in particular the manuscript of a novel about the Second World War entitled *War and The Smiths*.

4. In *Culture and Crisis in Britain in the 30s*, ed Clark, Heinemann, Margolies and Snee, Lawrence and Wishart, London, 1979.

# CHAPTER I

DURING the whole of the morning heavy clouds raced from the west, dulling, when they came between the sun moving imperceptibly through the far-set blue of the April sky and the Derbyshire field down which Arthur Gardner was walking in the afternoon, the even bosom of the stream lazing about the valley bottoms. But by this time the wind had backed to south-west, pouring out of 'Derby Hole' and bringing continuous masses, rain-laden, to blot out for long periods the spring sunshine streaming to the steep, freshening meadows on the valley-side. Arthur did not cross at once the narrow wooden footbridge, but went down to the water-side to wash his hands. As he leaned over, a sudden burst of sunshine drenched the shallow depths, and for a few seconds the bare, betwigged branches of a near-by tree and the young man's head and shoulders were reflected in vivid detail. Thin grey lines, where the perspiration had trickled from his hair and down the lean cheeks, cut through the mask of black dust his face had collected in the mine he had left ten minutes ago. The only arresting feature in the regularly formed face, but one strikingly obvious in spite of the obscuring grime and the worn look due to physical fatigue, was the firmness of the mouth-line. But it gave no hardness to the general tone, merely holding it in tranquil confidence; it seemed capable of expressing the grimmer attributes of his character. His eyes saved him from set severity of countenance; they were soft and generous when no need arose to agree in spirit with the mouth-line. They seemed to show he was pulled or driven by soul-urgings, as well as to indicate that the mind behind was capable of clean, sure thinking.

Arthur dabbled his hands in the water, breaking the glass-smooth surface and distorting his own and the tree's reflection. As he rose again, clapping his hands together and making drops of water fly in all directions, a cloud-shadow rode over the valley, thickening the light in the waters, wiping the gloss from the slanting meadows. He crossed the bridge and climbed steadily for half a mile, his head and trunk forward, arms hanging as if incapable of use. On the rim of the valley he paused, and turned to face the strong stream of wind which had dipped into the bottoms and now rushed, humming, up the dull slope. A mile away to the south-west a stubby chimney and thin steel headgear rose above the engine-houses, workshops, screens of the mine which had kept him hidden eight hours from this fresh spring day. But he had not turned for the express purpose of gazing at the squat huddle of dingy build-ings; he was peering far beyond, into the very heart of the wind, marking the labouring heaviness of the sky lifting itself from behind the rim of the world. A sug-gestion of disappointment moved his brows, then he drew in his gaze to the mine. A smile, cynical, confident, lightened the strong line of his mouth as he watched a sudden billowing of thick smoke flow from the top of the chimney and begin to ride towards him on the wind. He turned, and walked away over the high, flat land; the wind, roaring through the trees, humming through the hedges, helped him as he grasped the corners of his coat and extending his arms, formed a kind of sail.

On his right, now, ploughland and meadow sloped into the sky, except where the long black mass of Devil's Wood fringed it. To the left, a mile away, Pirley squatted about its three tallest buildings—the Town Hall, the Waterworks Tower and the Co-operative Society's office buildings. Behind Pirley, far back, the dim lines of Steep tors cut a dark patch into the afternoon haze.

The land became more humpy, and closed about him as he walked on, past the brickworks, up Red Lane, by the disused colliery. Below him, now, was the village where he lived, Wingrove, one house-clustered slope half a mile long, with short side lanes jutting out—Top Street, Pit Lane, Little Lane. He dropped down steadily for a hundred yards, then wound about the Corners on to Back Lane, which ran parallel with Main Street, and joined Top Street. When Arthur had climbed Back Lane, walked clippingly along the level Top Street, he turned up Main Street for twenty yards or so, and pushed open the garden gate swinging slowly in the wind. He went noisily along the asphalt path dividing the house-side from the smooth, clean garden, then turned on to the yard and through the kitchen door. As he stood pulling off his coat and scarf, his mother reached a chair from the fireside and set it before a plate of steaming vegetables laid on the white cloth. Her quick gaze made certain that everything necessary was on the table before she rested against the sink, watching her son.

'Looks like rain, mum,' Arthur remarked casually as he sat down.

'It will rain if the wind drops,' she replied. 'Going to Nessfield to-night?'

'Why, yes.' He looked up. 'I worked hard all last night, and Monday night too, so that I could go with an easy conscience.' He laughed, and became busy over his plate again. 'I shall do a bit of my history essay before I go, though.'

'Your exam's getting near, now, Arthur,' she said, removing his empty plate and setting another full of rice pudding. 'You can't afford to waste too much time between now and July.'

He marked the trace of concern in her voice, and was quick to touch her hand as she left the plate.

'Don't you worry, mum,' he said strongly, and the strength was there to prove himself not sentimental. 'I'm on top of my work. In October I s'll say good-bye to the black hole and be a black-gowned undergrad.' He laughed at his emphasized confidence.

'Don't you harp on that. You never know what might happen.' But she smiled as she began filling the porcelain sink with a mixture of hot and cold water. He left the table at once, and stripped to the waist, washing himself while she cleared away his plate and set three other empty ones. She glanced at times to note her son's progress, and when he groped with closed eyes to where he knew the towel hung, she moved quickly and met his hands with it. His clean vest and shirt warmed over the fire, and she reached them for him a moment before he put down the towel.

'Thanks, mum.' He smiled, took the garments and slipped them over his head, then moved into the 'house', as the middle room was called, when he heard slurring nailed boots on the yard. She watched him go, her eyes were warm, the spirit in her face reached out as if to fuse with his in some kind of victorious peace. But she cleaned her face of all expression when her husband and other two sons clattered into the kitchen and clinked their tin drums on to the back of the sink, then threw their coats, caps and scarves on to Arthur's by the fireplace. That expression never shone from her eyes except on the occasions when she was alone with her eldest son. It was not that she loved him more than the others.

'Arth come?' Sidney, the younger youth, asked, as he sat down.

'It's Nessfield night,' Albert cut in. 'Bet he's washed and changed by now. Eh, mum?'

No reply came from his mother, who was busy over the fire. She brought a plate of meat and vegetables and set it before her husband.

'Here you are, dad,' she said cheerfully. 'A drink first?'

The man shook his head, and began eating. She set plates before the two youths. Albert marked the soft, away expression on his mother's face as she bent over his shoulder.

'I'll 'ave a drink, mum,' he said. Albert knew his father's curt negative with his head was the slamming down of a shutter upon himself; the mere mention of his stepson's name seemed to bring that mood upon him now. Sidney knew, too, and felt that Albert had asked for a drink to strengthen his mother in the isolation into which the father had flung her. He glanced at his brother, his mother, was quick to join.

'Pour me one, too, mum,' he said.

She poured out two mugs of tea and set them by the

youths' plates, then leaned on the sink until all three were ready for pudding. She glanced at her husband occasionally. A certain refinement was in him in spite of the grime and dirty, patched clothing; and his manner was not of the born collier. Upon these superficialities was founded the appellation by which in idle pleasantry the villagers were wont to refer to him—'the gentleman coal-cutter'. Until his early twenties he had held a good position in a large co-operative society, but, because of some misdemeanour, had been compelled to seek a livelihood at an occupation where an exemplary moral character was no essential. He had come to Wingrove, a stranger, in 1912, went into the pit, and so escaped the war. Mrs Shirley's first husband, Arthur Gardner, was killed before Christmas 1914, and Albert Shirley married her two years later, when her son Arthur was three. He was twenty-three now; his half-brothers, Albert and Sidney, Shirley's own sons, were nineteen and seventeen. All three were intelligent, their mother's endowment, yet the two Shirleys lacked drive and the capacity to reach forward, aware of the moment only, though filling each richly but without point. Albert could discuss the music-masters and their works comprehensively; he listened with rapt attention to symphony concerts and the Foundation of Music series. He had large opportunity and ample hours to practise, yet he remained fiddling on the piano with one finger, lingering over slow movements, making unintelligible attempts at *allegrettos*. Sidney could read fairly easily the plainer-mannered authors of France. Those, however, which could not offer him straightforward, concrete narrative, were skipped as being too mind-straining. Impatient of grammars and exercises, he preferred to grope and misconstrue, indifferent to the pleasant gibes of Arthur.

Immediately she had removed the empty plates and set pudding before the three, Mrs Shirley went into the middle room, where Arthur was pulling on his shoes. Already he had been upstairs and changed into a navy-blue suit.

'What time are you going?' she asked.

'Oh, about the same time. Sixish.'

She went into the kitchen again, and filled the sink for her husband to wash himself, then came back, but her son was not there. She walked into the front room overlooking the street; he was at the small table under the window, and she stood at his side while he wrote the title of his essay across the top of a sheet of foolscap.

'I hope to get Alpha plus for this,' he said humorously, as he felt her body pressing lightly against him. 'The Scotch tutor's never given it any one yet.'

She put her hand to the side of his head, pressed it gently to her body. He did not respond with any physical movement, except to bring his teeth together more firmly. A spiritual hunger swelled about him, paining him; it had its point in the woman at his side, not as a woman, not as a mother, it was some kind of thankfulness, gratefulness for love expressed, demonstrated. He was incapable of more outward show than that he was thrust into in the moment before his brain controlled rushing emotion. He was too self-critical; he felt a fool if some one, in greeting him, held his hand for a moment after the mutual grip. He had wanted to embrace his mother many times, to hold her and let

her know how much he loved her, how they were bound
together wholly not only to resist that which each
knew beat against them, but in the simple resting of
love. But he couldn't, he knew he couldn't—he
wouldn't if she were ill. And the idea of kissing her
shuddered him. It was different with Nancy, though
even with her he was restrained. But his mother
understood. He wished he wasn't like this. She stood
beside him now, pressing his head to her, and he wanted
to put his hand on hers. He couldn't; he would start
thinking what he was doing. Many a time in the loneliness of fields, he had repeated aloud, over and over
again,

　　　'But I have that within which passeth show',

but he found no relief from the emotion pressing outwards, straining to escape through the physical. He
felt it now, in his chest, his throat; one could measure
it if one marked the pressed mouth-line, the pained
eyes.

'I must get on,' he said. 'Half to-night, half to-morrow. Hope I get this question in the exam.'

She withdrew her hand and left him. He sat for a
few moments with empty eyes, then shook himself
angrily and gave himself to his task. Two foolscap
sheets, filled with bold, clear writing, rested to the right
of the one on which he was working when the sound
of lilting music came from the middle room. Quarter-
past five. No day, except Sunday, and sometimes
Saturday, did Sidney miss the forty-five minutes' dance
music on the wireless. Arthur worked on. Once
Sidney's voice joined loudly with the vocalist's in an
attempt to croon a chorus, but was cut short by a curt

word from his mother. Arthur knew she was thinking of him.

Soon came a few moments' silence, then the sharp pips from Greenwich. He finished the paragraph, then laid down his pen and looked through the window. The wind had eased and rain was falling. He watched the thick water-lines beat against the house opposite, and marked the troubled surface of the gutter stream hurrying to the lower village. He turned away with features unmoved from evenness, and took a raincoat down from behind the door, then passed into the house.

'You're not starting in this storm, are you?' his mother asked quietly.

'I'll wait a few minutes; it may abate.' He sat on the chair at the foot of the stairs.

'Why don't you stay in, Arth, and listen to the Emperor Concerto?' Albert said. He moved to the wireless and cut off the fat stock prices. 'We'll let that go past.'

'Who's playing it?'

'Solomon. Best concerto ever written.'

'I'm not stoppin' in to listen to that saw,' Sidney said, cheerfully but definitely. 'No fear.'

'Well, get off out—to your billiard pals at the institute,' his father said, from behind the newspaper. 'That variety and dance-slosh you 'ave on every night's gettin' on my nerves.'

'There's a cup of tea and a bit of cake on the kitchen table, Arthur,' Mrs. Shirley said, into the silence which her husband's curt words had cut in the conversation. 'Get it before you go.' Her son went into the kitchen; she followed. 'Nancy won't expect you a night like this.' He smiled into her face as he stood with the cup in his hand.

'No. Maybe not.'

'And going all that way after a day at work. And work in the morning.'

'I shan't be late. Half-past ten.' He went to the door. 'Wind's getting up again. Not raining so fast, now. Think I'll get off.' He pushed the last bit of cake into his mouth. 'Shall just catch the seven bus in Pirley.'

The wind shrieked as he went out, impatient of the unyielding house walls. On the quarter-of-a-mile road between Wingrove and Peathill it rushed with a sea-sound through the trees about the fields on either side. Weakling twigs snapped and fell, slurring on the smooth tarmac. Arthur strained against it, piercing it with bent trunk, then walked freely between the houses in Peat-hill, to struggle again along the field-path to Pirley. He looked at his wrist-watch under the light—an electric lamp hung high up a telegraph-pole to help night travellers safely over the railway-lines—near Pirley Colliery, and found that the wind was beating him. He turned again to his striving, and almost ran when the violent force was constrained to let him be and climb the high masses of the town buildings, but even as he rounded the bank at the bottom of Peak Street the Belford bus was moving like a room of light from the top on to High Street. He ran a few paces involun-tarily, stopped, pulsing with empty anger, then walked on again, feeling foolish. He'd have to walk, and, instead of being where Nancy would be waiting at ten minutes past seven, it would be half-past; gone half-past, against this wind. Still, she'd wait.

Arthur hurried through the gusty emptiness of the wide market square, between the post office and the Town Hall, along the outer streets of Pirley, then had perforce to slacken on the open level to the top of Nessfield Hill. Below him, now, was the night-filled bowl of the Lea Valley; cold pin-points of light pricked here and there the vast darkness, some on the right-hand ridge from the grey houses set among the damson orchards of Pentland, on the left from the first houses in Overdale, far ahead isolated ones in the streets of Steep squatting on its high tors. Brighter ones looked up from Nessfield at the foot of the long hill.

It was gone half-past when he had passed through Nessfield and was leaning against the wall where the road swept round to Pentland Hollow. The wind and the darkness were the only things about him. After a few minutes, he crossed the road and walked along a cart-track between fields, and in five minutes was pushing open the garden gate of a house, lonely among straining trees.

'Good evening, Mrs. Maugham,' he said to the middle-aged woman who opened the door to his knocking. She peered forward.

'It's you, Arthur, is it? Haven't you seen Nancy?'

'Why, isn't she in?'

'She went out about seven. Wasn't she coming to meet you?'

'I missed the bus. I thought she would come home again.'

'No.' A pause. 'If you come in, she might be back soon. Come on in.' Arthur followed her. 'Maybe she's walked on to Fanny's in the Hollow.'

'Perhaps she wouldn't expect me when the bus did not bring me. Good evening, Mr. Maugham. Been working to-day at your pit?'

'Aye. Look like makin' a full week.' He yawned. 'Just bin 'avin' a nap. Facin' that wind comin' 'ome made me worse tired than all t'shift.'

'I faced it coming here. Made me later.'

He sat down, and the conversation lagged, the woman soon took up her knitting; her husband seemed anxious to take up the evening paper, his fingers toyed with it as it lay beside him on the sofa. He took it up definitely at last.

'Put wireless on a bit, lad, if tha wants.' He put on his glasses and looked over them. 'Me an' t'missis doesn't bother it a deal. Nancy's allus this dance stuff on.' He watched the young man move to the cabinet, then settled to his paper.

The clock hands were moving with irritating speed while the symphony orchestra played *Rosamunde*, then a short piece by a modern composer. Even while Solomon triumphed through the Emperor Concerto, his mind was half off the music; he felt a sickening sense of waste, he had waited emptily for two hours. It was just unfulfilled expectancy which held him, he did not wonder suspiciously where Nancy was, did not hope or reach forward to her coming, he merely held himself emptily. The clapping, a minute or so before nine-thirty, roared through the speaker, and it seemed to scrape Arthur's mind. He rose as the noise faded, and the man and wife looked up. The Greenwich 'pips' sounded.

'I shall have to go now,' he said. The woman put down her knitting, and fetched his raincoat from the other room. 'I might meet Nancy in the fields. If I don't, would you tell her I will be at Pirley Hippodrome at six on Saturday?'

'You won't have a bit of supper?'

'No, thank you. I must get off.' He took his coat and scarf. 'Tell Nancy, will you? Thanks for having me all the evening.'

'All right—all right,' the man said. 'Come any time. 'Ow's your schoolin' goin'?'

'Oh, very well. My exam's in July. I shall leave the pit, I think, if I get through.'

'Good. Good.' The man rose and shook Arthur's hand. 'Don't miss thee bus. Good night.'

'Good night,' he gave back, and went.

The wind had calmed and rain was falling in thick lines. He splashed through pools and sunk sole-deep in mud along the cart-road. Only the sound of the rain on the trees, on the tarmac road, pattering about his raincoat, came to him standing in the pitch darkness. Nessfield lights quarter of a mile away were hidden by a bend in the road. He struck a match, and held it near his watch. Surely the bus hadn't gone. He turned his head suddenly towards the darkness blacking out Pentland Hollow; an increasing rumble quickened in a moment to a roar as a bus swung from behind a mound the road circled. Arthur stepped into the road and held out his arm, but the bus was already slowing. It stopped where he stood, and Nancy got down.

'Hello, Arthur.' There was surprise in her voice, a gladness too. 'Are you going on this bus?' She was still holding the hand-bar of the bus, the young man's hand was on the other. 'Don't go till the next.' She moved from the bus.

2

'Comin', or not, sir?' the conductor asked, his fingers on the bell-push.

Arthur looked into Nancy's face, then withdrew his hand, and the bus roared away. An emptiness was in his eyes for a moment. He had, in a moment of indecision, fled to his mother; he had seen her look of concern, heard her gentle scolding for staying so late. Tired in the morning, tired when he came home to tackle his studying. He switched back to the girl half-angrily.

'It'll be late when I get home, now,' he said. But he smiled and took her arm, and they walked a few yards along the road and leaned against the low stone wall. 'Put up your umbrella, you'll be wet through.' He kissed her, pulling her to him, forgetting all other things.

'I saw the seven bus go, and thought you weren't coming,' Nancy said. 'Fanny and I have been to Belford pictures.' They stood for a while in silence, the rain splattered heavily on to the umbrella. 'We must go to the Hipp on Saturday.'

'Yes, I told your mother I'd see you there.'

'It's Fred Astaire and Ginger Rogers.'

'Oo. I wish it was summer.' He shivered. 'This weather gives one the creeps. Outside, I mean.'

'I don't want to be stuck in an office another summer.' She hesitated, though her voice had broken off in no finality. 'Why don't we get married? I'm sick of scratching down shorthand and tapping a typewriter and the humdrum nine to five regularly.'

'We can't get married yet, you know that—you know that, Nancy.' His tone smoothed from firmness to gentle reasoning. 'I'm working night and day to get away from the pit on to a more secure level. I want more money as well.'

'You could get a better job now. You've got Matric.'

'Yes, but if I left the pit now, I should have to chuck college. I should lose my scholarship.'

'What would that matter? You could study at night. And if you got an office job, you wouldn't be so tired.'

'Come on. I'll walk a little way down the fields with you. My bus'll be here in ten minutes.'

They stood together in the darkness of the fields; she rested easily in his arms for a while, her smooth, cold cheek to his. Arthur held her, as if satisfied, finding nothing to say. Suddenly she became tense, then alive, and her arms gripped fast about him. He responded with like holding, and she moved her face round to kiss him with open lips. But after a moment she relaxed, took away her lips, and stood silent as one knowing futility.

'How long will it be before you're out of the pit?'

'Oh, in October,' he said, brightly, quickly, 'if I get Inter—and I should do that. I reckon I'm on top of my work, the stuff the syllabus covers, that is.'

'And how long is it after that—two years?'

'Well, I could get a job then, but not a teaching job—not in a Secondary, or Elementary even.'

'Why not? You didn't say that before. You said two years.'

'Well. You have a year at least in the Training Department after you've got your degree.'

'Three years.'

'Oh, I'm not forced to do that. There's plenty of other jobs going. I daresay I should get on the staff in our department. Not many of our chaps take

English—they're more for Economics and History.' She did not answer. 'There's good jobs going as well in the Social Service. One of our chaps with an Economics degree's just gone to Sheffield. Three hundred pounds a year. My bus'll be about due.' He kissed her, but she was merely passive until the moment he was breaking away. 'I'll see——' But she smothered his speech with a sudden, passionate kiss.

'I do love you, Arthur, but——'

'Never mind. See you on Sat. Outside the Hipp at six. Must go now.'

He left her, sliding his hand down her arm, pressed her hand for a moment. She tried to hold him, but he pulled away with a happy laugh.

'Good night,' he said; but she did not answer, and he went. She turned, too, then stood and looked again the way Arthur had gone; waiting, before she did begin moving towards home, to see the bus stop, then continue on towards Nessfield and Pirley.

'You're late—and wet—and cold,' Mrs. Shirley greeted as her son walked in at eleven. 'Fancy being out till this time.'

'Not cold, mum, I've hurried from Pirley. My feet are soaked, though.'

'I've put a bottle in your bed.' She took the steaming kettle from the fire, and poured water into a cup on the table. 'Get that hot cocoa and those onions. I'm going. Time you were in bed too; you'll be no good to-morrow. Good night.'

''Night, mum.'

His brothers and their father were up before him next morning; Sidney had to call him twice before he came down, yawning. Mr. Shirley was pushing his arm through his snap-bag string and taking up his water-bottle. He always went early, twenty minutes before the youths.

'Come on, dozy,' Albert said. 'It'll be last bantle for you again. Gaffer'll be on to you.' Arthur went to his heap of clothes, and pulled on his trousers. Like most other miners, the Shirleys dressed for the pit downstairs before the fire.

'Shan't be far behind you.'

'Courtin' till eleven's no good for anybody,' the other chaffed, good-humouredly, and Arthur smiled. 'Time you were married when it gets to that.'

The remark seemed to damp the elder brother. He swept mentally at once to Nancy; he walked through the fresh spring morning thinking of her, of her impatience to be married—he knew it was merely to be free from the irksome office routine. She was light, airy, not the sort to be pinned to a dry line; she wanted variety—shopping, dressing a child, working in a home in the morning, walking out in the afternoon, content with him in the evening. She had talked of these things to him, and in these moments was her most lovely self. What could he do, though? All this was quite impossible for two years at the least. He wondered, with a touch of fear, whether he could hold her as long.

He hurried the last two hundred yards to the pit-head when he heard the steam hooter rush in a long curve to its screaming line, marking ten minutes to seven. There was a line of men and youths at the lamp-house, a small crowd at the pit-top a yard or so from the whirring ropes, but Arthur managed to get on to the cage before the last, on which the under-manager always rode.

'Sun just comin' up,' a youth who stood next to Arthur on the cage said to him, as they waited for the signal from the pit bottom.

'It'll be going down when we're here again.' The bell rang, and, when the cage lifted for the onsetter to pull out the props, all the men on the cage bowed their heads to avoid the swift cut between light and the dark wall of the shaft, as well as to miss experiencing the stomach-turning of the sudden dropping. The cage moved downwards, the wooden gates guarding the shaft crashed to rest. From twilight into lamplight the men were rushed; the up-cage sighed to them, rattled emptily for a moment, sighed upwards, and its sounding was lost. All bent their knees to the sudden, arresting bump on the pit bottom.

A deputy went through most of the men's pockets as they spread about the wide bottom; the stallmen walked down the roads, gangers turned into the stables for their ponies. Arthur hurried ahead down the long brick-arch incline, up which eighteen loaded trams would soon be pulled by the rope driven from a jig-house on the surface, along a stint to his work at the bottom of a short, steep jig. Nine full trams stood on one set of rails; the night-shift had used up all the empties, and he would have to wait until the ganger came before he could start work. He hung his snap-bag on a nail, took a short pull from his water-bottle, then hung his coat, waistcoat and scarf over his snap-bag. He sat in the manhole, waiting; lights twinkled along the stint, swinging a little, grew from a pin-point to a glow, passed him, and those that bore them greeted him with ''Mornin'', or ''Ow do, Arthur'.

Soon the ganger rumbled along the stint with three

empties. Arthur got to his feet, and began work. He hung the three empties to a rope, pulled hard at a bell-wire running through staples fastened into the props lining the steep jig slope. He heard the bell chink at the top. The man there knocked out the block in front of the first of three loaded ones, and they began running down, pulling up the empties Arthur had hung on. Another ganger had come with empties, was turning his horse to hang on to three loaded ones.

"Owta gooin' on, Arthur? Splodgin' last night?'

'Oh yes,' he laughed, and pushed the empties to where the rope-end reached. He hung them to it, and rang the bell. The empties and loaded trams roared in the darkness, and Arthur turned to the three which had come down last time, pushed the first down the track to a plate, and turned it about. The trams in this district were open at one end; they had to come down this jig open-end last so that the lumps packed there would not fall out. Arthur had to turn the trams so they could go up the long incline open-end first. It was only because of the heaviness of this part of the work that Arthur had the job; a boy could have hung on the empties and pushed down the loaded ones to where the ganger hung on to them.

The gangers came and went, the empties and loaded trams rushed in and out of the light-circle of Arthur's lamp. By snap-time at eleven o'clock, he was waiting for coal, and he sat in the manhole for short periods. Each time he rested, he fetched a small note-book from the inside pocket of his coat, and bent over its pages, holding his lamp on one knee. He mumbled the lists of Latin verbs, turned over, examined different gram-

matical constructions, turned over and, with a small
pencil from his waistcoat pocket, attempted a translation of a passage he had written out the previous day.
All this was done in spasms; when the ganger came he
left it, when the deputy or the under-manager passed,
he was busy over something if not actually working at
the trams. In other intervals, he wrote logical symbols
on a smooth piece of rock in the man-hole side, and
mumbled, as he looked at them:

> 'SaP   SiP   SeP   SoP.'

He recited aloud poems and chunks from Shakespeare and Chaucer, all within the limits of the Inter
Arts Syllabus. The gangers heard him sometimes.

'Wot the 'ell are yer mumblin' and grumblin' about,
Gardner? Learnin' a piece for t'chapel anniversary?'

Once when he sat in the man-hole—it was getting on
for 'loose-all'—he bent over, elbow on knee, his cheek
moulded to his hand, staring with empty eyes at the
glow about his lamp, which he had put on the floor.
He was thinking of the evening's homework. Finish
his History essay. A chapter of Logic. The ganger was
rumbling into the top of the jig; he heard it sub-
consciously, knew that he must turn to work again in
a few moments. Voices sounded faintly.

'Come ower, Roger.' That was the ganger.

'Is that bloody block on?' The jigger was shouting
to the boy who helped him. 'It isn't. Damn thee,
throw it in t'road. Quick. 'Old this second un. They're
goin'. Look out.' He raised his voice, almost
screamed. 'Ay up, Arthur. Look out.'

Arthur jumped up, kicked over his lamp, grabbed at
it, but the flame leapt suddenly from the wick. A

rumbling in the darkness up the jig; in a moment it was a rushing, a quick clicking over rail-joints.

'Look out, Gardner! Look——'

The jigger's voice was drowned in the roar. Arthur ran with head bent and, as fast as he dared in the darkness, ran with hand outstretched on to the empty road, or where he thought the empty road was. A ganger was coming slowly along the stint, singing. The roar, the rushing was nearer, the quick clicking. Arthur flattened himself against the empty-road wall, afraid suddenly. There was a bump, a crash. The tram had leapt the track, smashed into the side, overturned. Now sounded only the slow rumbling of the gang coming up, the voice of the driver singing. Arthur groped back to the bottom of the jig. Lights were swinging down the steep.

'A'right, Gardner?' a voice called down, slightly concerned, maybe, at seeing no light.

'All right,' Arthur called back. He moved quicker towards their lamp-glow, was by the overturned tram first. 'I kicked my lamp over when I jumped out of seat-hole.'

'Hell! There'd 'ave been a mess if it 'ad 'it that prop,' the jigger, Hawley, said.

'We should 'ave 'ad the bloody jig in,' his mate said. 'Just missed it. Come on, let's get it right else we s'll be 'ere at three o'clock.'

'Wot's goin' off?' The stint ganger came up. ''Ad a runner?'

'Yes. Give us a hand.'

They heaved the tram on to the rails, scotched it, then loaded the coal into it, examining each lump to find the stall mark.

'It's one of fifty-one's,' Arthur said. 'Lend's a bit of chalk; I'll mark it.'

They lowered the tram steadily to the bottom of the jig, five yards or so of the incline, and work began again. There was no interval of rest and waiting now until 'loose-all'.

'Ar've put in for one a' them scholarships, Arthur,' a youth said, going up the long jig. He had hold of his horse's tail, and Arthur grasped it, too, when he had bobbed in a man-hole to let it pass him. 'I'm on t'short list. Wot do you do when you go to Trentingham? Write an essay or something?'

'Yes. But there's an interview afterwards. If there's an essay on Adult Education, have a go at that. There's a choice of about six.' The youth went into the stables with his horse. Arthur continued towards the cage. 'I'll give you a hand if you get one,' he called.

'Right. Thanks.'

Arthur went home slowly; he was tired, the long pull up Gorsey Lumb made his legs ache. When he turned into Back Lane he saw a figure at the top limping to the corner of Top Street. He puckered his brows suddenly. Surely it wasn't Albert. When he got in, however, his brother was sitting in the kitchen with his boot and stocking off, and his mother was bathing Albert's instep.

'Hello. What's the matter, Albert?'

''Ad a bit of bind on my foot,' the other said. 'Nowt much, is it, mum?'

'I don't know. Just a bruise. If you rest to-night and to-morrow, it might be right.'

'Nay, I shall try and go to-morrow, and rest durin' the week-end. We might 'ave three 'olidays next week.'

'Hold your foot in that while I give Arthur his dinner,' his mother said, and got from her knees, wiping her hands on her apron.

'Yes,' Arthur said, 'I want to get a lot done to-night, and go to bed early.'

He fed and washed, changed and went at once into the front room before his father and Sidney came in. His mother came in when he had been working at his history essay for about half an hour.

'You'd better come and give your dad and Sid a hand in the garden. They're going to put some potatoes in.'

'Crikes,' he said, with a touch of bewilderment and disappointment. 'It'll throw me all behind.' He looked into her face, then at his papers. 'No Logic to-night. I s'll be too tired.'

'There'll be a row if you don't. Come on. Albert can't do any. You shouldn't stay out so late, you wouldn't be so tired then.' A touch of anger was in her voice, not at him directly, but that such a circumstance had arisen through what she felt could have been avoided. Her emotion was with him, really; she was angry that he would fall short of the point he had aimed at.

'I shall stay up and finish this, anyway.'

He followed her out and put on his pit shoes again, turned up the bottoms of his shifting trousers, then went into the garden. His father and Sidney were digging; neither had washed.

'Where's the other spade?' he asked.

'You can use the fork. You can put the manure in the rows, then cover up after 'e's put the potatoes in.' Arthur went to where the fork stuck from the soil. His father was cutting out the row; his brother was filling his cap with whole and half potatoes all with sprits sticking from them. Arthur spread forkfuls of manure, which he carried from heaps standing about the garden; his brother stuck in potatoes eighteen inches apart along the row. 'You thought of gettin' out of it nicely, didn't you?' the father continued, when Arthur came with the last spread of manure. The man was standing at the end of the row, his face slightly pale with the exertion just ended. He spoke with a suggestion of a sneer. 'Runnin' into t'parlour every night.'

'What are you talking about?' Arthur looked the man straight in the eyes, after momentary surprise had waved across his face. 'I didn't know you were coming into the garden to-night.'

'Didn't want to know.' Arthur walked away to the other end of the row, and began covering up the potatoes. Sidney had stuck in the last potato, and was looking up with frightened eyes. 'Nothink else but books and women. Other folks can sludge-bump.' The young man did not reply; he knew where these weak bickerings could lead. He saw in a flash of remembrance, his mother looking grey-cheeked and old, saw Sidney crying, big youth that he was.

They worked in silence for a while. When Arthur or his father did speak, Sidney was always the mark of it, and the youth answered guardedly, his mind at once centred on the one who had not spoken.

'I'll take the tools in, Arthur,' he said, when the light had thickened and they could see to work no more. His brother went in, and he carried the spades and the fork to the toolshed at the bottom of the garden. Mr. Shirley followed with the bowl, holding the few potatoes that were left.

'If you'd put your readin' and studyin' to some end, you'd beat him easily,' the man said to his son.

'I don't feel like it after I've been to t'pit,' the youth replied. 'Besides, I wanted to go to the Tech when I was a lad, but you banged me off to t'pit.'

'Oh, shut up whinin'. You could do as 'e's doing, couldn't you?'

Sidney walked up the garden and into the kitchen. Arthur had changed his boots again, and was washing his hands, a set, impatient straining about his eyes and mouth. He went at once into the parlour, lit the gas, and sat down to his work.

'Are you coming for a bit of supper?' His mother came in at half-past nine, and stood by him.

'I've got on awful to-night,' he burst out impatiently. 'Awful. I'd a good mind to scrap the whole essay.' He bent over the last sheet he had written, read a paragraph. 'Oh lor'.'

'Why, what's the matter?' She spoke softly, nervously.

'He——' He stopped suddenly. 'I suppose it was being interrupted that upset me. And I stayed out too late last night.' He looked at his papers again. 'But I'll finish this to-night. Right, I will come and have a bit of supper.'

'You should go to bed.'

'I s'll finish it.'

He followed her out, and sat to some cocoa and bread and cheese. The other three had just finished. Sidney was by the wireless under the little side-window; Albert in a chair, his foot resting in another. The father was on the sofa as usual.

'Going in the morning, Albert?' Arthur asked, as he sat down. The Greenwich 'pips' were sounding.

'This is the National——'

'Oh, we've heard the news before,' Sidney said, and switched on to a Regional. Music streamed in sharply.

'Put news on again,' his father said at once.

'He isn't going, I should think,' the mother was saying. 'He couldn't manage to work; he can hardly walk.'

'Oh, if I can get to the pit I s'll be all right. Don't think everybody who goes down the pit slaves 'is guts out. I don't, and I'm going to nurse my job as long as I can.'

'Don't be so ass-'eaded,' his father said reprovingly. It was rarely he spoke other than conciliatorily to Albert; the youth was obviously a favourite, and felt a fool at times, even angry. 'Rest this week-end, and it'll be all right for Monday.'

'I'll see in t'mornin',' Albert said.

'I don't think I'll go out to-night,' Mr. Shirley said, looking at the clock. 'Fetch me a pint of beer, Nell,' he ended, addressing his wife.

She looked across at him, quick bewilderment shot into her eyes. It wasn't often he missed going for a drink; usually he spent the half-hour between nine-thirty and closing time in the taproom of the Miners' Arms at the corner of Top Street. Sometimes he took a jug and brought the beer home to drink with his supper. He had had no cocoa, and they expected him to go out at once. Arthur and Sidney both looked at her the moment the father spoke; they knew she hated the job of fetching beer.

'I'll fetch you some, dad,' Arthur said genially. 'I

could do with a blow before I begin again.' The man
did not reply. 'Give me a jug and some money, mum.'

'I'll go, Arthur, if you want to get on,' Sidney said, as
his brother wound a scarf about his neck.

'It's all right, I'll go.'

He took the money and the jug his mother laid on the
table, and went out whistling. Immediately he came
in, he put down the jug and the change, and walked
into the front room again.

'Can't he turn that light off when he comes out?'
he heard his father say. 'Wastin' gas. We might find
money on the road.'

Arthur had gone into the parlour brighter and in a
fitter mood for work after the short break and the walk,
but his father's remark when he had pushed open the
door rushed him back into the unsettled state of mind,
angry and disappointed to be behind in his schedule of
study. The man was getting worse. It was mere negative envy, an anger directed at him because his own
sons were standing while he plodded ahead; he was
angry with his sons, yet spilled it over his stepson.
Arthur sat down grimly. He felt a faint sneer run
through him, though it was not expressed at his mouth
or nostril. But he wouldn't hold him back; except
that he might block him through his mother. Fear
chilled about him, then he set his mouth-line straight,
straining to dismiss all matters irrelevant to that his
eyes were holding fast to on the sheet before him. He
began writing; he forgot other things, forgot his weariness until his mother came in at half-past ten.

'I'm going to bed,' she said. 'The others have
gone.'

'I'm finishing this,' he told her quietly. 'Shan't be

more than twenty minutes.' He bent over the sheet again.

She went without saying more, and he heard her go upstairs. He felt heavy suddenly, and got up at once when he knew he was sitting stupidly. He went into the kitchen and sluiced his face with cold water.

The clock struck eleven as he went upstairs. He heard his father mumbling as he passed the bedroom door. When he came down in the morning his father had gone. Sidney was standing ready, watching Albert hobble about the floor, trying his foot.

'Go back to bed, you fathead. You'll never manage.'

'Shut yer face. Who's foot is it?'

'Don't be a clown, Albert,' Arthur joined in. He was dressing hurriedly, glancing at the clock with quick jerks of his head. 'Put kettle on for me, Sid. You'd never get to the pit for seven.'

Their mother came down; it was unusual for her to get up until they had gone. The youths would not have her; they could see to themselves without her slaving so early in the morning. She came to the fire, watching Albert.

'Go back to bed, and don't be so silly,' she bade him.

'I'll draw 'is money,' Sidney said, 'and tell the gaffer.'

Albert stood for a while, then began taking off his pit clothes, an excruciatingly painful thing morally for him to do. The woman turned swiftly to Arthur, who was lacing his boots.

'You'll be late if you don't get off quick. I'll make you a bit of breakfast. Have you had any, Albert?' He nodded. 'You get off, Sidney.' He went. Albert went upstairs again. Arthur stood up to drink his tea and eat a bacon sandwich. Half-past six buzzed, and he set down his cup and hurried out.

''Mornin', mum.'

''Morning,' she replied, and went to the window, standing by the back window until she had seen him pass over a short space of Top Street which lay between two houses. Then she went upstairs again to examine Albert's foot.

# CHAPTER II

'WE'LL walk down, shall we?'

'Yes, if you like,' Nancy said. 'Wasn't it a grand picture. I like those two together. Can't Fred Astaire dance?'

'He can. Would you like some chocolates?'

They were passing the market stalls; men and boys were crying fish, fruit, meat, sweets, mingling voice-levels and strengths. Arthur bought chocolates from a stall on the top row, then the two passed over the top of the market-place where the pot man stood with his crockery and ornaments about him on the floor. He clinked together two cups, shouted a price three times, spat, then poured cynical abuse on the laughing crowd, ringing his ware. The linoleum man thwacked a rolled piece of his stuff with a stick, called a price, and said, 'Lady over there' to his attendant, who carried the roll to the edge of the crowd where the stick pointed.

'Now, sir.' The pot man turned to Arthur, who was passing close behind him. 'What about this tea service for the lady? All right for when you get married.'

'They'd be old-fashioned by then,' Arthur laughed.

'Three years,' Nancy added, and did not smile.

'Good God.' The man turned back to the crowd. 'Courtin' three years. Why, I married my missis after I'd known her a month. Still, that's how you are in these slow country towns. Now, who'll gimme a pound for this tea-service?' His voice and the clinking of the cups faded as the two passed the post office and turned out of the town towards Nessfield Hill.

'Don't you be nasty about the three years,' Arthur said, and squeezed her arm to make her certain he was joking.

'I wasn't nasty. I felt angry—well, disappointed. I thought it would be two years at the outside. And that seemed a foolishly long time. It's old-fashioned to court—and for three years. It'll be four in another three years. I like you and you like me.' She paused. 'That should be enough.'

'You're not talking sense, now. Do you want to be a miner's wife? Me bringing dirt into your home. Me coming home tired most days and wanting to do nothing but sit about all evening. Do you? If you do, I can chuck my studying to-day and ask the gaffer to let me go in the stall on Monday—he would do—then I should get enough money to keep us.' He waited for her to answer, but began speaking as another thought flooded him. 'And who knows how I might come home one day. Do you know, the first day I went down the pit a stretcher came back from the pit bottom and I had to handle it, change it from one tram to another. The day before, a dead man had ridden to the pit bottom on it.'

'You know I don't want a miner for a husband,' she broke in fiercely. 'Should I go with you if you weren't trying to be something different? But you're taking your own time about it. You could meet me, couldn't you? There are two men clerks in our office who aren't half as clever as you. They just copy figures from a day-book into a ledger. Well, one of them does that; the other writes out invoices and enters them in the day-book. Anybody could do that. They haven't got Matric, either. Never went to a secondary school.'

'No. But they began in the office as kids. That's just it. I began in the pit and it'll take me all my time to escape, work as hard as I will. People think that those who are in the pit are capable of nothing but manual labour. I know. I've been after jobs—in offices, as a storekeeper, a timekeeper. When they asked me where I was working, and I told them the pit—well, I don't know what it was, but that fact made them tone down anything good they'd said about my having matriculation.'

'You don't go the right way about it. Get to know somebody—a doctor, a parson. You could get a job through them if you got them interested in you as a scholar.'

'I've no time to go hunting out doctors and parsons. It took me every night of three years to get Matric. I've taken two years over Inter. College youths do it in one. They get three or four lectures a day, then go and sit in the library.' He stopped and pulled her to face him, pulled her body close to his. The wide, empty darkness at the very brow of Nessfield Hill sung about them. 'I love you as much as my studying, Nancy. I do. At times I feel like chucking it all just to have every night with you.'

'Look out, there's a bus.'

They walked to the side of the road, and continued down the hill in silence.

'It's no good quarrelling,' Nancy said soberly. 'I think it a waste of life to stick your nose in books for hours on end. Still, I know you like it, just as I like pictures and dances and nice clothes. I know you think it the only way to get out of the pit, but I reckon if you got to know people, as I said before, you'd get out quicker.'

'I'll see. I'll think about that.'

'You won't do it.' She laughed and he pressed her arm. He was glad to hear it. 'But I'm not going to sit knitting at home while I'm waiting three years for you.'

'You've been reading about Penelope.'

'Who's she?'

'Oh, she knitted or something while she waited for her husband more than three years. Chaps came and said he was dead, and wanted to marry her. She said she would when she had finished whatever she was knitting. But she undid every night what she put together in the day.' He laughed. 'You see?'

'Hm,' was her comment. He puckered his brows for a moment, but failed to understand the tone of her short murmur.

At the foot of the hill, they turned left, on to the towing-path of the canal, and left it again at the bridge over which the cart-road from Overdale passed and ran by the Maugham's house to the Nessfield road. They stood for a while in the fields, warming to forgetfulness of things other than the straining to know the utter fusing of mind and body. Nancy was never from him. At times he gazed into the darkness over her shoulder, and physically she was lost to him, though his arms were as tight about her. When he came back to her on these occasions, he seemed as if he would speak solemnly, but always he roused and rushed into demonstrations of love.

'Your bus'll be about due,' Nancy said suddenly,

and they broke from each other slowly. 'Are you coming to tea to-morrow?'

'Well—yes, I will.' He seemed to be pushing through a barrier to agree.

'Were you going to say you couldn't because you'd a lot of work to do?'

'You will be nasty,' he laughed and hugged her playfully until she pleaded to be freed. 'I shall be here about four.'

After tea next day they walked into Lingfall Park up to the Manor. Arthur thought of beginning a conversation about Mary of Scots who was imprisoned here for a while, and of Anthony Babington who had worked to help her, from Dethick a few miles away, but he let the thought slide. He permitted Nancy to move in channels congenial to her—the cinema, light novels, the coming summer. She had read a good deal, was intelligent, quick and easy in thought. He glanced at her as she reached forward eagerly to the summer, to hikes, country dancing, tennis. Her face was alive, rich, it seemed to bring the summer about him. He always felt a dry, stodgy being when she was like this; he knew he really was inclined to be more serious than the tone of the circumstance moulding him at any moment. He knew the girl was what he was not, and that was why he loved her. She had a living beauty, was irresponsible within decent limits. Now, he could see her dancing about him on the smooth, sun-warmed grass in the fields lost between Matlock and Ashover, her white arms flung to the skies while she was off the ground, her slim, supple body turning, bending in graceful line. He had stood by, feeling heavy physically, his emotions streaming richly to her, his brain telling him he was something of the clod.

'We'll go on the hikers' train every Sunday morning, rain or shine. I can see Lathkill Dale, now. It's marvellous; I think it's as lovely as Dovedale.'

'If I get through my exam, we will—I mean we will be the happiest pair in the Peak.   There'll be something to be happy about.' They were coming out of the park by Pentland Hollow, and, while he was speaking, Arthur became somewhat timorously fearful. He took hold of her arm and looked away from her for a moment towards the line of limes, and beyond where the slow Lea wound under low arches of alders. 'Nancy, I've been thinking.' She looked at him as he turned back to her. 'I think it would be better if I stuck to my study, now, and only came to see you on Saturdays.' His voice quickened. 'If we holidayed on Wednesday any week, I would come then, because I should have most of the day at my books after I had signed at the Exchange.'

She answered at once, digging her elbow in his ribs.

'Well, you needn't look so glum about it.' Her tone was generous. 'I shall find plenty to do.' They left the park by a narrow bridge over the river, and were forced to walk singly. Nancy felt away from him at once now they were physically apart. She was emotion-full in contact, when the object of her love was by to feed on, but away, even physically away by a yard, she was not held to him. She was not warmed by any knowledge that she had in her keeping to cherish the very essence of the youth who walked behind her. On the other hand, he held most secondly the physical delight of her; away from her, he was aware of her more. He glowed richly in moments down the pit, at home, in the lecture-rooms and grounds of Trentingham University College. He was glad for her, that she was beautiful, happy, living. He was content to know of their love; she must feel the outward edges of its thrusting, like one who must handle and crush to her senses blossoms perfect in themselves and satisfying richly the rest of those about her. 'There'll be tennis coming soon. There'll be country dancing.' She was away from him, satisfying herself.

'Yes, you'll be all right,' he agreed with a touch of eagerness, but the rush of words did not come wholly from the desire to keep her content; he was satisfied within himself. There was selfishness within them both; each recognised it in the other, neither in themselves.

'I shan't see you till Saturday, then,' the girl said, when they parted in the fields near her home. 'Don't be surprised if you hear of me at the pictures with Fanny on Wednesday, or even strolling round Pirley on Sunday nights. I can't stay in, it'd kill me.'

'Of course I shan't be surprised. You do as you like, of course. I'm not the jealous sort, wondering where you are every minute, whether you're talking to some other chap or not. I shall work, and it'll be for both of us. That's when I shall think of you—when I feel satisfied that I've done a good evening's work, and it's a step nearer what I want for us both.' He took her in his arms again, carefully. 'And on Saturdays we'll do just what you want to do—go to any pictures, any place.' She returned no pressure to his kiss. 'I shall come on Wednesdays when I can.' He released her again. 'Good night, dear.'

'Good night,' she said softly and turned away as he

did, and kept on, did not wait to see the bus take him away.

He went home satisfied. Nancy had not mentioned getting married all the afternoon and evening; she must have taken heed of the things he had said last night. Still, he knew she hated being pinned in the office; she had said she could scream the place down when sheets and sheets of figures were laid by the side of her type-writer, enough to last her all day. Still, she should get another job—yes, he'd never thought of that—get a job in a smaller office where there was more variety in the work. He'd tell her; she'd perhaps never thought of that.

Albert's foot had improved enough by Monday for him to go to work. Arthur did not get up until the three others had gone. There was no need this morning or Tuesday; he was going to Trentingham, and the eight-o'clock 'bus from Hillcross, half a mile, away, was soon enough. It was always seven at the earliest when he got back again, and he noticed on both evenings when he walked on the 'end', as the asphalt path dividing the house from the garden was called, that no more potatoes had been set, no more of the garden had been touched. He usually did little or no homework these evenings, the day-work was sufficient. He always felt more tired than after a shift at the pit.

'We'll have some more potatoes in,' the father said on the Wednesday, when he and the two younger sons had sat for about half an hour after their dinner. Arthur had come into the kitchen from the parlour to wash out his fountain-pen. His stepfather had said the words into the part of the newspaper he was reading. He had the news pages; Albert was reading the short story; Sidney the only part he ever looked at—the sport section.

'I'll go in to-night,' Albert said. 'Don't think I can dig, though. But I can put 'em in and spread t'muck.'

'Shall you need me?' Arthur asked.

'Yes. You must all take your whack. If one goes in, you can all go in.'

The young man turned away, went into the parlour and laid down his pen. He had felt cynically resigned until he saw how little he had written. Now a sudden nervous fear worked him. He hadn't reckoned on this; he couldn't afford to have gaps in his studying now the Inter exam was so near. It seemed as if his stepfather was doing it on purpose. Still, he'd say nothing; it would only mean a row, and his mother suffered most though she never took part in any. He changed into his boots again, and followed the others into the garden. His mother did not look at him as he passed through the middle room; she had turned to gaze through the 'little window' over the garden on to the village street. His teeth came together as he slurred over the yard, and sudden anger weakened him, pulling at his brows and mouth.

'What yer lookin' so sulky at, Arth?' Albert asked. 'More of us in, sooner we s'll get garden done, and you can be at your books in peace.'

'Who was looking sulky?' Arthur jerked his head from spades to forks, at the bowl of potatoes. 'Come on, what are we doing. Have I to dig, or what?'

'You take your time,' the father said, and pulled complacently at his pipe. 'Not so much of your rushin'. We 'aven't got a kid's job 'angin' empties on at the bottom of a jig. There's plenty of time, and we're goin' to take it steady. You can dig with me and you can cut some of the rows out as well. Sid can carry the manure, and Albert stick them in.'

Arthur began digging at once, impatiently. The father and Sidney began, too, but they worked steadily, resting at times for five minutes at a stretch, talking, smoking. Arthur had to rest as well, unless he cared to take on the whole process himself—cutting out the row, manuring, putting in potatoes and covering them up. But that would have been foolishness; he wouldn't have got away any sooner. Besides, they were taking it easily, as they should do. Still, they needn't have such long breaks. It seemed that his stepfather was holding the work up longer than was necessary.

'Why 'aven't you gone to Nessfield to-night, Arth?' Sidney asked, when they were at the end of a row together; the other two had gone to the shed for another bowl of potatoes.

'Oh, I'm not going again in the week until after July. I must stick at my work. Not going Sundays, either. But I shan't get much benefit from it at this rattle. Why didn't you come in last night and Monday?'

'I dunno,' the youth said innocently. 'Dad sat about all night and never said nothink.'

The others came back and the gardening continued desultorily until seven. It was half-past before Arthur settled down again in the parlour. He had intended having a full evening at logic, but his mind was in no fit state to examine the exercises he had set himself to analyse. He could not get a nervous anger out of himself; fierce thoughts would rise in his brain and run out to fasten themselves on the man talking loudly in the other room. He put Dr. Stebbing on one side, and

began running through the Virgil book set for the
examination. But he could not satisfy himself. If he
had a weak subject it was Logic, and he ought to have
stuck at it.

They all were in the garden again the next night and
Friday, and not a great deal was done. There were
two fairly big stretches—one bordering Main Street,
another Top Street; half of the former was done by
Friday. Arthur worked all day Saturday until five
o'clock, then shaved and had his tea, and went to meet
Nancy in Pirley.

'Do you want to go to the pictures?' Arthur asked
her, when she came to him at the top of King Street
across from the Hippodrome. 'I've been stuck at my
books all day, and a walk would do me good.'

'I don't want to walk about in the dark three or four
hours,' she said definitely. 'Besides, there's a good picture on here.'

'All right,' he replied, and they went in. 'I'll walk
down with you after.'

'Are you coming to-morrow?' she asked, when they
were down Nessfield Hill. 'If you've been working all
to-day, I should think you could do with a break.'

'No, I shan't come. No.' He was silent for a while.
'I've had to go in the garden every night this week,
and I'm behind. I've done no Roman history at all
this week.'

'*Had* to go in the garden,' she repeated. 'Who made
you? You're old enough to please yourself, aren't you?'

He was silent again, not knowing what to say. It
would mean bringing his mother into it, her helpless
misery, if he said his step-father made him go in the
garden. Nancy would say, 'You're not afraid of him,

are you?' He wasn't afraid of him, but the girl would want to know why, then, he went in the garden at his bidding. Oh, he didn't know what to say.

'Well, we all have to take our whack,' he said, at length. 'More in, sooner the thing's finished.' He felt ashamed somehow of this utterance. Both thoughts were mere echoes of what had been said to him. 'But when we have a holiday on a Wednesday, I shall come. I told you so, you know.' Silence again. 'We might have one next Wednesday. Did you go out in the week?'

'No. I didn't. Fanny came up on Wednesday, but we stayed in. I thought you might come.'

'If I do come on Wednesdays and Sundays, Nancy, I shan't get through.' He blurted the words uncontrolledly.

'Don't come, then, you silly,' she told him, evenly. 'I'm all right. I shall be here when you do.'

'Good. I like you for saying that. I'll love you a lot down the fields.'

She laughed and he was glad. He pulled her to him and kissed her impulsively. In the fields he held her close, silent, richly soothed. She was not content with his resting.

'I thought you were going to love me a lot,' she whispered.

'I am doing, really.'

'Well, I'm not enjoying it.'

Her body movements made him daring. He was weaker than usual and she was easy in helping. When he was leaving her she clung for a moment.

'Couldn't you come to-morrow?'

He was angry at himself and did not answer.

'Never mind,' she continued, with brave consideration. 'I know you would if you could.' She laughed
at her words. 'I shall manage a week, now.' She kissed
him fiercely. 'That is, if you love me like that again.'

He went after he had forced himself to return her
kiss.

'Good night, dear,' he said, but was still angry, even
though he spoke gently.

He sat in the bus wondering at his new experience.
It kept him alone over the fields from Pirley to Peathill
and along the hard highway to Wingrove. Fear sprang
to his throat at intervals, and he attempted to get rid
of it with a slight turn of his lip and a shrug. He tried
to be as he usually was, walking home, concentrating
on some likely question in the examination; but it was
hopeless to-night, bigger things surged, surging and
drowning the dry lines of thought.

At Trentingham the next Monday, he felt the inter-
ference and was astounded. He forced himself to the
routine of note-taking in the lecture-rooms and library,
but in the afternoon he came to himself, staring at a
window where the rain beat. When he left at five-
thirty, students hurried past him down the long, curving
drive between the mounds and the flats of bright,
freshened grass. He sauntered through the rain, not
caring; the world was upside down, the garden, his
step-father, Nancy, all pulling him away from his
studying just when the last strong effort was needed.
And the pit was making full-time when he could have
done with a holiday or two.

The next day, Tuesday, he had recovered most of his
confidence, and satisfied himself in his work at college
and the three hours he put in when he got home. On

Wednesday, Thursday and Friday, he was in the garden
again with his brothers and their father. The man did
not help with the potato-setting. He spent the whole
evening on Wednesday at the seed-beds, Thursday with
beans and peas. He began straightening the hedge-
bottom at the end of the garden on Friday for the first
half-hour, but a man looked over and spoke to him,
stopped, and the two stood talking for almost an hour.
Arthur was doing most of the digging. Sidney helped
when he was not carrying manure and covering-up.
Albert merely stuck in the potatoes.

'Why the devil doesn't he come and help a bit?'
Arthur burst out at length to nobody in particular, but
loud enough for his stepfather to hear. 'We s'll never
get the damn garden finished.' Anger flung out the
words; it had been pressing them outwards for a long
time, until he had been weak enough to let them escape.

'Good night, Sam,' Mr. Shirley said, after a few
minutes. His conversation had deteriorated to mere
monosyllables after his stepson's words had shot
between him and the man on the road. It was a quick
'good night'; the youths felt a relief in it, as if their
father was half away already.

'Good night,' the man said, and Mr. Shirley came
across to the gardeners. Arthur felt somewhat scared
for a moment. He had said too much, too strongly.

'What the hell do you reckon you're sayin', eh?' He
was close to Arthur; angry because he had felt a fool
before Sam Braithwaite; strong in the knowledge that
the young man's peace of mind was dependent on him.
Albert was grinning slyly. Sidney glanced nervously at
the two. 'What's it got to do with you what I do?
Mind your own damn business.'

'Well, I don't want to be stuck in here every night till July. I'm getting behind with my work.' Arthur's tone was strong, though not pugnacious. He felt he must stand his ground, yet allow the other his authority. 'If we all set into it we could have both gardens finished in a week.'

'We've got to suit you, eh?'

'You didn't come in on Monday or Tuesday. Seems as if you wait for me.'

'It rained on Monday, you know that, Arth,' Albert said. 'It wasn't fit until Wednesday.'

'You needn't make excuses,' his father snapped. 'We come in when we like, and 'e comes in when 'e's told.'

'And what if I didn't come in?'

'Yes, my lad. I want to see you do that. You'd do no more studyin' in the parlour. I'd break every gas mantle, and there'd be no more put on. There'd be no fire in, either.' Arthur was digging the whole time. He was thrusting his anger down with each foot-pressing on the spade. He was beaten, the fool had the victory every time. The man had always his studies or his mother as weapons to thrash him with.

'Hm. You would,' the young man muttered.

'Yes, I should. And if you wanted to study, you could get some digs where they'd supply you with fire and light till midnight.'

'Oh, come on, dad,' Sidney broke in fearfully. 'Let's get this row in.'

'Tryin' to work at the pit, and go to college, and see to a woman. 'E'll 'ave nothing when it's all weighed up —it'll be madhouse sooner than the University.'

'We'll see,' Arthur commented.

They worked on, no one spoke; only the scraping of the nailed pit-boots on the spades, the dry shuffling about the soil sounded. When they went in, Arthur changed his boots, washed his hands, and walked into the parlour at once. Sidney came in while his father and Albert took away the tools.

'Arth and my dad's been on again,' he told his mother.

'What about?' she asked quickly, her lips tightening.

'Oh. Arth started about 'im gossipin' over the 'edge with Mr. Braithwaite instead of 'elpin' us. An' my dad swore at 'im. Said he'd break gas mantles in t'parlour and not let 'im 'ave a fire if 'e grumbled about comin' in the garden.'

She turned from the youth and went to Arthur in the front room. Fear and anger pulled her features tense.

'You've been on again, have you?' She was condemning him fiercely. Love was driving her, was insulted that one where it rested in sacredness and comfort should have so illogically, so foolishly sprung pain through it. 'You ought to have had more sense. Bickering and doing. You'll never have any peace.' Her features closed again tensely. 'Besides, can't you see you're pulling me in two?' It was in her mind to say what she felt at the moment as her living-level fell suddenly. 'Can't you see it's killing me?' But she pulled herself upwards again from the melting feel of sentimentalism and closed her mouth tightly.

'I can stand so much and no more,' he replied impatiently. 'He's dragging out the gardening to keep me from my studying. I'm sure he is.'

'You can't say that. The garden has to be done and

4

every one has to do a share. You don't mind that, surely.'

'He didn't make me go in when I was swotting for Matric. He doesn't like the idea of me getting out of the pit. I know.'

'Well. You be careful. He'll have the first word and the last. You'll gain nothing by rowing.'

'I s'll gain nothing by letting go all that I've done.'

She left him and he turned to his work. He was in the parlour all Saturday morning and afternoon. His brothers went to a football match, the father pottered about the garden. He looked up from the bean-row when Arthur walked on the 'end' at five o'clock to meet Nancy in Pirley. The youth knew the meaning of the glance.

# CHAPTER III

IT was twenty minutes to eight on a Monday morning in late May. Arthur Gardner picked up the small attaché case he had packed with books the night before, and stood ready to go. His mother was bent to the fire, the sun shooting narrowly through the small south window glinted her hair, and he marked the grey streaks along the straight hair drawn from her forehead, winding among the 'bun' at the nape of her neck. The tone of his mood fell suddenly, heavy thoughts rolled through him, damping the wide, cheerful air which was his usual emotional atmosphere on the mornings when he was setting out for Trentingham, pressing the quick cheerfulness into a painful anger. Many centres shot into the embracing ugliness holding him, and he flashed from one to the other—his mother was one, his stepfather, Nancy, the pit—and each particularly, all generally, were pulling at him, pulling back as he strained forward towards a smooth level of content. His anger was not fastened on to any of these centres; he was merely impatient of the pit and his step-father; he loved his mother and Nancy, but it was the obstructing emotions which he was compelled to experience because they were all important streams washing through him. All that the greyness in his mother's hair implied shot anger through him, his helplessness before them pained him.

'I'm going, then, mum,' he said abruptly. She looked up. 'Back about seven. 'Morning.'

''Morning,' she replied, and looked him up and down quickly. 'Your shoes aren't extra clean.'

'They'll do,' he gave back, and went.

He walked down the empty, silent village, in and out of the rosy flood of sunlight splashing between houses, up the slow slope to Hillcross where he would wait for the bus from Pirley and Condor. He faced the sun all the way. He stood across from the hundred years' old church, glancing occasionally up Condor Hill for the bus. It came, and when the conductor had collected his fare, he opened his case and took out a book. Invariably he read parts of a history or literary history book during the hour's jolting ride to Trentingham. But this morning he let the book rest idly in his hands. He couldn't read, couldn't think straight. Everything seemed to be attacking him at once. A month in the garden, almost every evening for a month. He'd jibbed once or twice, and there'd been a row between him and his step-father. Yet it was his mother who seemed to feel the worst effects of it. He couldn't study when she was suffering. Still, the garden was finished, now; that was one thing out of the way. But Nancy. He glanced through the window. They were running down from Heanor into the valley of dirty rows of houses. Up, now, to Eastwood. The bus stopped in the market-place. Arthur looked through a gap in the buildings, down a steep hill opening into the wide valley of woods and fields of 'Sons and Lovers'. The bus moved on. He glanced down the street where Lawrence was born; a shabby street with flat-faced houses and a grimy chapel. All the adult students in his group at Trentingham were crazy over Lawrence. Nancy was like some of the women in his books—well, she had been lately—sex-driven out of all balance. She could think of nothing but the pictures on Saturday evenings at one time. Now he couldn't get her near, except about once a month. They must go and lie in the fields, or prop themselves up against stiles and fences. And last Saturday she had asked him to tea, and her father and mother had gone out at six o'clock. It would have to stop. He'd stand no earthly chance of passing the exam, feeling as he did. What with that and the heavy work at the pit and his late studying at night.

They ran on towards Kimberley. On the right, the 'Rainbow' country spread in flats and ugly lumps up to Ilkeston on the hill. Lawrence doubtless roamed about here, feeling penned-in by his existence as a student and teacher, driven or pulled to another expression, the real expression of himself. He felt the same about his pit life: it was an obstruction to his real self. He must get free, must get to a satisfying level of all books and continuous teaching. He had to be aware of the other side of it, for Nancy's sake—the security, the raised social tone; but that didn't matter, really. He was no snob; he seemed to realise even as he thought, and was content to know, that, however far he reached from the practical atmosphere of his class, he would still be one of them, no better than the miner conscious of life. He didn't want to be, either. Examples of climbing deputies and under-managers shot to his mind and shuddered him.

The bus ran into the city, he changed over to a tram, and in ten minutes was at the college gates. Quarter-past nine rung from the thin tower as he passed from the sun-glowing drive into the chill shadow of the building, then down the steps into the cloakroom and the

thick warmth of the men's common-room. It was long
and narrow, overlooking the lake and the boulevard.
Two doors let into it, each immediately by the short
wall of the room. Arthur went through the first he
came to, and walked close by the wall to the window
where a group of young and middle-aged men sat about
a small table. The rest of the long stretch gowned
youths filled, moving about, sitting awkwardly without
thought of resting, books in their hands or on the table
near, laughing, talking. The men Arthur approached
seemed less alive.

''Morning, Gardner,' some of them greeted, the
others were engrossed in conversation, some talking
politics, some about the day's lectures.

''Morning. Hello, Dave,' he said, to a stocky Welshman who sat with his back to him and had not seen him
come up. 'Still harping on going to the barricades?'

''Morning, Arthur. You'd be a damn sight more
help if you'd more fire in you,' he laughed. 'No, I'm
not on about the barricades, but they're the only things
that'll put us where we belong. I was just telling
Bob, here, a thing or two about Matric. He takes it
in June, and thinks he'll walk through.'

'It's not so easy,' Arthur commented.

'I've learned three hundred French words this week-
end,' Bob said. He was swarthy, had a fine mop of
hair, and a hanging under lip. 'Logic's only common
sense; I'm not frightened of that.'

'You'll not find your common sense carry you far if
it's a paper like I had,' Arthur said. 'It's all memory
stuff.'

'Coming, Arthur?' David Neil said, as he left his
chair. 'It's time. What's yours—Latin?' Gardner

nodded. 'Mine's Economic History.' They climbed the stairs to B corridor. Bob Peel was behind, loud with an idea important to himself.

'If I get through Matric, I reckon it wouldn't be a bad idea to get on the dole for a year and sock at Inter. Then I could come here full-time, and soon have my degree.'

'Oh, give it a rest, Bob,' Neil said, turning his head. 'Get through Matric first.' He was continuing up the next flight to C level. Gardner's room was on B. 'See you at eleven, then, Gardner.'

Arthur turned with others into the Latin lecture-room, and there was a scramble for the back row of chairs. He never dashed about; he felt faintly out of it among these young, soft-skinned youths and maidens who seemed always to be laughing and playing. Yet they came to the lectures with easy, intelligent discussion and plainly pertinent difficulties to be solved. He had watched some of them in the library and he liked them better there, their young faces composed and alone, beautiful they all were in study. There was pain in his studying, always something waiting on the fringes of his mind to disturb him. Most of these would move easily through Inter, through Finals. He was hacking his way, every step, but he neither felt nor saw anything heroic in it; he was moving towards his satisfaction. There was a sort of gladness, though, in the reaching forward. To have mastered a phase of Logic—this week he had stuck at the chapter on Causation and could think intelligently about it—was to have given his being a good, sound meal, and to be conscious of it as a strengthening of his growth. But he would be glad when all the examinations he had to take were over, and he could take off the blinkers which forced his attention to set things. Then——

'Good morning, Mr. Gardner.'

A girl was in the chair next, and she was smiling when Arthur looked up. She was a doctor's daughter, a settled type of girl, not a 'swot', but one who seemed to be unable to loose herself from a certain quiet dignity. She was not handsome, but in her eyes and mouth was that incomprehensible attraction of the essential woman; in others the physical allurements must have fallen away before such could shine from them. In her it was there at once, always; people fused with her immediately or not at all. Arthur liked her; she did not disturb as did the others with their boisterousness, though he liked them, too, and joked with them. He was the only one of the male adult group who did mix with some sort of freedom among the full-time students. The rest kept to their corner in the common-room, apparently not heeding the younger members of the college, but there was a feeling of antagonism pricking each individually. It pained one so badly on a certain afternoon, that he complained to the others about it, and there was a common, secret crying. In the discussion class on Tuesday afternoon they poured out the bitterness to the head of their department, bringing a concern to his face—rather a sad concern. Not on account of the circumstance that the college youths and girls 'cold-shouldered' them, and would not 'mix'— he dismissed the thought at once, knowing it to be utterly false—but that the men, the working men from the pit and factory, whom he was attempting to help to deserved higher levels of life, were moving upwards with their brains only; the realness of them was holding back in awkwardness and suspicion. He told them plainly and at once they were mistaken; they themselves were holding away from the younger students, perhaps. Arthur had said he could not imagine them thinking such things, and the head seemed glad of his support. But the adult group kept to themselves, kept to their corner in the common-room, clung together round a couple of tables in the refectory at lunch-time, or walked in a bunch to the public-house in Dunchurch.

'You'd a rare neck telling the head that, I must say,' Arthur laughed to some of the others when the meeting broke up. 'The three women looked flabbergasted. And he didn't know what to say, either.'

'It's true, whether he didn't know what to say or not,' a thin, croaky-voiced man said. 'They look sideways at us sittin' in that corner. When they run into you they apologise as if it was a stranger.'

'Nay, Tom. You think that,' David Neil said. 'Head was right, it's we who hold away from them. Still, we've all got a touch of the inferiority in us. We're frightened of them.'

'They're more afraid of you, of us,' Arthur broke in. 'Besides, most of 'em think us marvellous slogging in the pit all day and then swotting for the same exams as them.'

'They all call us "Mister"; they don't think of us as being the same as them. We're away from 'em, I tell you—we're dirty colliers.' This was Green croaking again.

'That's all rubbish,' Arthur butted in impatiently. 'You're the snob. I get on all right with them, both sexes. And they call me "Mister".' He laughed.

It was Miss Fleming saying, 'Good morning, Mr.

Gardner', which had flashed these remembrances through his mind. His smile responding to her's was rather more humorous than he was wont to greet with; the 'Mister' seemed to tickle him slightly.

'Good morning.' The silver-haired professor was swishing through the door and on to the dais. 'Hope you've got the next hundred lines off. It'll be sure to be our turn to construe this morning.' He nodded towards the old man arranging his books and opening the register. 'He ticks them off in the register as they construe. Only about four of us left.'

She laughed, and turned her face forward, waiting for her name to be called.

'*Adsuu*,' she cried softly, then turned to Arthur again. 'I hope he doesn't call on me. I've skipped my Latin this week.'

'Mr. Gardner.'

'*Adsum.*'

'Mr. Williams.'

'*Adsum.*'

The tutor closed the register and rustled open his Virgil. The students in the chairs below rattled theirs on to the desks.

'Let me see. Line four hundred and two, I think. Yes. Would you begin, Miss Plant?'

Arthur followed the text for a few lines as the girl jerked it into 'crib' English, revealing how Corœbus, seeing Cassandra taken, rushed at the foe and died. Then he glanced sideways at Miss Fleming, marked the quiet repose of her mouth and understanding eyes bent down to her book. She had taken off her gown; it hung over the back of her chair. Her red knitted jumper clung to the curves of her back and breast, the tweed skirt shaped her smoothly. Arthur suddenly saw the naked body pressing outward into the clothes, and life leapt through him vividly. Then he jerked away his eyes angrily, ashamed. He glanced about the room, at the other girls. He strained with himself to see them in true perspective, but he could not tone down the emphasis his eyes carried to his mind. He had to mark the postures, the dignified which needed breaking, the careless, inviting. All the phrases of the worst kind of 'pit-talk' flooded swiftly through him and he felt sick. He was a fool, this new experience with Nancy had unbalanced him, the obstructionist attitude of his stepfather, his mother's frightened eyes and tense mouth. He'd have to pull himself together or——

'Mr. Gardner, would you continue, please?'

He swept his eyes to the open book before him, but there seemed a haze clotting the characters of each word. He blinked strongly twice, and got purpose in his gaze.

'What line is it?' he muttered, to the girl beside him.

'Four-three-one.'

His glance ran down the page where the morning work had begun. He felt a warmth thicken his flesh as he fumbled to turn over.

"O Ilian ashes, and funeral fires of my kin . . ."

Arthur knew the text almost by heart, and translated easily. But his tone was hurried, nervous, the splendid and affecting rhetoric of Aeneas was almost galloped. He was glad when the quiet 'Thank you' came from the dais, though it gave leave for the burning confusion, the shame, the anger to flush him again. He was full of bitterness, self-condemnation. Nothing had ever been allowed to intrude into his periods of study,

whether at home or college; no hour spent with Nancy
had been stolen from his mapped-out syllabus. But
everything seemed to be going wrong. Still, it was his
own fault. There was his individual line stretching
ahead through life, and if he didn't keep strongly to it,
he'd have to suffer, and that was all there was to it.
But it was agonising to think away his contacts, Nancy,
his mother. . . .

The low time-buzzer on the wall bored into his
mind; books closing brought him back to his own.
He took it up and waited for the usual Roman history
question to be given.

'Write a short account of Jugurtha and Roman
politics, and hand it in next Monday. Thank you.'

The professor collected his books and left the room,
the students crowding after him. Arthur went along to
the top corridor where the Logic lecture would begin
in ten minutes. He was glad to find some of the adult
students there. They had just finished a first-year Logic
lecture, and would be leaving in a few minutes.

'Hello, Gardner. Come and give us a few hints.
What are these Laws of Thought?' A man of forty
had looked up from a note-book with a puzzled
expression to ask the question.

'Why, they're easy,' Bob Peel broke in confidently,
his under lip hanging when he had spoken. 'A cannot
be both X and not X. That's the Law of—of——
See?' The others burst into laughter as he fumbled in
the pages of his notes.

'Have three tries, Bob,' Arthur said. 'You're
bound to be right.'

Four full-time students came into the room, two of
each sex, free, laughing easily. Their conversation

continued without loss of tone and brightness in face of
the men suddenly confronting them. They passed with
unmeaning glances and flopped their books on to desks,
then went to the window still vivid and full of talk.
The adult students fell silent, seemingly damped by the
living unconcern of youth; even Arthur was, with them,
awkward in spirit. The others went out; Arthur sat at
a desk, and the tall, thin lecturer came in followed by
more students. Stott, the lecturer, invariably splashed
the long theory of his talk with comic examples.
The class was certain of entertainment at every lecture,
and friends of the members, especially those who had
been under Stott the previous year for Logic, and those
who attended him for Psychology and Philosophy
looked forward to some amusement at the lunch or
tea-table. Occasionally, the senior Logic students
grimaced. 'We had that one last year.'

Arthur enjoyed the lectures; Stott's style suited him.
The man himself was approachable: he had his eye
always on the examination syllabus. Early in the
session the old Latin lecturer had taken them for a few
lectures, and he had talked of nothing but George
Santuyana and 'essences'. The students had groaned
spiritually, then become seriously alarmed. 'We shall
never pass the exam at this rate.' To their great relief—
Arthur's especially, who got one lecture less each week
than the rest of the class—Stott resumed. He seemed
rather pleased at the circumstance and his manner
for a while was warmer than generally. To-day he
began by stressing the importance of the matter of the
lecture he would deliver—the validity of the major
premise of the syllogism—and Arthur set himself to be
single-minded. Nancy rushed into his mind even at the

moment of his resolve; he saw her in her lightest, laughing mood in the summer fields. He was a fool, he was making too much of something not abnormal, not unnatural, not extraordinary. If he were to be whole, to live wholly, he must take these things as complementing that side of his living he felt bound to emphasize. He felt more cheerful as the lecture proceeded; the atmosphere of learning soaked into him. He was as comfortable as if he had already reached the undisturbed last levels of his forward reaching. Each new thought the lecturer gave delighted him; he took it down in the note-book before him. He was conscious that by the same time next week this knowledge would be part of him. He laughed with the others at Stott's examples; he used political, social and church names in ridiculous situations. He closed his small mouth and swallowed down his long thin neck while the students' minds were on the superficiality of the example and were laughing. His wit was never studied, the examples were happy liftings in the stream of his easy and brilliant discourse. They lit up the truth he was conveying; the truth was important to him, not the example. Arthur revelled in his lectures. The young man knew he could never be as brilliant, but was not disheartened.

David Neil was in the refectory when he walked to the usual table. Bob Peel was there and other adult students.

'Stripped to the waist, your muscles not hampered by clothes, sweat pouring out of you—fit—you feel fit. It's a real feeling, you know that you exist—you're vivid, alive.'

Bob's lips were moving quickly, they were moist;

his hand beat the table emphatically. Neil's lip was curling.

'Why, Bob, you make me ill. You can have the bloody pit. I know what they can do with it if I've a chance to get away. What do you say, Gardner? Here, I've got you a coffee.'

'Same here,' Arthur said. 'I shouldn't be working as hard as I am if I didn't. Bob's gone all Lawrence, that's about it.'

'If I get Inter,' Neil said definitely, 'I've finished at Kirby in October. With a college scholarship and a class one night a week, I could manage. Have you ever asked for a class, Arthur? It's a quid a time.'

'No, I haven't. I don't know that I could manage one.'

'Manage.' Dave laughed cynically. 'I've had one this last winter, you know. Twenty-four lectures on "Some Modern Problems". It was easy. Only general stuff. These village classes aren't brain-strainers. You have to humour them, and they'll eat out of your hand. Give 'em an hour lecture, then let 'em talk. I'm digging up local history this summer—that's a cert. Tell 'em something about their own village and you're made. You could do some English, couldn't you? Literary history.' He laughed. 'I know a chap who's just done six lectures on the history of the drama—covered from the Greek to the modern in six lectures.'

'I shall ask for one next winter,' Peel said. 'There's lots wanting Economics.'

'You'd never hold 'em, Bob,' Neil said. 'They soon drop off if you don't humour them. And you've got to qualify so many for the grant.'

'How many classes are there which qualify and don't

qualify?' Peel shot out quickly. 'I can mark a register as well as anyone. I've been to classes for years —I know.'

'They're running a three years' history course in a town near us,' Arthur said. 'There's fourteen or fifteen thousand folks in the place, and the tutor couldn't get a dozen. He's an M.A., and a good chap generally. He had to go round himself with hand-bills, write to a heap of people and go and see them before he got enough to start. I can see no good in that. My idea of adult education was that you put out a notice and people flocked to the lecture, athirst for knowledge.'

'They don't,' Neil said, a trifle grimly. 'Towards the end of my course I'd got eleven to qualify, and I wanted twelve. There was one woman who could qualify, but she began to miss. I'd got to get her to the last four, so I went to the place earlier than usual and called on her, sat with her and talked nicely to her. She was flattered enough to come, and I got the grant. Shouldn't have got any more lectures if I hadn't.'

'I went to classes,' Tom Green, the croaky-voiced one, said. 'I went because I knew these Miners' Welfare Scholarships were goin'. I'm not takin' Matric— couldn't get it if I did. But it's two days' rest from t'pit every week, and a good chance of a free week at a summer school.'

'You're a fine specimen of an adult student,' Neil laughed. 'You know what the ideal of these scholarships is, don't you? That after one of these courses a man can go back into industry better equipped for his work, not then having only a work-outlook but a living-outlook.'

'That's what you got a scholarship for, isn't it?'

Green gave back in equal humour. 'You're going to get Inter and chuck the pit—Gardner is, Bob is. Why don't you go back and use it in t'trade union work?'

'I would if I could get county secretary job, or the treasurer's, but I'm not slogging my guts out at the coal face. I do want to help my class. If I get a lecturing job, I shall preach communism and trade unionism, but I'm looking after myself first.'

'I can't see as they do want helping,' a comfortable, complaining-toned man said across from Neil and Arthur. 'All chaps I've worked with seem satisfied enough. But if somebody said, "We'll go on strike for more money", they'd come out. If they had their wages dropped, and the same "leader", as they call him, says, "Nothing can be done"—well, they'd just keep on workin'.'

'Well, I'm not arguing with you,' Neil said evenly, but with obvious biting anger. 'When you said that, I felt as if I'd throw all exams on one side and go shout about the god-awful system until I went crazy. Why, you . . .' He pushed his chair away. 'Come on, Gardner, let's get out into the fresh air. Ugh.' They went through the long refectory window on the sloping lawns and down to the water's edge. 'What do you reckon of a sod like him?' Neil was writhing.

'I know why you're angry, Dave but I couldn't be angry at a remark like that—I couldn't, really. I can't grasp the idea of class, somehow. I never know a man as a miner or a coal-owner; they're just individuals to me, pushing forward through life.'

'We know they are, you damned fool,' Neil said. 'But if one man had no bread and another was kicking loaves about, what then?'

5

'Oh, I know, Dave. There's a lot in that. There's something in what Langley said as well. I'm glad I'm not like either of you with your emphasized feels of indifference on the one hand, and contact on the other. What he won't recognize is that there are others besides himself; you that there are others besides your particular clique. There are poets and painters and authors in each of the classes you divide men into; there are Labour men who have money enough to be Tories, and there are working-class Tories. You say the rich Labour men are "real" men, you sneer cynically at the working-class Tories. I can't understand it at all.'

'Working-class Tories are creepers, that's all there is to be said for them.'

'Could you think that the rich Labour men have come down knowing they can satisfy their itch for importance and authority—a thing they couldn't get in their own class?'

'You're going to justify MacDonald and Jimmy Thomas soon.' Neil stopped and leaned over the stone veranda ; the breeze-driven water beneath them glinted in the sunlight, it sloshed unmusically against the smooth concrete. 'We'll chuck talking about it.'

'I'm justifying nobody—I'm condemning nobody. You have your politics and divide men into whatever classes you like. I know how I divide them. There are the wise and the not-wise, those whose beings are emphasized towards consideration for others, those who lean more to themselves. It may sound pessimistic, even fatalistic, but I think a person is born into one of these classes, and—well, he's in it. According to my theory, you see what a hell of a struggle's going on——'

'And you think you're one of the wise, eh?'

'Now, Dave don't be nasty. If you think about it, you might see how all your superficial party and class wars have their roots in my theory. And the toleration —and the attempts at peace by the wise.' Arthur laughed, and broke off as a young man came up.

'How are you feeling about July, you two?' he asked.

'I don't know,' Neil said. 'I've gone through all my stuff, now, and am going to rush through a revision of it. I'm beginning to see things, though. Diagrams and chapter headings dancing along the coal-face. Think I s'll go on the club until a week or so before the exam.'

The young man laughed. He was clean and smooth; Neil said he always reminded him of Harry Wharton in the *Magnet*. He was an adult student; had been a clerk until a year ago, when he took an Economics degree and was put on the Adult Education Department staff. He lectured Monday and Tuesday in college, to the adult students; the rest of the week he prepared lectures in the day-time, and in the evening went to some village or town and lectured to a class.

'I shouldn't overdo it these last few weeks,' he said. 'My firm were pretty decent over my finals. They let me have a fortnight off before the exam, and paid me for it.'

'Different from mine,' Arthur said at once. 'When I got the scholarship the first year, one of the directors was glad, he said, and sent word to our pit that my wages should be paid for the two days I came here. But the boss never put it in, and when I mentioned it, he said he had to keep the working costs down and couldn't afford it.'

'Why didn't you go and see the director?' Neil burst out.

'I wrote to him, but my letters never seemed to reach him. Besides, the boss never liked the idea of having a spare man down the pit especially for me. When I'm away—and I should think all the others are in the same boat—another chap has to do my job, and then there's one to spare the rest of the week. I daresay some bosses are all right. Mine isn't. I have to be careful, and rather subdued, when he's about. S'll be glad when I'm out of it. I thought your job was guaranteed when you had one of these scholarships, but it isn't, I can see that.'

'Well, I shall have to go,' the graduate said. 'Got a lecture. So long.'

The two leaned over the water in silence for a few moments. Neil took a packet of cigarettes from his pocket, gave Arthur one and lit them both, then threw the empty packet in the water. Two girls were standing a few yards away. David glanced sideways at them, then spat at the small box floating beneath them.

'Bit o' nice stuff there. Shouldn't mind stickin' that far-side one up against a stile. Look at her, how quick she is, every bit of her moving. She'll be like that until some chap takes to her, then she'll be as still as a mouse.' He threw his cigarette in the water. 'Still, I couldn't do her much good as I feel, now. Slogging at the pit, sitting up half the night, smoking and drinking coffee to keep me waken.'

'I dip my head in a bucket of cold water about ten if I intend staying up,' Arthur said.

'Look at her, she's climbing all over her pal. Christ!

Look at her. She's almost eating that chap who's coming towards her. Bet she stops him. I knew.' He felt against his pocket for a cigarette-packet. 'Must get some fags, then we'll go in the library until lunch.' They turned and climbed back to the refectory window. 'Do you have anything to do with women, Gardner?'

'I've got a girl, if that's what you mean. I'm not promiscuous like you.' He laughed shortly.

'I thought you were one of these true-love blokes. Just a bit of cling in you. Might have been a Methodist parson with a quiet, wistful wife and a careful number of kids. Still, you can't help it. I'm condemning nobody for what they are. I sometimes wish I'd got this certain steadiness which holds one to one thing.'

'And I wish, sometimes, that I hadn't a tie in the world. But I know I shall always have.'

'Don't you be too sure about that,' Neil said quickly, and there was something in his tone which suggested that all his strength was false, was not of his essence, that his vaunted sure aloneness was surface stuff. 'You're one of those who, if ever they're turned off their track'll put a barrier up that nobody will break through—become the most pig-headed, hateful swine alive, or the most cheerful hermit God made.' They passed through the long french window into the coffee-stained air of the refectory. 'You'd either go crazy at once or not at all.' 'Ten Players,' he said to the woman at the buffet, and put a sixpence on the counter. They walked out and up the stairs to the library. 'And if I were you, I should leave women alone till I was through with my degree. I shall, although there's a woman chases me about all week-end. Not a bad tart, and her folks have a bit of money. But I'm getting out of the pit first.'

Arthur pushed open the library door and they passed in. Their feet at once lost the stepping sound; students sat like statues at tables by the windows in the section alcoves round the walls.

'I'll get Bradley and come over to you there,' he said, motioning to an empty alcove. 'Must get a question up on Shakespearian tragedy in general.'

'I'll get Trevelyan, though I'll bet somebody's got it.'

Some one had, but he brought a substitute which he swore about, and they worked till lunch-time. In the afternoon both went to the History lecture over which the Scotch tutor presided. He sat comfortably at his task, and gave out historical information with a complete detachment. After a series of dry facts about some point, he would cut himself off into silence and sit looking at the group with half-closed eyes, and with a sort of smile on closed lips. Then with a sound, beginning low and curving into an almost feminine tone which sounded like 'We-ell', he began another series of facts. He amused Arthur, irritated Neil, who wanted every lecture rich with facts for examination.

'I tell you things which have not yet been put between the covers of history books,' the lecturer was fond of saying. 'Here is something.' Then, with quiet importance, he would begin on a long ramble which made Neil groan.

Facts, important, incidental, humorous, cynical, all came out on one slow, bland tone. He knew his subject thoroughly, covered every inquiry with a fullness and point which called up admiration in some of the students. Sometimes he was plain in language, almost to the point of embarrassment for one or two of the feminine members. To-day, in his revision of the course, he was dealing with the Black Death and its economic results.

'The huge death-rate was not such an amazing thing. The people invited the plague, and fed it when it was among them. Throwing their slops through the bedroom window into the middle of the road. What could they expect?'

He was looking over the class with the whimsical air; most of the students held their eyes to note-books before them, grinning silently. Arthur glanced sideways at Miss Fleming. Her eyelids were moving strongly, her head was bent and her cheeks hung, making her mouth open and heavy with disgust. She took no more notes, and when she walked out and along the corridor with Gardner and Neil, she turned to them with open face, the corners of her mouth moving slightly.

'I shall go to no more of his lectures,' she said definitely. 'He says such unnecessary things—he's disgusting.'

'That's the sort you get here, you see, Gardner,' David said, when she had left them and they were moving past the refectory doors to the cloak-room. 'It seems to justify our sticking to our own table here and our corner in the common-room. We have to be on our guard always when we mix with these kids— there's something funny comes over their faces if we let ourselves go as we do in the pit.' His tone was becoming warmer, a touch of cynicism slowed it. 'They look away and laugh from their throats for a moment, and they're soon off. They know all about things we talk about, and they might be free among themselves about them, but I doubt it—sex, and everything off family-table talk'll be individual to them all their lives. It's the class. To them the working class is coarse.'

'Why, most of them come from working-class families,' Arthur said. 'And, besides, they don't understand themselves yet. I'm not much for dirty talk, either, if you mean it is that which makes them look funny in the face.'

'There's no such thing as "dirty talk", in fact. What he said was dirty talk to the Fleming dame—it seemed polite to me.'

'Ah, well. She's rather more particular than the majority.' They collected their clothes from the cloakroom and walked together down the curving drive.

'I don't think Miss Fleming's worrying about getting Inter. She told me she's trying to get to Oxford.'

'S'truth. Some of these bourgeoisie don't know what they do want. Nibbling at six or seven things at once and not bothering about any. And here Inter's life or death to us. There's something frightening about the thought of failing and going back to the pit the morning after the result, without hope of ever getting away.' His voice became serious. 'You know, if we fail, they'll not renew our scholarships again.'

'I know that. There's plenty more miners wanting a chance.'

They continued to the 'bus in silence, rode to the city and parted. The thought remained with Arthur; he concentrated desperately on a book all the long bus ride to Hillcross. Riding to Trentingham next morning, he was single-minded to his study, and when he got home in the evening, and his mother told him that Shenton pit, where he worked, was holidaying the next day, he began an essay and worked at his Latin grammar exercises, which kept him up till midnight.

'Have we to "sign" this morning?' he asked of Sidney at breakfast.

'No. It's no good. If we holiday on Friday they'll let us sign back.'

'Good,' Arthur said, with pleasure. 'I'll stick at my Logic this morning, my History this afternoon, and go out a bit to-night.'

'Come down on to the Park with me and Albert and have a knock at cricket.'

'No. Think I shall walk to Nessfield.'

But when he had had tea, he thought of the five hours until ten o'clock, of the pages he could cover, the questions he could get up; it pulled him away from Nancy. Not that she was banished from all thought; he merely set her apart, waiting while he worked for her, worked for them both. At half-past ten, when he closed the book in which he had answered two literary history questions he had set himself, he went to bed satisfied. He felt almost as if Nancy was rejoicing with him over the good night's work.

The girl was waiting for him when he reached the top of King Street at six o'clock on Saturday evening. He smiled and grasped her hand as he stood at her side; he saw her physically to a greater degree than ever before. Like a flash the clear vision of himself and David Neil on the terrace at college swept across his mind, the 'bit of nice stuff' the Welshman had pointed out, her climbings about her friend.

'Hello, darling,' he said. 'Pictures to-night?'

'Nothing on, either here'—she turned and nodded towards the Hippodrome—'or the Empire. Been round to see.'

'We'll go a walk, then.' They moved towards the market. 'Chocolates?' She nodded. 'We'll go round Pentland and back through the Hollow.'

They went down a street and into the fields by the vicarage, then over the canal up to Pentland, a still, clean village of stone houses and blossoming damson orchards. Nancy had held him about the waist coming up the fields; she loosed him as they gained the village street, and seemed away from him in manner almost with the physical breaking.

'Your pit had a holiday on Wednesday, didn't it? Had you to go?'

He was taken aback for a moment, not gauging the mood behind her tone. Her countenance was plain, when he shot a side-glance at her. He laughed suddenly, apologetically.

'You're getting at me for not coming, eh?' He squeezed her to him, but she did not respond. 'You're not angry, are you?' He bent to look into her face. 'I felt just like doing some real work. I worked hard in the morning and afternoon, intending to come in the evening.' He laughed shortly. 'But—well——'

'But what.' Her voice was even, no anger, no disappointment was in it. 'It didn't matter that I waited in all night.'

'I'm sorry, dear.' He said nothing more; he hoped that conveyed to her the sentiment he had uttered many times before.

'O.K.' Her reply was short, her arm tightened about his, and they walked into the open parkland. He felt that she was washed utterly of any ill-feeling which could have been with her, was clean of any malice. His love worked richly as they stood under a lonely tree and she guided his demonstrativeness to her own way. He was angry suddenly as they walked on, a flashing suspicion dashed upon his mind that she had worked for love in that way. And he had meant to withstand her, to keep himself strong and easy in conscience.

'What are you so glum about?' she asked, as he kept silent down the hill into the Hollow.

'Oh, nothing. I'm not glum; I was thinking.'

'What about?'

'Oh, nothing.' He brightened. 'Shall come on Wednesday if we holiday. Or it might be Thursday: the pit might holiday Tuesday and Thursday. I'll let you know.'

They stood in the darkness near the Maugham home. The girl was strong about him again. He held himself in silence.

'I'll go,' he said at length. 'My bus's about due.'

'Wait till the next.'

'No.'

'All right.' She broke from him at once, and walked away for a dozen paces, sensed that he had not moved, turned and came back. He held her close, and she kissed him purely. 'All right. Good night. See you on Sat. if not before.'

'Good night, Nancy.'

He went up the fields, his head bent, thinking vaguely. He was a fool, somehow. She was moving along the ordinary course of love and courtship, and he was both on it and off it at the same time. He was a funny bloke. He was hungry for her, was hungry for learning; he suffered for his mother. He needed three whole lives, and he was trying to push them all into one. He was accursed in some peculiar way; he'd never be happy. His spirits began to fall as these thoughts pulled at him walking up the dim fields to Peathill. He was conscious that his limbs were heavy, his eyes hard, his brain burning a little. He tripped over a stone in the uneven path and almost fell head-long. Anger flooded him quickly at the shock. It was all his own fault; he ought to be as selfish as hell; he ought to cut himself off from everything until after the exam. David Neil could have done; the majority of the others could have done, too. They had not so much of the 'soft' in them; they were not turned in upon themselves like he was. He was conscious that Nancy was rooted to him, that his mother was, that there was tragedy for his being if he should betray any relation. But if he could only rest on those relations with Nancy and his mother, and not be always disturbed by them, if they could be there and certain while he fulfilled himself in his essential drive. It seemed impossible, though, and he must take them as they were, the girl with her humanness, the woman with her environment. He wanted them both as much as he wanted the self-satisfaction. He was born to burn for things he loved, and the burning drove him on, fastening him to these things. But the burning, even as it drove, strengthened him, weakened him.

# CHAPTER IV

As soon as he walked into the house from college on Tuesday, Arthur asked his mother if the pit was holidaying the next day.

'Yes,' she replied. 'Why?' Though, even as she asked, she seemed to sense the reason for his question.

'I'll drop Nancy a postcard telling her I'll go along to-morrow night.' He set down his case, and snapped the pen from his pocket, then went to the sideboard drawer for a post card.

'What about your tea?' she demanded, with a touch of envious concern. 'It's ready.'

'I'll have it when I've run down to the post. Shall only just catch it.' He sat at the table, and scribbled on both sides the card, reached a stamp from his wallet, and licked it as he went out. 'The postman was at the box,' he said, when he came back quarter of an hour later. 'And he was late at that.'

'Racing about all over the place,' she said with warmth. 'You're trying to do too much, my lad. You'll see. Pit, college, courting. I'm surprised at you. Nancy knows what you've got on these next few weeks; she'll not mind if you don't go.'

'Now, look here, mum,' he said pleasantly, his gladness was in that he had caught the post. 'I shall work until eleven to-night, get up about nine in the morning and . . . ' He broke off. 'Have we to sign?' he continued quickly, with patent uncertainty of mind.

'No, you haven't. Get that tea.'

'Oh. Good.' He began his meal. 'I shall work from ten till half-past five. Look what a lot I shall have got through by then; I s'll need a break.'

'Your mind will, perhaps, but it'll do you no good racing eight or nine miles at night, then having to go to work next day.'

'I shall go on the bus, and come back on it, you know that. Where's Albert and Sid?'

'They're at cricket practice. Yes, and how many times have you missed the bus? I know——'

Whatever she knew was not said; her husband came in at that moment with the evening paper, and she broke off and went into the kitchen.

'How's Derbyshire going, dad?' Arthur asked genially.

'They've won by six wickets.' He laid the paper on the table as if indicating that the youth could seek any other information himself. His tone of voice had faint begrudging in it over the question he did answer.

Arthur took up the newspaper, looked through it while he fed, then went into the parlour with his case of books. The next afternoon at a quarter-past five, when dance music sounded from the wireless in the middle room, and Sidney began crooning, he left his study and went into the kitchen, where his mother was ironing.

'I've done all my home-work and covered fifty pages of the History set book,' he told her with satisfaction. 'I deserve a break. I feel like a walk, now.' She did not reply, but turned from him and bent down to the fire, exchanging her cool iron for a hot one. She straightened again, held the iron near her cheek, wet her finger and touched for a second the smooth face, then she resumed her ironing.

'Well, see as you're home in decent time. I shall leave your supper. I've had a big wash and feel ready for bed, now.'

He did not answer; he felt some of the joy flow from him, driven out by a mild, impatient anger. Coming from the narrow, confined atmosphere of studying, he had been large and free, light with satisfaction. He had felt that essential contacts of his should be free and rejoicing, too—his mother, Nancy, his brothers. And yet she was weighing on to him, dulling the brightness of his mood. He was angrily impatient of the causes of her disharmony with him, not with her. But he could not pity her, feel any sympathy at all: he could only be angry at those things pulling at her. He went into the other room, and came back with his raincoat folded over his arm.

'Shan't be late, then. And you go to bed early.' He went before he might mark the effect of his last words on her face.

He reached the Maugham's house at a quarter to seven.

'Good evening, Arthur,' Mrs. Maugham said, opening the door to his knock. 'I'm afraid Nancy isn't in, and won't be until very late.'

'Didn't she get my postcard?'

'Well, she goes before the post comes, and she takes her lunch, you know. But come in a minute.' The young man followed her in. Her husband was asleep on the sofa. 'He's been in the garden all day. But I had to go into Belford this afternoon,' she continued, in the voice she had used at the door, 'and I took the card down to Nancy at the office. But she said she wouldn't be home till late; her, and Jane had had a ticket each given them for Derby Theatre Royal. That's all. She said that she'd see you on Saturday as usual.' She paused, and looked at Arthur with head slightly on one side and eyes opened widely, mouth pursed, wondering how he would take the news, sympathizing over his disappointment.

'Oh, well, I'll get back, then.' He had not sat down, and he moved a foot or so, suiting his resolve.

'It isn't nice to come all this way for nothing,' Mrs. Maugham said sadly. 'Won't you stay a minute or two?'

'No, thanks. I'll walk steadily back, it's a pleasant night.' The man on the sofa stirred, and Arthur moved to the door; it would be murder to have to talk, now, especially with a sleepy man, and in this silent, deadening atmosphere. 'Well, good night. Tell her I've been, won't you?'

He was in Nessfield when the bus for Pirley stopped to pick up passengers, but he let it go, he had plenty of time and would be home by nine, easily. Besides, he felt faintly disturbed; he didn't know why. Maybe he had sensed that Nancy's mother seemed to be riding with some artificial sort of brightness and a too-eager directness over the tale of her daughter's absence. A walk would get this feeling out of him, would tone him up. At the foot of Nessfield Hill, which began too steeply for cyclists to ride, a youth dropped off a bicycle at his side, and walked with him.

'Hello, Arthur,' he said affably. 'Where've you been? Walkin' round a bit?'

'Well—yes. We've had a holiday to-day.'

'Oo. Thy girl lives down 'ere, doesn't she? Been to

see 'er?' His voice lifted. 'W'y, I've seen 'er. Yes, I saw 'er in Belford about six. I'm sure it was 'er. Does she work at Walker's Mill?'

'Yes, she's in the office.'

'Yes. They were outside the office; 'er and that Jane W'o-is-it. They were gettin' in a car wi' two chaps. I know it were them.'

'Yes, they were going to the theatre at Derby.' Arthur's voice was steady, the tone of it casual. 'Where are you working, now?'

'I'm signin' on at present. It is a damn game an' a'. I ride about all week except Wednesday and Friday mornin's; them two days I start after dinner. I'm just comin' back, now. Been round Dovedale an' come back through Matlock.'

The youth lived in Pirley, and Arthur was glad to be free of him. He tried to keep his thoughts from Nancy in relation to what Ernest Needham had said, but he couldn't. The youth would not have been mistaken, he knew Nancy and Jane well enough. Still, what was there to worry about even if two men were in the car with them. But——

He hurried from Peathill home. His mother, who sat at the supper-table alone, looked quickly into his face as he came into the gas-light. She glanced at the clock, then back at him quickly.

'Nancy not in, eh?' she said, then looked about the table. 'You'd better have a bit of supper while it's about. Was she out?'

'Yes, she'd gone to the theatre at Derby. She'd booked, I should think.'

'She ought to have told you, then. She'd know a day or two ago that she was going. Letting you tramp there

6

for nothing.' She seemed to be expressing anger at his disappointment. 'I don't think Nancy's as steady as she might be. She's too fluffy-brained.'

'Now, don't say that, mum. She would have let me know if she had booked before to-day and thought that I might go.'

'Get this.' She set food before him. Sidney and Albert came in and sat down at the table; the mother bustled about with some impatience, bringing them food too.

'What you doin' 'ome so early?' Albert asked. 'Nancy chucked you?'

'No. She'd gone out.'

'It's a fine game, courtin'. No girl'll have me on a string like that.' He laughed, and began eating. 'You should 'ave come down to the Park with us, shouldn't 'e, Sid?'

''E does as he likes, I suppose.' Sidney was always with Arthur; he looked up to the other in some peculiarly sentimental way, had often gone upstairs and wept silently for his step-brother when Arthur and his father had 'been on'.

Arthur left the table and fetched a book from the parlour, and began reading. Mr. Shirley came in just before half-past nine.

'Put the news on, Albert,' he said. 'Let's 'ear close-of-play scores.' He began his supper as the jangling interval signal sprang into the easy silence. Arthur left the sofa at once and put down his book, then took off his coat, collar and tie, kicked off his shoes, and went upstairs, taking the book again as he went. ''E might as well 'ave said, "Shut the bloody wireless off", as do that,' the father burst out angrily. 'Does 'e think the damned 'ouse is made for 'im and 'is studyin'?'

'Surely he can go where it's quiet without asking leave, I should think,' his wife said, with heat. 'You've had the wireless shut off many a time when you were reading.'

'Hm. It didn't mean burnin' two lights, did it? And it'll 'ave to stop with 'im. 'E's 'ad the parlour going all winter.'

'You don't begrudge the lad getting on, do you?'

''E's so damned perky over it, though.'

The 'pips' sounded, and they were silent. The woman began packing up the snap-bags with sandwiches of bread and bacon; she took them into the pantry out of the warm, dry air. Then she washed out the tin water-drums, and put them by the tap in the kitchen. She looked over the pit-clothes as she took them from a box under the sofa, felt the shirts and the waists of the trousers to see they were perfectly dry, then laid them in separate heaps about the kitchen fireplace.

'I'm going,' she said, when all this was done. 'Been a big wash-day, and I'm ready for bed.'

No one spoke as she went upstairs. She went into the room Arthur had for his own; the other two youths slept together.

'Don't have the light on much longer, Arthur,' she said. 'Your dad's been grumbling about so many burning.'

'Right. I'll just finish this chapter. Good night.'

'Good night. You ought to have had your pit boots mended to-day while you've been at home. Remember to take them next time you holiday. Good night.'

He put down the book almost as soon as she had gone, and turned out the light. For an hour he lay thinking, first of the examination, then sliding off to Nancy. The two topics began to exchange importance in his mind more quickly; soon they were jumbled inextricably, and he fell asleep. But he took them to work next day. They slowed him, quickened him, through the fields and the bright May morning, brought him with surprising shortness of time to the bustle of the pithead, dragged at him straining to reverse the trams on the metal plate, kept him distant to the gangers, the corporals, deputies. He would be glad when Saturday came, and he could see Nancy meet him in Pirley with the same free smile and easy movement. It was no suspicion or jealous gnawing; he was experiencing foolishly disaster smashing into him and shattering the possible future for them both; he was keenly conscious to what regretful things mind-drowning pleasure could lead; how, with a girl like Nancy, the moment was only that richly crowded into it. She must have been thrilled to go to the theatre. Even his going could not hold her from it. There would be many moments after for him; she must live this one while it was here.

He was impatiently early in Pirley on Saturday night, and when Nancy approached him from the top of Peak Street, he looked straight into her face. Her lips, usually parted slightly in freedom, rested together quietly; her eyes were steadier than she was wont to keep them. When she was up to him, a quick smile broke the corners of her mouth, her eyes melted faintly.

'Hello, Nancy,' he said brightly. 'Where are we going?' He was attempting to fuse at once, though a strange wonder touched his mind and stomach.

'We'll go to the pictures, if you like,' she replied, as if leaving the decision with him.

'If you prefer a walk, I don't mind.' He kept his voice bright. Each knew, however, that there was something to bridge before they were in each other again, acting, speaking unconscious of self or the other.

'We'll go to the pictures, then.' She laughed shortly, without pleasure. 'Sorry you came for nothing on Wednesday.'

'Oh, I enjoyed the walk back. I needed a break. Did you like the show at Derby?' They walked across to the Hippodrome. 'Do you want to come here?' She nodded strongly.

'It was all right. I've seen better.' Her utterance was quick; it seemed she wanted to be away from the topic. 'I'll go and wait in the lounge.'

He got the tickets, and they went in, and sat in silence through the show. They seemed unable to find contact on the way down to Nessfield.

'What's the matter, Nancy? Aren't you very well?' They stood in the dusk fields, and Arthur suddenly felt the hunger of knowing her in his arms. She quickened at once when he held her, laughed suddenly in the old, free way, and kissed him.

'Have you worked hard this week?' she asked. 'I'll bet you have. I'll bet you were glad I was out on Wednesday so that you could run off home and get a book again.'

'Oh no, I wasn't. I'll bet you never thought of me while you watched the smooth-haired actor doing the love-stuff.'

She fell silent, was heavier in his arms.

'Your bus'll be about due, won't it?' she asked, at

length, brightly. He nodded his chin to her shoulder.
'We'll be good, now, until after your exam, eh?'

He kissed her gladly, released her; they held each
other at arm's length. He was happy for the moment.
He said he would come on Wednesday. She forbade
him and told him to stick to his books. They laughed
happily, then he went. But immediately the warmth of
her went from him a holding uncertainty kept his face
to one expression, kept his eyes blinking as if to wash
the thought-pictures clean which flowed along his
mind. She did not want to talk of Wednesday; had
not mentioned the car, the men; had lost some strength
and definiteness of her personality; made him and his
affairs important, as if in an atonement of some kind.
The bus was rushing under the bridge when he came
to the road. A sudden surge in him held him from
putting out his arm. He'd walk home in the darkness.
No he wouldn't. He shot out his hand. No, the walk
would be dreadful. The bus swept past him, roaring,
pulled up twenty yards along the road and he ran and
climbed on. Oh, he was glad he'd not walked.

For the next three weeks he saw her each Saturday,
and she always chose the pictures. They walked along
to Nessfield after, and stood in the fields. Nancy
seemed away from him for long periods, then came to
him with rushing love, holding him, kissing him with
more passion than he had conceived her capable.
Arthur could not keep from himself the feeling that
fear was driving her to the rich expression, for nothing
of the physical was in it. He wondered vaguely,
faintly fearful himself. A heavy shower came on as they
stood one night. It began immediately they reached
the fields about nine o'clock, and he suggested that they

should hurry the hundred yards to her home and pass the next hour; but she quickly said they would hurry the three hundred yards to the bridge on the highway. And so they stood there, for an hour, while cars and buses lighted them vividly every few minutes, and drenched, singing cyclists returning from the Peak greeted them with calls, suggestive advice. But they stood with faces buried in each other, speaking at times.

He sat in the bus with still features; he was worried. Nancy was different, somehow, though when he had asked her if anything was the matter, she had brightened at once and told him she was restraining herself to please him, but let him wait until after his exam. He could not feel convinced, however, that this was the out-flowing of her essence. She seemed to force herself into the brightness, and he took his solemn thoughts to bed, to the pit. When the 'turn' slackened, and he could sit in the seat-hole waiting for coal to come to the top of the jig, he took out his note-book, but soon put it back impatiently. He stared at the logic symbols scrawled on the rock; his brain would not hold them; he blinked and cursed mildly, forcing himself to work on them.

'Bloody fool,' he muttered. 'Bothering like this over nothing. I s'll pass some exam at this rate.' With sudden anger he brought out his book again, bent over it, leaning slightly towards his lamp hung on a prop. The ganger was rumbling along the stint; the empties he had hung on to the jig-rope were rattling away into the lifting tunnel of dark. A light suddenly shone into his face and he looked up with a start.

'What ta readin', Gardner, some love stuff?' The deputy was bending to the note-book.

'No.' Arthur laughed apologetically. 'Just looking over a few things for my exam. It's in a month and I want to be ready.'

'Hmm.' The thin man held up his lamp and looked about the jig bottom, the far track lined with empties, down the 'loaden' road unoccupied and strewn with slack and cobbles fallen from the trams banging into each other. 'Tha might be better put to to clean up this bloody place; somebody'll be gettin' lamed ovver this coal lyin' about.' He walked away down the stint. Arthur had risen quickly, surprised and afraid somewhat by the tone of the deputy. He picked up a shovel, and began scraping the floor noisily so that the man could hear as he walked away. But the jig had run in and he was compelled to attend to it, take off the rope, swing it over and hang it on to the three empties already coupled together, push the loaded trams to the plate in turn, and swing them round and lower them to where the ganger was waiting with his horse. He'd never been caught before, never let the ganger see him studying his note-book. He did not mind them seeing the logic signs; they'd probably think he'd been amusing himself, which wouldn't have mattered even to the gaffer. Youths wrote and drew anything, anywhere, in spare moments. He was a fool, a damned fool; he ought to have made sure no one was coming, because he couldn't hear with the ganger coming and the jig running. He was careful after that, always busy cleaning round when the deputy or gaffer walked past.

He saw Nancy the next Saturday. Her mood was the same; she kept to herself for long periods, laughed harshly at times, but was always rich with love for him when they were alone. The flesh of her lips seemed pressed closer to her teeth, her eyes seemed larger, somehow.

'There is something the matter with you, Nancy,' he said, firmly, to her as they walked down after the pictures. 'And you can tell me what it is. I'm doing no work that's worth anything, worrying over you. Come on, what is it?'

'There's nothing the matter with me,' she replied sharply. 'It's you who are looking at me differently, perhaps. Don't you like me like this? You were always grumbling when I was all over you, wanting other things.'

'All right—all right. Don't snap my head off. Shall I come on Wednesday?' He pressed her arm to show there was no reality in his quick, seeming-angry tone. 'I will, if you'd like me to.'

'No.' She was definite, quickly definite.

'O.K. That's enough for me.'

He worked more easily until the next Saturday, when he got a card from her.

'Am going out for the week-end. See you Wednesday.'

He was puzzled, and when he went to his desk in the front room, he sat silent, pulled away from his work. He read paragraphs from a history book but the matter dissolved from his mind even as his eyes travelled. He went into the garden.

'Anything I can do, dad?' he asked, halting where his stepfather was sorting out pea-sticks. The man looked up wonderingly, blinked a few times, then stood upright.

'You can stick some of these rods along the pea row, if you like.' He turned to the bundle again, and Arthur

took some in his arms and carried them to where the
fresh green of the pea row ran across the garden.
The man, who had intended doing the job himself,
walked away to the bottom of the stretch and busied
himself with other things.

After dinner Arthur tried the front room again, and
forced himself to study until half-past two. Sidney came
in, then, clean and shining in his cricket attire.

'Comin' down to-day, Arth? Stickin' in a grand
afternoon like this. Come on.' When his brother rose
from the chair he stared in astonishment. 'Comin'?'
he cried quickly, his eyes shining with pleasure.

'I may as well. I can do some work to-night.' He
saw the other about to speak. 'I'm not going out;
Nancy's away for the week-end. Is Albert playing as
well.'

'Yes, come on.'

He sat and watched the village team through the
shining afternoon. The Park ran level from the dark
wood to fifty yards beyond the wicket, then rose steadily
to the old Hall shoulder high in trees. Groups of youths
and men lay about the dry grass, talking of the game,
horses, women, praising shots, sneering at times over a
wicket foolishly thrown away, but always living in the
moment, their emotions, opinions, swinging superficially, dying, reviving again suddenly. Arthur sat
near two groups, a holding heaviness keeping his
features in glum seriousness. He was angry at himself;
he would have sacrificed everything at the moment to
be as free from himself as they were. None of these
seemed to be dragged forward by some straining thing
in themselves, to be warmed and worried by hitches
and hindrances cutting in and across a deeper sense of

living. One of his brothers was at the wicket now; was running, after a vigorous pull, was running again, standing up now to face another ball. Damn it, he ought to have relaxed at this sort of stuff instead of hanging himself on to a woman. But even as the thought came, he knew it would have been impossible.

When Wingrove had batted and half the other team was out, he got up suddenly and went home. Even though he recognized that at the cricket match, in the bright, warm sun and the wide sound-dotted silence of the Park, there could be rich content, the positive freedom and resting from pulling, weighing toil, he had suddenly felt that time was uncoiling for him unprofitably, that an end of some kind was rushing towards him, and he was turned aside from the labour of fulfilling himself. It had made him afraid, startled him, and he had hurried on to the forward-moving line again. He was in the front room until ten o'clock; he had pressed Nancy from him and worked in freedom. For an hour after that he walked about Condor Common, and inevitably she flowed into him until he turned home again impatiently and went to bed.

On Wednesday evening he reached the stile as she was coming up the fields, and he stopped, leaning on the crooked post. But she had stopped, too, and he walked on down the field-path. He had thought she would prefer walking in Lingfall Park. Obviously she wanted to go the other way, or take him home for something.

'Well, stranger,' he began, when he was almost up to her. Then he stopped, his mouth held at the next word. She was looking straight into his face, her eyes burned, the flesh about her mouth was pulled taut and dry, it seemed dead. 'Why, Nancy——' He was afraid.

'I'm not ill, Arthur.' She did not respond to the pressure his arms made about her. 'I thought of writing and telling you not to come. But I'm no coward.' The corners of her mouth turned down pitiably for a moment. The pressure of his arms relaxed, an uncertainty took him from the physical.

'What's the matter?' His voice held fear, not wholly for her, his fingers tightened on her arm unconsciously.

She looked at him steadily, silent for a moment. There was no craving for pity in her eyes and mouth.

'We've finished, Arthur.' Her utterance quickened. 'I'm going to have a baby—I'm getting married.' She did not change in spite of the incredibility pulling him straight and his head away from her. 'It was when we went to the theatre——' She broke off, knowing her words were flowing past him. There was no attention in his face; he was away from her completely, his eyes empty and staring. His fingers were rubbing about the silk sleeve of her dress, off the round smoothness of her arm. She put out her hand, pressing his. The gesture brought his head sharply to face her; he looked into her eyes steadily; his mouth-line was firm but suggested no anger. For a moment each held the other's gaze. Then he broke contact and without a word turned and walked towards the Nessfield road.

# CHAPTER V

'I SHALL have to ask the gaffer to let me off some time this week,' Arthur said to his mother, as he sat at the table in his pit-dirt one day towards the end of June. 'The exam starts a week on Monday.'

'You ought to have asked him before. It's silly leaving it so late. What if he says he can't spare you?'

'He's good enough, but I don't think he will. Anyway, I will ask him to-morrow. I may as well have the whole week off; shall be at Trentingham, Monday, Tuesday, Wednesday and Friday. I shan't go in on Thursday, I can get at my Logic then, ready for Friday.'

She watched him at his meal, and gradually her eyes emptied and she stared as if through him. She had watched him closely since he had told her of Nancy; had seen him at times blink strongly and quickly as if beating at his mind to summon it from some vague wandering. There had been no outward sign of his reaction to the sudden crash in his love affair, but she knew what had happened to him. He was like her, incapable of grieving before calamity, of thrilling at pleasure, but he was filled with or drained of something other than emotion, the quality of intelligent being was vivified or dulled.

'What did you do when Nancy told you?' she had asked him.

'I just walked away,' he had answered. 'I wasn't disgusted; I wasn't sorry for her or myself. I don't know.' He had seemed at a loss to account for his state of mind. 'I know that I was different from what I had been before. I don't remember ever walking home, yet I never thought of anything all the way. I wish I was like other folks.'

She had walked out, then, her attitude was akin to that with which her son had walked away from the girl the day before, suffering, but not emotionally. She was remembering this, now, as she watched him eat, and was wondering vaguely whether strength and full-ness of living had come back to him, whether he had sealed up the rent torn in him so that all power could flow to feed and uphold the labouring for his examina-tion. But she could not tell and he gave no sign; he worked in the front room as he had before, and seemed satisfied with what he did.

'Yes, I'll ask him to-morrow. He'll be down our district.'

The under-manager came along the double-road stint about nine o'clock. Arthur rang the jig to go, when the man was near enough to be recognized. He was small, and his lamp almost touched the ground; it gleamed on his yard-stick and knee-pads as he walked along. The trams were roaring in the darkness when he reached where Arthur stood at the bottom of the incline, and he stopped until they should come to rest.

'I say, Mr. Lander.' The official turned and looked into his face. 'I start my exam a week on Monday and it'll last a week. Do you mind if I have that week off?'

'Exam. See.' He looked at the loaded trams slowing to the level track at his side. 'Oh. Mr. Redfern was telling me you'd got some books here readin'. And the place slattered about with coal.' He looked about the tracks. 'That's not how to go on; you come here to get coal out, not study.' He began moving up the jig. 'Yes, I should think you can have the week off.' His tone was not begrudging, but in it was a firm reproving. Gardner's inattention to work was not forgotten.

'Thank you.' The young man's gratitude was humble as he turned to his work. Then anger rushed through him, anger turned upon himself, against the sneaking deputy. But he was the fool, letting that miserable cow of a deputy catch him. Still, he'd be careful for the next week.

Every half a dozen jigs or so, now, he cleaned up the coal which had fallen off the trams; he swept the tracks with a besom after going along them with the shovel. The deputy, Redfern, came down the jig about eleven.

'Keep this jig goin'; they're stocked out with coal up there and stalls are waitin' of empties.'

'Right,' Arthur replied. 'We've been waiting, too. They must be letting 'em all go up Stone Head.'

'I'll bloody well see into that.' He hurried away along the stint, his stick tapping quickly.

A heaviness hung about him all through the morning: the gaffer's attitude, the dissatisfaction with himself, took the rich life from him. He hated uncertainty, nothing gnawed him like half-revealed attitudes; if he knew where he was with people, he could be content. When Nancy was strange for those few weeks, he was all out of gear, but immediately she had told him what was wrong, he had adjusted himself instinctively. The moment he walked away from her, he was content in being, not in mind, though that must inevitably follow. He had not been miserable over the break; he never felt miserable when his mother suffered because of his stepfather. What he did experience was some sort of anger, not of the quality that could ever move him physically, though he knew he would meet violence with violence if ever it was needed in the cause of someone to whom he was attached; rather did it take his strength and hold him away from all other matters, a sort of spiritual sulking. Not mental, for he held no object in his mind to brood on; not emotional, for he was detached from all circumstance. But in uncertainty he suffered acutely; in that he was pushed off his path, lost in a bewildering maze and conscious of the waste it all meant. He felt this mood pulling at him this morning, taking his strength, shadowing his attention in moments. But he kept himself aware, he must watch for the under-manager coming back.

At half-past eleven a light swung down the jig. Arthur thought it was the gaffer, and took up the shovel, but it was a man going out at half-day to a funeral.

'Gaffer's at other end o' t'jig stint,' he told Arthur as he passed. ''E'll be 'ere in about ten minutes.'

'Are they waiting of empties up there, yet?'

'Yes. An' they look like waitin' to-day. Chock-full o' coal, every turn-out.'

'Hm.' Arthur turned to his work again, pushing the three loaded ones he had taken off the jig-rope into the six already up to the block. The ganger was rumbling along the stint, singing. 'What the hell's up wi' t'incline?' he demanded. Not often did he fall into dialect, only on occasions when the atmosphere was wholly pit or village and his mind was pulled into vagueness by the conflicting thoughts of uncertainty. 'Is it holdin' empties out, or are they sendin' 'em a up Stone Head?'

'Oh, shut thee bloody rattle about empties,' the ganger said. 'Every bloody gang tha'rt on. It's as bad as if it were thy damn pit.'

'Who the bloody hell dosta reckon tha'rt talkin' to?' Arthur burst out angrily, and took a step towards the ganger. 'Ar'll make thee bloody ear-hole clink if tha doesna have less o' thee cheek.'

'Thee keep thee paws to thisen.' He lifted the shaft iron he was handling to change his horse from empties to loaded trams. 'Ar s'll conk thee wi' this.' They glared at each other in the light of the two lamps. Arthur put down his hands, and the ganger hung on his horse. 'Ar s'll tell 'em down 'ere tha'rt 'inderin' me if tha touches me.'

Arthur left him and pushed the empties to the jig rope. The ganger was clicking to his horse.

'Go on, you bloody college swank. Thinks tha'rt iverybody cos tha goos ta—— Goo on, Captain.' He was looking round, and had seen Arthur rush to the bell-wire and pull it, then begin coming after him. 'Comm on.' The horse broke into a trot, and when Gardner stopped, the ganger gave out a great guffaw and leapt on the shaft-iron.

But Arthur had not stopped because he considered the chase hopeless; he was arrested by the thin dragging up the jig. A chill seemed to lift his scalp, a weakness seemed to loosen all his inside right to his throat.

'Heavens!'

For a moment he stood, cold in the hot air, fear-stricken and unable to move though conscious of danger. The jig was running, yet the empties had not moved, the iron tail of the rope rushed drily over the dirt floor and sleepers, clanked at times against a rail.

7

He'd rung off and not cottered the rope to the empties! The three loaded ones were rushing unrestrained down the steep decline, the jigger couldn't possibly hold them with the brake on the wheel. There'd be a hell of a mess. The roar started him. He turned and ran wildly down the stint, stumbling. A mighty crash, splintering wood sounded suddenly, a moment's awful silence, then a dull thud and a rain-like splattering of falling roof. He stopped, breathless, sobbing drily with his breathing, then began to walk slowly back. Lights were coming down the jig and voices sounded.

'Wot the 'ell 'as tha bin doin', Gardner?' one called, when Arthur's light appeared. 'Keep back, there's goin' to be a bloody mess 'ere before it's done.' It was the corporal shouting, a man responsible for the smooth-running of the section of road he was over; his was from the top of the jig to the stalls.

Arthur halted a short way from where the trams had rested, two on their sides, the other reared into the wall, standing on end. Three props lay poking across the tracks, two from one side, one from the other ; another, broken in the middle, was held to the wall by the rearing tram. Two bars which had stretched from prop to prop were almost buried now by the falling rock and bind. The heap was half-way to the roof-level already, small pieces and dust were pouring on to it; big, ugly lumps thudded down and rolled towards Arthur or the men on the other side.

'Look out,' the corporal shouted, 'another bar's goin'.' The jigger, a ganger and the corporal himself backed hastily. Arthur stood as if paralysed. 'Get back, you bloody fool. Tha'll be under.' Arthur jumped back as a twelve-foot bar crashed down. 'Go an' send a ganger to find t'deputy,' Castledine, the corporal, yelled to Arthur as debris poured and thudded down, building up the heap and diminishing the opening between them. He turned away trembling inside with nervous fear. A ganger was hanging on to three loaded trams, unaware of what had happened.

'We've had a runner,' Arthur told him, in a voice foolishly loud with false strength. 'And the jig's running in. Castledine says you've got to get a deputy. Tell him what's happened,' he ended, after a slight pause in which he gulped.

'Ar'm goin' to 'ave a look,' the ganger said, and Arthur followed him to the jig. 'Bloody hell,' he said slowly with awed amazement. 'What a mess.' The fall was solid, now, hiding the men on the other side. 'We've done for to-day, an' 'appen for to-morrer as well. His utterance quickened. 'What 'appened?'

'Nay. Cotter must have come out or summat.'

'That never comes out. Tha couldn't 'ave 'ung it on.'

Gardner did not answer and the ganger walked away, leaving him alone. There was no sound about the fall now, but he knew all the earth would be alive above it. It might take two days to clear it. He gulped again, and went to the seat-hole and had a drink. He sat down, but rose again immediately; it seemed a crime to sit down. And the gaffer was on the other side: he'd be about crazy. He began biting his finger-nails, and waited, standing foolishly watching for a light to break through the darkness of the stint.

The ganger rumbled up with empties; a deputy and men with shovels were with him.

'What's tha been doin', Gardner?' the deputy asked

at once. 'Started jig without 'angin' t'empties on.' He was holding his light above the three empty trams which were coupled together. 'Looks like it.' He turned to the men behind. 'Bring a' empty up.' He walked forward the twenty yards to the fall. The men, there were four of them besides the ganger and Gardner, had uncoupled the first empty and were pushing it up the steep, loaded-side track. 'Hell,' he said, holding his lamp to the roof and tapping the bar next to where the break was. 'How many bars are out, Gardner?'

'Three, I think.'

'Good Lor'. Come on, scotch that tram and get it filled.'

Arthur fetched his shovel, and helped to load the tram, then they lowered it down, and the ganger took it away. Another was thrown across to the loaded track, pushed up and loaded. And so it went on for an hour until the under-manager came. Arthur felt suddenly sick as he heard his stick clicking quickly up the jig. He had to strain to keep control of his excretory organs, his whole inside was weak and trembling. He did not look up when the short man came up to the deputy.

'This's a bloody nice mess, isn't it?' he said angrily.

'Worse than I thought it would be,' Redfern, the deputy said. 'Can't see it bein' cleared for to-morrow mornin'. Have you come round by Stone 'Ead?'

'No. I've come round the air-way on the other side. Quicker. I've sent the men round there. Where's Gardner?'

'I'm here.' He stood up, resting on his shovel crutch.

'And what the bloody hell do you think you've been doin'?' He looked into the pale face of the young man. 'Made two days' stand in this district. You can get your clothes on and get off up the pit. You can't work down a pit and study as well. Go on.'

'I haven't——'

'Get thee bloody clothes on and get up pit. And tha needn't come and see me, tha'll not come down here again.' He turned to the deputy again. 'We s'll have to have extra men on this job to-night.'

Arthur had rested his shovel against the wall, and was walking away down to the seat-hole where his clothes hung. He was thirsty, his mouth clogged with dust, but though he heard the water in his drum as he put on his coat, he did not think of drinking.

'Where are tha goin'?' the ganger, whom he met in the stint, asked him, pulling up his horse. It was Gordon, the youth Arthur had begun to chase after he had rung off the unattached jig-rope.

'Home.'

'Sack. Crikes!' The youth fell silent suddenly, incapable of expressing the apologetic shame surging through him. But Gardner had walked on.

'Where's incline?' he asked of the corporal, when he reached the end of the stint, and entered a wide turn-out where another road branched away and from which a ganger was running in with three loaded trams.

''E'll be about startin' down, now. What's up? Poke?'

'Yes,' was the short reply. 'Can I go up?'

'Tha can if tha likes,' the corporal replied, in a tone which suggested plainly that the young man would go up at his own risk. The two gangers in the turn-out, and the youth who helped the corporal to see the incline off, looked curiously at him as he walked into the darkness up the slope leading into the pit-bottom. Then they turned again to coupling on the eighteen loaded trams which the main road jig, driven from an engine-house on the surface, would soon be fetching, bringing as many empties in exchange.

Half-way up the mile incline, Arthur heard a rumbling forward, and stepped aside into a man-hole, waiting. Eighteen empties rattled past, the jigger riding in the last to which the rope held. Gardner bluffed his light and the man did not see him, then he climbed to the pit-bottom.

'Ring me "hold-out",' he said to the onsetter.

'What's up, badly?'

'No. Sack.'

'Oh, tha was at bottom o' t'double-road, eh? Oh ay. Gardner, isn't it? Oh dear.' The man pulled the bell three times while the cages were in the shaft. Pit-top answered. When the cage rested, the man on the other side of the bottom pulled off the empty and Arthur walked on. The guards were fastened, the bell rung and answered, and he was whisked up into daylight.

He took in his lamp and motty. Everybody seemed to know why he had come out early; they stared but said nothing. Along the dry tarmac road, up the steep Lumb where the sun glossed the grass and flamed the gorse clumps, his mind churned incessantly, quick points of thought pressed painfully into importance in turn. At times two or more rushed up together, each demanding adjustment to the others—his mother, step-father, his examination, his brothers, the Unemployment Exchange, other places where he might try for a job. Shoots of pain lifted his head, brought his brows together, the whole jumbling and effort to think straight made his neck ache. When he walked along Red Lane and up Back Street, ten minutes from home, two streams of antagonistic lines of thought flooded him. A strong positive one: he must think of nothing but his exam this next week, use all the time at his books and keeping fit. As strong a negative one: his stepfather would pull down at him, getting at him through his mother. He closed his eyes in pain as he strained to persuade himself to the positive one, but the other inevitably thrust a weakening fear through the strength. He gritted his teeth as he walked on the yard.

'Hello,' his mother greeted, as he came into the kitchen. 'Knocked off?' She looked into his face. 'What's the matter, Arthur?' She thought suddenly of death in the pit.

'Got the sack. Started jig without hanging t'empties on. Made a run-in that's cut a district off.' He glanced at her while he pulled off his coat, saw her let go of herself and marked the worn age she had hidden. Her mouth was loose, her eyes dull, the hope she had carried because of him faded, her whole physical being drooped. He strengthened at once. 'Oh, don't bother. I s'll get another job.'

'Sack!' She was compelled to think away from him. 'What——?' But she did not say it, she must know that his own mind must be pulled in two by the mighty facts of his exam and her husband. 'Dinner isn't ready yet. You'd better wash and change.'

He sat in a chair by the table, got up again quickly

as if in anger, and washed and changed, then went into the front room. Neither had spoken all the time, nor did she come to him until it was to say that his meal was ready. He came and ate in silence for a while.

'I shall have to sign on to-morrow.'

'For heaven's sake don't be in that dole queue long. If you don't get another job quick, you'll be out all summer—perhaps longer.'

'If——' But he could not mention his exam. He moved from the table, and went into the front again and sat gazing on to the street. Soon pit-men passed up and down, in groups, odd ones. His brothers and father clattered on the 'end', and his stomach lightened suddenly. He stared for a while unseeing, then rose with resolve and walked into the kitchen.

'Tha's been doin' it, hasn't tha?' Albert said. He laughed without malice. 'Ringin' t'jig off an' no empties on. They're 'olidayin' to-morrow up that district.'

'Gaffer needn't 'ave sacked 'im,' Sid said mildly. 'It's been done before. There's been "runners" and run-ins. Why, they let four run down a jig up our road other week. It 'eld us up for 'alf a day, but they said nowt to Greening who knocked t'block off before 'e 'ung t'rope on.'

'No.' The father's tone held a sneer. 'But 'e 'adn't been caught readin' books an' usin' the side as a black-board. Gaffer's been tellin' me. Such folks deserve the sack.'

'Yes. P'raps they do.' Arthur's tone was hard. 'It all depends who it is when folks say that.'

'Well, you've got it, 'aven't you?' The man shot out

the words. 'An' it's dole, now. Fifteen shilling's a week. Is that goin' to keep you?'

'I shan't ask you for anything, that is a fact.' His mother was imploring for peace with her eyes, but he snatched his own away from hers.

'Well, you'll put twenty-five shillings down every Friday else clear out, and that's another fact.'

'I s'll do that, and when I can't I shall clear out. Who the hell are you?'

'An' who the hell are you?' The man rose from his chair, but Arthur did not flinch. 'You'll find your clothes and books chucked out on to t'yard if you don't 'ave less of your damned buck.' His arm came up, but lowered again as he saw the young man's mouth-line. 'Bloody young mon-funk. Thinks because 'e knows a bit o' blasted 'istory an' 'alf a dozen French words that 'e's too good for t'pit.'

'Oh, give it a rest. You're always on that tune.' He turned away in disgust, saw his mother leaning heavily on the table, her face grey even to her lips, a glazed, empty look was in her eyes which blinked as if the lids were hardly capable of function. He drew in breath sharply, and all heat was out of him in a moment and fear and a kind of shame weakened him. 'What's the matter, mum?' he said, stepping across to her. They were the only words he could say, but even as he uttered them, he felt like some criminal who is sympathizing with one he has desolated.

'Nothing,' she answered, bracing up. 'I'm all right.' She walked into the kitchen. Arthur stood for a moment, took a step towards the front room door, but turned again as a wave of sickness flowed through him, and he pulled on his coat and went out.

He walked about Condor Common for a while, then on to Pirley. A hopelessness dragged at him, over the fields going back ; he shook himself, strained to hold himself strong, but inevitably he fell back again. His mother was alone in the house when he entered ; she sat on the sofa in the fading light, her hands resting on her lap. She looked up like a sick animal.

'Don't bother, mum,' he said, but then dropped into a chair and became silent himself.

'You should say nothing back to him,' she said. There was no spirit in her tone. 'He's the master here, and he'll show it.' Her son did not reply. 'He's been on since you went out. He'll be on, now, for a week or more, especially if he gets in the pub every night.'

The young man remained silent. A block was full across his whole stream of thinking; he saw no way to reach comfortable living again as he had known until a few months back. There had been odd tiffs with his step-father, but lately the man had become unbearable, and he could see no reason for it except that the man begrudged his efforts to better himself while his own sons were content with the pit. And his mother was looking old, her husband bickered at her continually. Not that she did any more for her son than for his own. Arthur knew they were as much to her as he was, but, of course, her husband's slighting of her son might drive her to a secret siding with him. He didn't know what to do, the pulling apart was killing her, her husband's sneering and rowing was hastening her end. It was obvious, oh, so obvious. And what could be done? Nothing, nothing. He beat his brain to find a way. Only the father's death, but that wasn't likely.

'Mum.' He spoke suddenly, and she jerked to attention at his tone. 'I'll study this next week as hard as I can. I'll take my exam, then leave until I find a job. That'd be all right, wouldn't it?'

'Don't talk silly,' she said strongly. 'And where would you go? Tramping round and living on the wind. You'd soon be dead. And I should die if you did.' She had permitted these last words to come from her quickly ; she had not intended uttering them, it was a weak moment in her running strength.

'I shan't go,' he replied simply, then fell silent. She rose and began preparing supper. His brothers came in. Sidney walked across to the wireless and gave the knob a twist, then sat down, apparently not interested in the news which broke into the small silence of the room. 'Shall you bring my money to-morrow, Sid?' Arthur asked.

'What's your number?'

'One-eight-one. And you can pay my union. I might get on at another pit, and I should be in benefit, then.'

'O.K.' He sat at the table with Albert. 'Goin' to sign on in t'mornin'? I'd better call in t'office for your cards."

'Yes, do.' His mother came in with a jug of cocoa. 'I'll just have a drink, mum, and go to bed.'

'What are you having?' she asked the other two. 'Bread and cheese, or will you fetch yourselves some chips?'

'Oh, we'll have bread and cheese,' Sid said, noting his mother's weariness. 'An' I'll cut mine. You sit down.'

'Hm. Why couldn't you fry the cheese?' Albert

grumbled. 'Or do some chips over the fire? You know we only 'ave a bit o' bread and butter for breakfast. My belly'll think my throat's cut before nine in t'mornin'.'

She cut up some cheese without replying, and took it to the kitchen fire, standing there with the pan until it was cooked, then bringing it back and setting it before him.

'You'd better have some as well, Sid, as it's done.' The youth held his slice of bread. 'Will you have a bit, Arthur?'

'No. I'll go to bed when I've drunk this.'

He left his bedroom door open, and heard his step-father come in. There was some low conversation for a time, then the man's voice raised in slow sneering. He sounded as if he were partly drunk.

''E's sneaked off to bed, 'as 'e?'

'There's no "sneak" about it,' his mother said impatiently.

''E's sneaked off, 'as 'e?' He was obviously not sober. 'Never mind, Albert. We're not afraid of work, are we? No fear. We wouldn't stand in t'regular dole-queue, would we, Albert? No.'

He rambled on, and his wife closed the stair-foot door and Arthur could hear nothing. He got out of bed and shut his own door, lay thinking until long after the others had gone to bed.

In the morning he lay awake while his step-father and brothers clattered about the house in their pit-boots, jangled the pots, spurted water into their drums, and left the house. Then he got up at once, and set breakfast for himself and his mother. She came down obviously unrested, dry featured and burning. She moved about without interest in her work; it seemed as if there was a mist before the joy she could feel for his presence. They did not speak much. He helped her to straighten the rooms and wash up; then he got ready and walked to Pirley. Small groups were ahead and behind on the fields: they turned as he did at the edge of the town, and crossed a children's recreation pitch to the old school building serving as a Labour Exchange. A crowd stood in the yard, and he began sidling through.

'Eh. What's thy time?' A burly man barred his way at the foot of the stone steps leading into the school porch. 'We sign at 'alf-past.'

'I've no time,' Arthur told him. 'I've been signing at a pit-table. You're regulars, aren't you?'

The man stood aside without answering and Arthur pushed up the steps, through the crowded porch and into the room. He went to where a clerk was working at a table behind which a large square of cardboard with 'Shenton' printed in crude capitals hung on the wall. No line of men led to it, the pit was working to-day. Other tables backed by names of half a dozen other pits were empty, too. Only the long line of wholly unemployed stretched across the room, shuffling, muttering. As each signed, he took a slip and passed into another room, came out again in a few minutes counting money in his hand.

'I've finished at the pit,' Arthur told the clerk when he looked up from his work. 'Shall I have to sign on here or—where?'

'You'd better take your book and get transferred to the other box, then.' He slid his fingers along a file. 'See, what's your name?'

'Gardner. Arthur Gardner.' He watched the man

move his hand from one end of the file to the other, to the G compartment, flick a few books then bring out one. 'Which table shall I go to, did you say?' The man pointed to one along the room where a clerk sat. Arthur knew him, a somewhat testy sort of individual, especially in hot weather, for he was stout and his disability dragged heavily on him. His face was round and smooth, his eyes small and mouth thin. When Arthur reached him and stood close to the table, he continued working for some minutes before he looked up. 'I'm wholly unemployed, now,' the young man said, when the the clerk ceased writing and lifted his head. 'I worked at Shenton, and the man at that table said I was to come here and transfer or something.'

'Give me your book.' Arthur handed him the half-dozen leaves held together by an elastic band, and the man examined them for a moment or two. Then he took a slip of paper from the desk, and waved his pen over it, began copying from the front of the book. 'Have you your time-card?' he asked, when he had done. Arthur produced the yellow card, and the man tore it in half and dropped it in the waste-paper basket, then made out another showing the holder of it to be wholly unemployed. 'You'll sign on Wednesdays and Fridays at ten-thirty.' Arthur took the card and turned away. 'Here. Don't you want to sign for to-day? You can sign here this morning.' He watched while the young man took up the pencil fastened to the table by a piece of string, and wrote his name on the line where his own finger pointed. 'You'll sign at Mr. Round's table over by the door, there.'

The man dropped his head and forgot him. He

turned instinctively towards where the man had
nodded, saw the young clerk, stout and short, long hair
pulled carefully over the bald front of his head, shirt
sleeves rolled up uncovering white arms, his hands quick
and sure in diving among the box of books, stamping
'Excused' and 'Sign here' on each man's book he had
opened, turning it round for the signature, sweeping it
back into the box. He saw the men watching the clerk,
taking up the pencil and writing, then bringing the
pay-slip towards the door of the room where the
manager and a clerk sat behind a wire fence and pushed
money to them. The older men in the signing queue
seemed slower, quieter than they really ought to have
been. Some put on spectacles a moment or so before
their turn came to bend over the table, wrote carefully,
laid down the pencil silently. Most of the younger ones
spoke lightly to the clerk, laughed, scribbled their
names and tossed away the pencil, then strode down
the room to the pay door.

Arthur went home thinking deeply. He had not
taken much notice of the regulars before ; he knew some
of them, and they had been ordinary men, talking
cricket, football, billiards, horses, gardening. They
had laughed and joked with him, did laugh and joke
with him, now, if he happened to walk with any across
the fields from or to Pirley. They neither grumbled
nor groaned at their 'lot', as far as he knew. Those in
Wingrove seemed to fill in their time fully enough, at
the Social Centre, in the garden, getting coal from a
thin seam running along the face of the 'clay-hole' at
the brickworks, gossiping brightly at the street corners.
But in the Exchange they had seemed different, somehow. Lined up, subdued, solemnly pushing the pay-

check through the cage, and passing out from the presence of the manager with some sort of relief, but bright and normal again immediately they were from the building. He wondered how he would feel among the regulars; he certainly wouldn't waste his time. But it was that bloody man at home; if it wasn't for him he could study all day. There'd be no peace, though. It had been bad enough when he was at work, but now —he was a fool to ring off the jig without making sure the 'clivvy' was hung to the tug-hole.

He worked at his books all the afternoon, but he had to force his mind to the stuff; there seemed a lighter, weaker quality about it than before. He sat empty for minutes together, was pulled away quite easily into other, quite foolishly extraneous musings. When he went out for tea, his brothers and step-father were home. Sidney brought out a dirty packet and laid it before him as he dropped into a chair at the table.

'Your money.'

'Thanks.' He took it up and unfolded it. 'I should have three-quarters to draw next week. Remember to bring it. Here.' He put a pound note and two half-crowns on the corner of the table nearest the sofa where his stepfather sat. 'You said you wanted to see me pay my board. It's there.' The man looked across, glanced at the money, and resumed his newspaper. Arthur felt strong, somehow, when he was facing the man. It was when he was away, in the front room especially, that thoughts pulled at him, that he seemed to have to listen all the time he worked. His mother came in from the garden while he helped himself to food. She saw the money on the table, and at once life seemed to sink back from her face, out of her body.

When the meal was over, she did not at once begin clearing away the pots and taking up the cloth to shake it. She fidgetted about for a time, until she seemed unable to stand it any longer.

'What about this money?' She asked the question impatiently. 'I want to clear away.'

'You can pick it up, can't you. Think I want it?'

She moved the money on to the dresser, then took the pots into the kitchen. Arthur was on the yard. He saw her close her eyes and bend her head for a few moments as if being forced to rest mentally. Then she shook herself, and turned to the sink and began lading hot water from the boiler. He had thought of working again, but now he walked into the street and hurried on to the common.

'I shall have to see if I can draw for the days I'm at Trentingham,' Arthur said to his mother as they sat at breakfast on Wednesday. 'You see, I shan't be able to sign either Wednesday or Friday, I s'll have only Thursday off. Perhaps they'd let me sign, then, for all week; they'd know I'm not at work.'

'You can ask them.' There was no apparent interest in her voice. She stared for long intervals, blinking slowly, her body seemed slow to act on mental decisions and directions. 'You needn't bother about money. While I've bread, you'll eat.'

'Why don't you go to the doctor, ma?' He knew the foolishness of the thought even as it rushed from him. 'I s'll never pass the exam, I know I shan't.'

She strengthened at once, whipping herself to brightness. It was as if a challenge had been flung to her.

'Don't talk silly. If you can't put everything out of

8

your mind for a week, you're a poor fool.' Her tone was almost one of anger, though he knew it was directed not at him but at herself for showing weakness. He looked across at her, saw the firm mouth and bright eyes, but he saw the false strength behind them, too. 'You know what it means to you, don't you?'

'I know what it means to me,' he replied quietly, 'but I'm no super-man. I seem to have been thrown into another sort of world altogether and I can't adjust myself—not all at once, anyway. I don't feel sure of myself and my exam stuff. My Logic seems absolutely beyond me, somehow. If I look at one of the problems at the back of my Welton and Monahon, I can't bring any rule or canon to bear on it at all. I don't know.'

'If I were you, I shouldn't look at another book. You can't learn a deal more in any case. And I should walk about the country-side from morning till bedtime.'

'Mopse'd be a better word in my case.' He left the table strongly. 'I'll go.'

He walked slowly to Pirley, and stood in the school yard with a crowd of 'ten-thirty' men. A young clerk came to the top of the steps and called, 'Any more "ten-fifteen"?' No one pushed through, and he said, 'Ten-thirty', and dived into the porch again in front of the swarm moving up the stone steps. Arthur signed, and put down the pencil.

'I shan't be able to sign next Wednesday and Friday, I'm taking an exam.' The clerk looked at him with interest, men within hearing stared. 'Do you think I could draw for those days? I could sign on Thursday.'

'You'd better go and see the Supervisor. First door on the right. You can tell me on Friday what he says.'

'I'm taking an exam next week—Monday, Tuesday, Wednesday and Friday,' Arthur told the tall, bald man at the desk in the room he entered. Am I entitled to benefit for those days? I shan't be at work.'

'I'm afraid I don't know,' the man said. Arthur looked at him as he held up his face, looked at his eyes and mouth, but he was hidden away behind position, was quite dry and emotionless. 'If a man doesn't attend and sign that he is fit and available for work— well, we can't pay him for those days.' He made a note on a scrap-pad. 'Let me see your time-card.' Arthur laid it on the desk. 'What exam is it?'

'I'm taking Inter Arts at Trentingham. I've passed Matric. Oh. Don't you think that could be recorded on my book? You might then take it into consideration if some sort of job came along which preferred one who had got it.'

'I'm afraid it couldn't take you from your classification. You're a miner, and, as far as we're concerned, you must remain one. Still, it can go down. What were the subjects?'

'English, Maths, History, Latin and Geography.' He watched the man jot down the names, then look up as if the interview was over. 'I can't draw for the days I'm away, then?'

'Well, you could go before the Court of Referees and state your case. They might allow you the days. What do you say?' Arthur felt suddenly angry, for some reason he could not understand. 'You can lose nothing.'

'Right. I will. What do I do?'

'Oh, we'll see to that. You'll be notified.'

'Thank you.' He left, and walked home with a man who lived in the village. 'I say,' he ventured, as they crossed the pit fields, 'do you know anything about the Court of Referees? I'm going to see them about some days I shan't be able to sign.'

'Tha wants to get Tom Cocks to go wi' thee. 'E goes almost every week wi' somebody to Sooton, an' 'e gets 'em wot they want. W'en are tha goin'?'

'I don't know. I've only seen about it this morning.'

'Oh, it'll be about a month before they send for thee. But thee see Cocksy before tha goes. Does tha know 'im? 'E was a union official till they stopped 'im.'

'I know him. A month? I don't think I should have bothered if I'd have thought it'd be that long.'

'Gerrout. Thee get wot thee can out of 'em.' He lit a cigarette. 'They'll pay thee bus fare.'

The man continued down the village when Arthur turned in the gateway. He looked at his mother from the corners of his eyes. She did not lift her gaze to him, but seemed to be waiting for him with mind empty but fearing. Always, now, when he came in she was the same, holding herself in readiness for news of some kind—had he something gladdening like chance of a job, or startling to tell her? Never did she meet him with her mind.

'I've asked about the four days I can't sign,' he said, and then she looked across at him. 'I can't have them until I've been before the Court of Referees—and they might not allow them.'

'What's the Court of Referees?'

'I don't know. They sit at Sooton, and I might not have to go for a month.' She did not answer, though he waited. 'I'll draw two pounds from the Co-op. I s'll need that for this week and next to make up my board.'

'You mustn't draw any.' She was firm, there might have been anger in her tone. 'There's plenty of money coming in the house.'

'I shall give him twenty-five shillings every Friday while I can; then when it's gone from the bank—I'll talk to him.'

She saw his eyes and mouth-line and did not reply, but began setting the dinner. In the afternoon he sat in the front room, but he sat for long periods with his mouth closed and awry, his eyes staring emptily. His mother seemed to be holding herself from death, her half-closed eyes and the ugly droop of her whole face in moments when she let go of herself showed that plainly. He roused and sat straight, pushing out his mouth. But why should he bother, why should his mind go fuzzy? He was young, and everything depended on the next week—his whole future, the ease and satisfaction of his complete being. The expression of his sexual life had been dammed up, and that had unsettled him for a time. Nancy and what she stood for had lightened him, had given a rhythm to the drive of his mental and spiritual strength. He seemed to have recovered from its absence, though at times a longing swept him to rush away from what had become a dry line of study, and meet her, a body of brightness and warmth. But with his mother it was different; her circumstance pressed on him. Always he had one ear cocked expecting the slow sneering of his stepfather to push thinly through the front room door. Then he could see his mother plainly, could feel her heaviness weigh on him, her hopelessness drag him into hot emptiness. He couldn't thrust her out of him; it was crazy to think of, to try. In the evening when he was out, Arthur waited with her, though they were physically apart, for the man to come in muddled and nasty-tongued. Oh, it was bloody hopeless. The epithet was formed clearly in the thought. He was conscious of it; the knowledge brought a shade of shame to his anger. He left his desk, and stood by the window. Men were passing up and down from the pit, slurring their nailed boots on the pavement; youths and younger men in twos and threes talked loudly, laughed suddenly. A feeling pained him for a moment ; their freedom and careless-ness, now that their time was their own, brought sudden envy. He wished he was like them, essentially super-ficial, going to the pit, grumbling at times that 'they had to pull their guts out for eight or nine bob a day,' but forgetting it all when they left it, turning at once to sport of some kind, or walks through fields. His brothers were here, now ; his stepfather wouldn't be long behind them. Oh, he couldn't work. But if he did fail, or if this worry did do something to his mother, he'd give the man the damnedest hiding he'd ever had. He couldn't imagine why his brothers didn't see their mother's condition and know that their father was at fault, then all three of them could soon put him in his place. But Albert was either blind or didn't care, though, of course, his father always forced the youth into neutrality at least if not on to his side—with his, 'Don't we, Albert?', 'Aren't we, Albert?', hung on to every sneering remark emphasizing their own ordinari-ness against his stepson's 'difference'. And Sidney, the younger one, had not the strength to follow with himself the mere feel that his father was killing his mother; rather did he melt, become bewildered and fearful, keeping his reactions to the mood of each parent

separate. But he needn't blame them, he was as weak
himself, held back by circumstances. If he were true to
himself, he'd either go away where he could study in
peace, or attack his stepfather physically. In each case
it meant cutting himself from his mother, leaving her in
her own strength. And why not? It was every one for
himself; nobody got anywhere with half their mind
fastened sentimentally on to another. Nancy had given
him strength, his mother made him weak and away
from himself. Oh, it was all so crazy. And yet who
could see weariness and pain breaking up one's own
mother and not turn to her, especially when there was
something positive probing painfully into her from the
other side. But he himself, really, was the cause of it
all. Oh . . .

'We've a 'oliday to-morrow, Arth,' Albert said, when
he came into the kitchen and saw tea laid for him and
his mother. 'Are you goin' with me and Sid to Derby?
Sussex's there.'

'No.' His tone was definite, sharp almost.

'We'll stand some of your expenses,' Sidney said
invitingly. 'Eh, Albert?'

'Don't talk so crazy,' Arthur said hurriedly. The
father, behind the newspaper on the sofa in the middle
room, laughed shortly, loudly, showing he had seen the
same implications as his stepson.

'They'll let 'im go in 'alf-price if he shows 'is dole-
card,' he called humorously.

Silence fell immediately over the kitchen. Then
Albert began splashing water into the sink; Sidney
went into the garden; his mother upstairs. Arthur ate
his food with savage abstraction, then went out until
bedtime. Next morning his mother packed food for

Albert and Sidney, who took it and went off to sign. They would go to Derby from Pirley without coming home again.

'Why don't you go?' she said to Arthur, sitting over his breakfast.

'Oh, I don't want to go.'

'It'd be better than moping about. You'd feel better with your mind on something.'

'This being out of work's getting on my nerves. It's a good job it didn't happen sooner, I shouldn't have stood an earthly chance of getting through. Don't know that I shall as it is.'

'Get off to the cricket match and buck up, for heaven's sake.'

His stepfather came in from the garden, and Arthur put on his coat and went out, not returning until dinner. The three sat down for the meal, ate it in silence. The young man felt angry, guilty, hopeless by turns; felt the man was accusing him all the time, though of what he could not fix clearly in his mind. He left the table immediately he had finished, went out, deciding suddenly he would not go in the front room again. He signed on Friday, went up to the Co-op. offices and drew two pounds from his account. When his stepfather came in from the pit, he laid twenty-five shillings near him on the table and went out. The Wingrove cricket team was playing away on Saturday, and he went with his two brothers. On Sunday he asked his mother to pack him some food, and was out all day, walking to Matlock, and coming back through the wild, wide country about Tansley, Dethick and Crich.

'You think you'll be all right?' His mother had

bustled about for an hour, getting his breakfast, seeing
that his clothes were handy, cleaning his shoes. He
stood now with a thick note-book in his hand, ready to
go, and she leaned against the table looking at him, a
helplessness fidgeting her now she could find nothing
to spend herself on.

'I think so. I'm glad it's here, and I feel ready for
it. If I get three or four of the questions I've prepared,
I s'll be well away.'

'Well, you think about nothing while you're in the
room except what you're there for.' He did not answer,
but looked away. She glanced at the clock on the
mantelshelf, the ticking hit into the silence disturbingly.
"You'd better be off.'

'Yes. Good mornin'.'

'Good morning.' She tried to get all she felt for
him in the brief farewell, and he went through the
kitchen door quickly without looking at her, knowing
something of her mood. But not all. She watched him
through the small side window walking down the street,
until he passed suddenly behind the straight edge of a
house. She held her eyes open to see his heel rise and
disappear, his hand swing backwards and go, then she
turned suddenly, sat down on the sofa and sobbed
bitterly. All her being was loosened, she felt every part
of her contributing to the flooding tears and the shaking
sobs. She was in the yard when he came back in the
evening, and walked into the kitchen while he was on
the end. Her husband was in the garden, and he looked
at the young man for a moment without interest.

'How was it?' she asked, when he came in.

'I'm satisfied,' he replied, and sat down at the table
while she prepared his tea with a kind of gladness.

Next morning she was calmer, firmer, and sent him off with a brave show of happiness. He was not quite so confident at night.

'The contexts were rotten, and I didn't get a question I'd swotted. Still.' His voice brightened. 'I daresay I did as well as anybody. David Neil said it was an awful paper, and he's taking a History degree. He's a pessimist as well, though; he's sure he won't get through. But he was the same when he took Matric.'

'Get your tea.' She had fallen back and seemed away from everything.

'I think I've done all right,' he said brightly, as he sat down. 'Shall certainly do to-morrow. Should never be afraid of Latin.'

'That won't pull History up, will it?'

The next evening he came home, and she saw he was satisfied. His eyes were bright, his movements brisk, he did not seem to notice his stepfather sitting on the sofa, but turned at once in eagerness to his mother.

'Done excellently to-day. Checked every grammar question and every context, and got 'em all right.' He laughed. 'And the verse unseen was one I'd been through not a fortnight ago. Out of Ovid. Pure luck. And the prose came fairly easy to me.' He began his food. 'Shall sign in the morning, then go for a long walk in the afternoon and think over my Logic. Shall look up a few notes at night.' The woman saw the man on the sofa hold his eyes away from the paper for a space. He seemed as if he would speak, and she went into the kitchen and listened, but only the faint sound of the cup being placed in the saucer, the knife touching the plate as her son continued his meal, came to her ears.

Shenton pit was working the next day, and immediately the other three had clattered from the house, Arthur got up and walked about the garden for a while. Half the potato-patch was hoed neatly; his brothers and their father must have done it yesterday when they were at home. He'd do some when his exam was over; do it all, he'd have nothing else to do. He signed, brought a form home for one of his brothers to draw his money the next day, then walked on to the common and lay down all afternoon reading through his Logic notes. The long, receding trill of larks, the quick, rich sentences of tree-birds, the swerving hum of bees made alive the glowing peace. At times, buses and lorries climbing Condor or Wingrove pushed their roar faintly to him. He did not leave his book for many moments together, until for five minutes booming 'bulls' and thin, curving 'blowers' from the seven collieries set about the district, proclaimed at irregular intervals that it was half-past two. The young man stared emptily for a while after the last sank below the horizon of quiet, his teeth pressed together like a pulse, working visibly the jaw-muscles, the ends of his right thumb and forefinger rubbed each other. Then suddenly he jerked strongly to vivid living, angry at himself, he turned to the notes again and fastened himself into them. It was six when he looked at his watch. He rose at once and went into the village.

'Where have you been till now?' His mother's tone was petulant. 'I've been keeping your tea for more than an hour.'

'I've been on the common, going through my Logic notes. And there were lots I should have been at sea over. Almost like learning the stuff again.'

'Well, get your tea so I can clear away.'

'And I got through only half of them, then. Shall have to put an hour or two in after tea.' He rubbed the back of his neck. 'By gum, the sun's burnt my neck.' He began eating, paused to rub his neck again, lifted his head as far back as he could.

'Fancy lying in this broiling sun all afternoon,' she said quickly, with a kind of fear in her voice. 'And not having a hat on. I never knew such silly work.'

'I suppose you've decided already that I've got the sunstroke?' He laughed. 'Do you know, mum, I think you'd be angry if I was ill any time, or if any of the others were. Not sorry for them.' He looked startled suddenly. 'I'm like that.' She went into the kitchen as he paused in slight confusion, stayed there until he moved into the front room. He had looked through the evening paper, and had put it down quickly at half-past seven as if startled at the waste of time. He heard his stepfather come in at nine and begin talking loudly.

'Where's that lad o' yours?' A moment of silence. 'In t'parlour? 'E's always stuck in t'parlour. And what's 'e been doin' all day?'

'He had to sign this morning, you know that.' His mother's voice was stronger. 'It's his last day to-morrow, and it's his worst subject.'

'Who the 'ell's bothering about 'is subject? What I'm botherin' about's t'garden. 'Ere me an' other two were 'oein' an' weedin' all yesterday after we'd signed. Did 'alf o' t'garden, we did. An' what 'as 'e been doin' after 'e signed? 'E wasn't in t'parlour when we came 'ome.'

'He was out. He was studying then. On the Common.'

'Common. Common. We 'ave to slave in t'garden after we come from the pit, but 'e can go to sleep on t'Common when 'e could have been 'oein' a bit. Why, the bloody idle rat.' He was shouting, now. 'An' you're shieldin' 'im an' fattenin' 'im so 'e can get on, as you call it. Get on. If 'e dosn't get a job soon, 'e'll get out, never mind get on. 'E's not ridin' on my lads' backs much longer, nor mine—the bloody young snipe. I'd a good mind to fetch 'im out by the scruff an' rub 'is nose in t'garden. You wouldn't tell 'im he ought to take 'is whack. Let us do it, while 'e rides on us to a better job. But——' He stopped speaking as the parlour door opened and Arthur came through with bent mouth and narrowed eyes.

'Here's my scruff. You'd better get on with it.' He advanced slowly to where the man sat on the sofa.

'Arthur——' his mother began.

The man rose strongly, and cut her speech off with a glare, then faced the young man boldly. She was breathing quickly, pale and afraid.

'I'll Arthur 'im if 'e comes much nearer. Needn't think 'e can come 'is righteous stuff over me. What about that garden, you damned idle young skunk? Think we're goin' to carry you on our backs till you . . .'

'You've been carrying me on your backs for the last ten minutes,' he sneered. 'You want to get out and come back sober, then you might know what you're talking about.'

'Arthur.' Her voice was weak; she held her hand to her breast and swallowed quickly a few times. But neither of the men noticed her, the anger of each was fastening him to the other.

'Sober. An' who the bloody 'ell buys my beer?' He rushed at his stepson swinging his arms. The woman cried weakly. 'I'll knock your blasted 'ead off. Oo!' He recoiled as his cheek ran into the fist the other stuck out, then dashed forward again almost screaming. 'Take that you bastard. I'll—bloody—well—kill—you.' His arms were flying like windmill sails; he uttered words, one with the effort of each arm. Arthur grappled with him, they reeled, the son's head dashed downwards as the man swung him, and it thumped into his mother's breast. She was backing from them, and the impact sent her sharply backwards into the sharp edge of the dresser. She crumpled to the floor without a sound, and the struggling men broke at once. The elder stood swaying, and rubbed his forearm across his face. The son stooped to his mother, lifted her strongly and took her to the sofa.

'Get that brandy,' he said, but the man stood muddled, his mind occupied with some ugliness. 'Get that brandy, you fool. Do you hear?' He left the woman and went to the cupboard himself, forced the liquid between her lips, then began rubbing her hands. The other sons came in.

'What's up?' Sidney asked, with quick fear.

'Mum's fainted. Put the kettle on and fill the hot-water bottle.' The youth ran into the kitchen. Albert looked from his mother to the two men. 'You'd better put the snaps up.'

'You've been rowin' again, 'ave you? It's damned sickening.' He turned to the pantry. 'Why the 'ell don't you get a job? You'll kill 'er between you.'

Arthur bit back the angry words rushing to his tongue, and beat at his mother's hands, then jumped up and fetched cold water for her face. She revived in a few minutes and attempted to rise. Her husband came across and peered at her.

'Come on,' he said to her. 'I'll 'elp you to bed.'

'Get off,' the youth flashed. 'You're not capable of walking up the stairs yourself, never mind . . .'

'Don't begin again,' she said tremblingly. 'I'll sit here a minute. The snaps want putting up.'

'Come on to bed,' Arthur said. 'Albert's doing that.'

But she would not leave them, knowing the peace would be kept while she was among them. She strengthened quickly, but sat while the sons prepared supper and food for the pit, then she walked into the cool night air and breathed deeply. Her husband sat in the chair by the wireless under the narrow side-window, his mouth pushed out.

'We're not havin' this much longer,' he said suddenly, in a tone which seemed to transfer blame for what had happened outside himself. 'She'll be a wreck botherin' about that fool out of work.' He looked towards Albert, who had, a few minutes before, flung 'Why the 'ell don't you get a job?' at his stepbrother. 'And 'e could 'ave been in the garden to-day. She knows 'e ought to 'ave 'oed a row or two up.'

'She's botherin' about the way you're always on to me, you mean,' Arthur flared. 'Your garden stuff's just a handle.' The man jumped from his chair. 'Yes. You'll get more than you bargained for if you start again.' He fell silent at once as his mother came in with fear in her face. The man, too, sat down.

'Well, you could 'ave gone in the garden a bit. An hour wouldn't 'ave 'urt you. Done you good, I should say.' Albert faced Arthur squarely. 'You don't expect us to do it all and go to work as well.'

'After to-morrow none of you need go in again. I'll do all the damned garden.'

'It's easy to talk when it's all . . .'

'Don't start again, Bert,' the woman pleaded to her husband. She staggered backwards a pace and Sidney rushed behind her and held her steady. 'I think I s'll go to bed.'

'The bottle's in, mum,' the young son said eagerly. 'I'll 'elp you up. Shall you 'ave a drink of anything first?'

'I'll take her one when she's in bed,' Arthur said shortly.

'I'll take it,' the man said. 'You get to your damned books.' The man rose as he spoke. 'Put the kettle on, Albert.'

Arthur sat on the sofa; he felt a nervousness thrusting him away from life. They were cutting him from his mother, making him look a fool. His head ached, the back of his neck hurt him slightly, and he put his hand to it. The woman saw the movement as she went to the foot of the stairs with Sidney, and she hesitated a moment, quick strength flowing into her. But she sagged again and moved on. The youth holding her saw the eyes close in hopelessness. Albert made tea, and his father took it upstairs and stayed for awhile. Indeed he did not come down until he had seen, through the bedroom window, Arthur walk up towards the Common.

Immediately the three men had gone to work the

next morning, Arthur went to his mother's room. She was drawn and sunk into the bed.

'You haven't slept,' he said quietly. 'I know you haven't, 'cos I haven't. I've heard you. I've heard you.' He put his hand to his head, felt over his eyelids with his fingers. 'My head's like a bucket and my eyes feel like stones.'

'You shouldn't have stayed out in the sun so long. It's silly.' She moved. 'I'll get up and make you some breakfast.'

'You'll lie still. Don't get up till I've gone.' They looked at each other for a moment, both were conscious that the other remembered last night. 'I'll go. Haven't much time.' He left her and got his breakfast, eating in spite of no appetite. His mother came down just before he was ready to go. 'Why did you get up? You can do nothing.' His voice was complaining, yet he knew he was glad she had come down. He knew, too, that she had to see him before he went.

'Do you think you'll be all right?' she asked.

'If I can shake off this headache, I shall, I think.' He forced strength into his voice, and laughed. 'It'll depend on to-day, I reckon.' She did not speak. 'Well, I'll be off. Will you be all right? I should go back to bed.'

'Take two aspirins with you, and have one before you go in the room each time.'

'O.K. No, I'll get them.' He went to the cupboard, and she tore a piece from last night's paper and screwed the tablets into it. 'Well, I s'll have to go. 'Bye.'

'Good morning.'

When he turned in at the gate at seven in the evening

Q

his brothers were hoeing in the garden; the father was on the small flower-patch lying between the yard and the small block of buildings comprising coal-house, lavatory and tool-shed.

'How've you gone on, Arth?' Sid called. Albert and his father looked up, but bent again without speaking.

'Not bad,' he replied shortly, then went in. He heard movements upstairs. 'In bed, mum?'

'No. Be down in a minute.' She had seen him coming up the street, and a sudden nervous sickness had gripped her. She felt afraid of meeting him until both had adjusted themselves from some hidden distance. When she came down, she faced him brightly. 'Well. It's over, now. What do you think?'

'If I've got through to-day I shall be all right. But I might have done better.' He stood, turned from her now, looking through the side window. 'I hope it's no worse than "referred".'

'Get your tea.' Her movements as she filled the cup and served him with fruit seemed mechanical; the tone of her face, the half-open mouth, the delayed blinking of her eyelids, showed her away from all near considerations, even his present phase of living. She came back and looked down at him quietly. 'If ever . . .' She stopped. 'You mustn't forget that your father's people are somewhere down south—it's somewhere near Winchester, I'm sure of that.' She looked about the table. 'Will there be enough bread and butter there?'

'Yes.' He was staring at her, then looked at the table to answer, and she walked into the kitchen. He left his chair and followed, but she went on the yard and down the garden to where her husband bent to a border of flowers. 'Mum . . .' But she was already approaching the man and beginning to speak. He turned and sat at the table again, chewing mechanically.

# CHAPTER VI

'Well, that's every pit I've been to now. Why, it's hopeless. Though I knew before I went; there's a man who signs at the same time as me goes round on his bike most days. They tell him they'll be stopping sooner than setting on.' He sat down at the table; his mother put his dinner out without speaking. 'Every Company pit I went to asked me where I worked last, and when I told them, they asked me what I left for. What could I tell 'em?' He began eating. 'And the others—well, Pentland, where I've been this morning. He wanted to know if I'd been in the stall. They want nobody who isn't used to the coal-face work. I was a fool for stickin' on the roads till now.'

'You should 'ave told 'em you could do it,' Albert said. 'If I was out, I should tell 'em I could do anything in the pit—gang, jig, or work at the coal-face. I could, an' you could. You've ganged stalls, and you know what they do. You can load a tram or set a prop and make a pack. Nowt about it.'

The father came in and the young men fell silent. Arthur left the table as soon as he had finished, and went into the garden. He put one foot on the flower-beds, and reached for a thin bit of weed just showing. But there was nothing to do at all, all the hoeing done, everywhere clean and tidy. It was dreadful walking about unoccupied. A sudden thought rushed to his mind, and a short force of breath came down his nostrils, a cynical sound. He had resolved that as soon as

his Inter was over he'd start on the books set for English Honours, and begin mugging up Anglo-Saxon
grammar. But—well, it was ridiculous, the mere idea
of it. Impossible to work in the house with his mother
worrying over him, his step-father sneering before he
went to the pub, rowing after he'd been. Besides, he
was almost sure he'd gone down in Logic; it'd be a
miracle if he had got through. If he studied at all, it
would be more sensible to look through his Inter stuff
again. But if he took it into the fields, he was pulled from
his books to stare at nothing, thinking, thinking. No.
He ought to get with people and do something, somehow. Joe Turner had asked him to go to the Centre.
That'd be better than mopsing about. He would.

'Goin' to the Centre this afternoon, Joe?' he asked
the tall, thin youth, after they had signed and were
walking to Wingrove.

'Yes. Are you goin'? Call about two, if you are.'

'Do you have to pay anything?'

'Penny a week. An' a penny a 'undred at billiards
if you want to play at that. Other games are free.'

He and Turner walked along to the Centre at two
o'clock. Rain began to fall as they reached the building
on the outskirts of the village. It was a long, barn-like
room, and had been out of use until the company
which owned most of the pits in the district and the
brickyard near by had repaired and heated it and
lent it to the unemployed of Wingrove and Condor.
A three-quarter billiard-table stretched across the far
end ; on the walls were dart and ring boards. Men
and youths sat at small tables reading or playing cards;
others on long forms backed to all four walls talked
and smoked.

'If tha wants a game at anythink, Arthur, ar'll play thee. Darts, rings. There's draughts and ludo, dominoes.'

'Ar'll 'ave thee a go at billiards for who pays, Gardner,' a man said, when Arthur had sat down on a form. He was holding the minutest length of thin cigarette between his lips, drawing at it, sticking out his lips and attempting to see it. He spat it suddenly, and wiped his hand over his mouth. 'What does tha say?'

''E's on for a cheap game again, is 'e?' Turner said.

'No,' Arthur laughed. 'I can play, but I'm not backing myself to beat you.' The man turned away at once, and Arthur picked up a magazine—a May *Strand*; other weeklies and monthlies, some dating back a year, or more, lay about. Rain pattered on the slate roof, and a crowd of men and youths bustled in, their haste dying immediately. Soon the soft thudding of darts and rings sounded, the rattle of dice, the click of billiard balls. Arthur joined a 'side' at rings, then sat down again with a magazine. He couldn't help but 'think', a thing none of the others seemed to do at all. Their minds were on the games, the conversation, the moment seemed all; just like the normal miner at work, doing what he had to do and content. If work came to any of these to-morrow, they would go with the same evenness of attitude, adjusting themselves at once as they had to this play-life. They laughed and joked, talked seriously, but never seemed to *feel* the tragedy of their position. A group sat at a table near him. One man was bending right over, almost lying on the table, his head lifted, turning from one to the other of the

four about him, speaking in a confiding tone which now
and then slowed and curved deprecatingly.

'Ar s'll bring it up at meetin' to-night. If 'e won't
pay 'is penny, I say 'e should be stopped from gettin'
coal.'

'Who's goin' to stop 'im?' one asked without interest.

'Coal's for anybody in t'village who's out,' another
put in. 'Penny we pay was for keepin' plenty o'
games, I thought. 'E 'appen doesn't want to come up
'ere any moor talkin' an' readin' an' playin' games. I
get fed up wi' it myself, sometimes.'

'Well, 'e could pay 'is penny,' the bending man said.

'I'm sayin' nowt about that. It's not time to be
botherin' about trade union sort o' stuff when you've
got about five kids an' five bob to feed 'em with.
You——'

'I say, Bob.' The first man cut in again, and pulled
at the sleeve of another brushing past. Arthur knew
him as the driving force of the Centre. He had
interviewed the directorate of the colliery company
and gained the use of this building, the grant of coal
from the thin seam in the clay face at the brickyard, a
small field for sport, financial help for equipment. He
stopped at once, but when he knew who held him, he
began to sidle away again, as if from one who pestered
with unimportant things for the sake of being in the
light.

'I'll be back in a minute to have your money. Busy
just now.'

'Only a sec.' He kept hold of the man's sleeve until
he stood straight and listened. 'This's as important as
owt tha'rt busy about. I've been to Ike Burns again,
an' 'e's not paid. An' it's 'is turn for coal again to-

morrer. Is 'e goin' to get any?' He watched the secretary blink thoughtfully. 'I may as well collect off nobody if 'e's goin' to 'ave coal——'

'It's not our coal, an' I can't stop 'im,' was the reply. 'If we did an' 'e went to see Danks, we might a' get stopped. What did 'e say when you asked him?'

'It was 'is missis. Said 'e'd plenty to do in t'garden this weather, an' that it wasn't as if 'e could come 'ere an' mend kids' boots. 'E could play dominoes an' cards wi' 'er at night, she said. By God, I come away before she bit me.'

'Well, we'll see at meetin' to-night. I'm busy just now.' He walked away, and the man stared after him, pulling out a packet of Woodbines and lighting one mechanically. He began muttering to the others. Arthur left his chair, and walked over to the billiard-table, past men playing rings, darts, cards. All this seemed so useless, he couldn't stand a place like this.

'Are you goin' to be a member, Arthur?' He turned, and saw an official by him. 'Penny a week, an' you can use this place thirteen hours a day besides Sunday. We might get it open on Sunday, yet.'

'I'll see. May do, though I'm afraid playing games all day wouldn't suit me.'

'We've a cricket team.' He moved away. 'Well, see.'

Arthur nodded, watched the billiards game for a few minutes, then went home. He couldn't do with that place. Still, those there had seemed occupied pleasantly enough. It must pall sometimes, though ; bound to do. All too easy. No, he couldn't go there regularly. And he couldn't stick in the house, or walk about the country-side doing nothing. He'd tried both during the past week, and it was beginning to eat into him, taking something from him, some drive, strength of purpose. Before, it was as if his mind was pulling him on, bringing the other parts of him after. Now, he lumbered, conscious of all the irrelevances of living. He'd go melancholy if he did not find something to occupy himself with. There was a larger Centre in Belford, four miles away, supervised by an M.A. It had an occupational side, too. He'd go there, the walk each way would do him good. When he signed the next time, he waited outside for a youth who lived half-way between Pirley and Belford.

'You don't go to Belford Centre, do you, Harry?'

'Sometimes. Not very often, 'cos I'm not a member. It's a penny a week, an' if you miss goin' for about a month it's fourpence. Why? Are you goin'?'

'I thought of doin', but I don't like to go myself—not the first time.' He thought for a moment. 'Does Joe Harris go? You know, him who ganged forty-sixes and was off a good while badly. They wouldn't have him back. You know. Does he go?'

'Oh, 'e's a big noise there. Don't know what; but 'e's allus with the supervisor and the parson.'

'Parson! Is there a parson interested in it?'

'By gum, if it wasn't for t'parson it'd be a poor show. Got some tin as well, an' isn't skinny with it, either. Folks are allus at 'is door, 'coordin' to what they tell me.'

'I'll go an' see Joe. We were pals when we both ganged up forty-sixes.'

Arthur walked the next day to Overdale and called at the Harris' house, but the mother said her son had already gone to the Centre. He went every day after breakfast, came home for dinner, and she didn't see him until bedtime.

'Can't see what 'e wants there all day an' every day. 'E lives there, an' what good is it doin' 'im? An' what good is 'e doin'? I dunno. 'E bothers me. Is 'e goin' to do this all 'is life? 'E'll nivver get a job, an' 'is dad's beginnin' to grumble. Are you goin'?'

'Yes, I'm having a walk down. Haven't been before, so thought I'd call on Joe. I used to work with him. But I'll find him there.'

He left her, and walked over the high ridge, then dropped into Belford. A man directed him to the approach to the Centre—a narrow yard leading to the rear of a large public-house. He waited for a while until a youth turned from the street and walked past him.

'Are you going to the Centre?' Arthur asked.

'Yes. Did you want anybody? I'll tell 'em.'

'Yes. Well, I'll come in with you.' He stepped to the youth's side, and they went down the yard, under an archway, and climbed stone steps to the long 'clubroom', where voices and sudden laughter, the click of billiard balls and soft thuddings stabbed about them. The youth left him at the door, and Arthur stood looking about the room. To the left a group stood about the billiard-table watching two middle-aged men play. Others sat at tables playing cards. On the right the larger part of the room stretched to a glass partition. Near it two youths played table-tennis. Between them and the door others played cards, darts and bagatelle. Arthur's spirits fell a little; this seemed nothing more than a larger edition of the

Wingrove Centre: men adjusted to the play-life, fastened to each other by the game-interest which pulled them from their real present, complaining or patient wives, under-fed, under-clothed children, parents worrying over unmarried sons, young women hoping for an impossible wedding-day. He felt like turning at once and rushing away, but stayed, recognising he was of them. A few stared at him until he moved over among the group about the billiard-table.

"Ave you seen Joe yet?' The youth who had brought him was at his side. Arthur shook his head. "E'll be in t'office wi' Mester Cameron. 'Ave I to tell 'im?'

'No. I can wait until he comes out.'

The door on the other side of the billiard-table opened in ten minutes, and Joe came through. He was a tall, thin youth, fair, with bright eyes. Arthur went across to him at once.

'Hello, Arthur,' he greeted cordially. 'What are you doin' here?'

'I don't know. Came to see you. And the place.'

'Out of work?'

'I got the poke for making a run-in on the double-road jig. You know, I was spinning there. Can't get a job anywhere, so thought I'd see if this would interest me.'

'Have you done studyin'? Don't you go to college now?'

'No. The session's finished, and I've sat for my exam. Nothing to do until the result comes out.'

'Come on an' see Cameron.' His eyes sparkled, and he began to move towards the door he had come through. "E'll be glad to 'ave you 'ere.' They went

into a long, narrow office. A lean man sat at a desk
holding the pipe he smoked; his hair was iron grey, the
face he turned to them as they entered, thoughtful and
wise. 'I say, Mr. Cameron, there's a friend of mine
'ere who'd be a good 'elp, I reckon. Arthur Gardner.
This is Mr. Cameron, our organiser, Arthur.' The two
shook hands and greeted simply. ''E's out of work.
'E's been to college, and got—— What is it?'

'Well, I've passed London Matric, and took Inter a
fortnight ago, that's all.'

'While you've been working?' Arthur nodded. 'At
the pit?'

'Yes. I went to Trentingham two days a week on
a scholarship. I want an English degree, if I can manage
it.'

'Good man.' His tone was sincere. 'And would you
like to come and help us until the next job comes along
—or until you begin to study for finals?'

'I haven't got through Inter yet.' Arthur smiled a
little doubtingly, then his face swept into brightness.
'Yes, I should like to help. But—if . . .' Sudden
strength pulled his features into seriousness, drawing
back his eagerness; it was as if he knew he was reaching
to agree with something which might prove to be other
than he had thought. 'Isn't there something more here
than just playing—than games?'

'Oh yes.' The man laughed. 'We are making big
preparations for the winter. We're getting a library
together. You're just the man we need for that; and
to help with the dramatic society we think of starting.
Wouldn't you like that?'

'I certainly should. Yes, I would.'

'Good. There are other things you'll be interested

in, too. Come in on Friday; Mr. Forrester, the vicar, will be in. That is, if you can get, of course. You perhaps sign in the afternoon.'

'Oh no. Wednesday and Friday mornings. I'm free all the week except then.'

'Oh, well, we shall be glad, very glad, to see you any time.' He looked on his desk, and took up a sheet of paper. 'I must be off, now. Joe, show him where we're fitting up for the library, will you?' Joe nodded with a smile. 'You know, Mr. Gardner, Joe's a good man here, an excellent worker. He's recreation-room steward and indoor games organizer. And, besides that, he represents the men on the Council. Why, last winter there was never one dull evening in the room there.' He swung his head to one side, indicating. 'And you know what a room looks like with a crowd of bored men half-lying about the seats and tables.' Life came into Arthur's eyes as the man said this, his mind jerked more to attention. Cameron seemed to be expressing a repugnance to uselessness in men, a feeling akin to his own, and he moved close in spirit to the organizer. 'But Joe kept them alive, making them fight at darts and dominoes and billiards every night, didn't you, Joe? And you could perhaps help to keep alive another part of them.' He made hurried movements. 'But I must go.'

Cameron passed from the building by the office door, and down steps on the opposite side to those Arthur had climbed to enter. The two young men went through the long room to the far end, and Joe led the way behind the glass partition. Newly painted shelves lined three parts the length of the wall; in the far corner was a small fireplace and a table.

'This is goin' to be the libr'y.' Joe waved to the shelves. 'Over there we're goin' to make a what-is-it. You know. We s'll make tea an' cocoa, and sell it a penny or a 'alfpenny a cup, an' sell buns an' san'-wiches.' He pointed to a hatch in the partition. 'We s'll 'and it through there. Be a' right, won't it?'

'It will.' They looked about the place for a few minutes. 'I say, Joe. Is there anything occupational here—you know, boot-mending and woodwork?'

'Yes. Come on, I'll show you.' He was eager, and they walked quickly across the room to the door and down the stone steps.

'This's cobblin' place.' Three men looked from the bench where each had seemed wrapped around a last, then began hammering or cutting again. 'They can bring their own and their family's boots. They pay about a shilling a pair for their own, ninepence for women's, and sixpence for their kids. That's to sole an' heel them, mind. Cheap.' They moved from the place which was beneath the recreation-room, as was the carpentry shop they entered next. 'There's some tried to do it across us, though,' Joe murmured. 'Bringin' other folks's an' makin' a bit on t'sly.'

'What do you do if you get to know?'

'They 'ave to clear out. But there's not many like that. This's woodwork shop.' A young man was planing a short piece of wood; two others stood watching him, one smoking. 'I say, Bill, you want to be careful, smokin' wi' them shavin's about.'

'Ger out.' The youth, heavy, slow and dirty, exhaled smoke and spurted saliva. 'Wot's up wi' thee, bossin' about. There'd be a bloody notice up if we 'adn't to smoke.' His tone was slow, sleering, as one who hated authority. 'Besides, tha'rt not shop steward. Thee go up theer an' polish the bloody tiddley-winks.'

'Those who want to make anythink pay so much for t'wood. We pay t'rest and supply tools.' Joe was not heeding the one who smoked, but had turned to Arthur again, and led the way round the benches, picking up tools. 'They've made that partition where libr'y is, an' t'shelves. Some's made wheel-barrers for the'selves, an' furniture.' They went outside again. 'There's not many use the places, though, they'd rather sit up there. We s'll 'ave a instructor in winter if some more'll take to it. There's men comes who won't try to mend their own boots—they pay another chap to do it.' He began climbing the steps again. 'I'm not very 'andy, but I've managed to sole an' 'eel mine.'

'I shan't come up again, Joe,' Arthur said, as the other stopped and turned. 'Think I'll walk steadily home, now.'

'O.K. When shall tha come again?'

'Oh, most days. I think it'll be all right helping with the library and such-like.'

He was there again at two o'clock on Friday after-noon. Cameron stood in the yard with another man, and Arthur greeted him, then moved to the archway to climb the steps.

'I say, Gardner.' Arthur turned and walked to him. 'Come up this way.' Cameron had left the man, and was at the foot of the office steps. 'You don't want to be stuck in the recreation-room all the time, do you? Must be a boring job for anybody who thinks the least bit.' He laughed silently, opening his mouth and stretching his lips against his teeth. 'Come up with me. You'll be interested this afternoon.' They climbed to the office, and found a huge round cleric sitting in a chair, and as near to the window as he could get. A cigarette at the end of a long, thin holder stuck comically from his large, sweltering face. 'Hello, Forrester,' Cameron said actively. 'Here first, eh?' He drew a little to one side, discovering Arthur to the parson. 'There's a young man here who will be a good help to us this next winter. Mr. Gardner. This is Mr. Forrester, the vicar of Belford and our chairman. Without him, as you'll learn if you are here ·very long, the Centre wouldn't be a centre.'

'We shall be glad to have you, Mr. Gardner.' Forrester pushed himself from his chair, and held out his hand. 'I believe anything Cameron says, except those things he says about me.' The three laughed; Arthur shortly, the organizer without sound, Forrester bubbling deeply. 'And where have you been working?'

Arthur told them of himself until steps sounded outside the door, and he broke off at once when the two seemed suddenly torn from attention.

'You're just the man we need, Gardner,' the parson said quickly. 'When we've done with the Rate Club I'll take you to my house and we'll go through my books. But we must see to these people, now.'

Cameron had already placed two chairs behind the table, and fetched out a ledger and some foolscap sheets. He went to the door and opened it.

'Ready,' he said. 'But come in one at a time, it's so hot in here.'

Men began to file in, each standing before the parson

and putting down a card and a coin. Most of them
seemed to bring in a kind of innocent shame with them,
and a readiness to come out of themselves quickly at
the words the cleric offered cheerfully to them. To a
few he was stern.

'Only a shilling? Why, you've paid nothing this
last three weeks.' The man mumbled some excuse.
'Well, it's no good, you know. We shall have to let
the summons go through if you can't be regular in your
payments.'

'I've 'ad a gel bad for a month. I can't see to every-
think, mester. But I'll pay two bob next week—'appen
three. Don't let that summons go through. I've never
bin to prison, yet.'

'What's the matter with the child?'

'I dunno. She seems to 'ave no life in 'er. She's
twelve, an' growin' fast. Doctor says she wants good
food. But there's three more besides 'er wantin'
it.'

'Tell your wife to come up to the vicarage to-night.'
There was no hint of sympathy in his voice. 'And don't
forget, the Council will be wanting to know why your
rates are behind.' The man went, no other came in,
and the parson leaned back. 'This is a rotten job, you
know, Gardner.' He was angry. 'We've collected
nearly a thousand pounds from these poor'—he
checked himself—'folks.' He turned to Cameron.
'And how many have we saved from doing time?'

'Scores.' Cameron was looking down, a peculiar
expression on his face; a kind of detached, pleasantly
cynical smiling. 'But you have to make them think the
police are waiting for them to miss a payment. It's
rotten. And we're fighting every day to make the

10

landlords put the rates on to the rent.' A woman came in boldly. She smiled at the two behind the desk, and put down her card and half a crown. 'Hello. Here again, Mrs. Twine?'

'Why don't you send your husband?' smiled the parson, banteringly.

'You know why, Mester Forrester. Would 'e land 'ere wi' it? I'm not far off dole place when 'e draws it.' She laughed. 'An' I spend it.' She took up her card. 'Got owt, to-day?'

'Yes. Have a look.' Cameron waved his hand to a side-table. 'Some good bargains, to-day.' The woman walked to the table and began rummaging among a heap of clothes. She picked up pairs of children's shoes from the floor, examined them, then turned to the clothes again.

'Missis Perkins hasn't been yet,' the parson called. 'She'll be here any minute, so you'd better look sharp and trade.'

''Ow much?' She held up a pair of boy's knickers and a jersey. 'Don't say above ninepence, else I'm droppin' 'em.'

'I've never heard such a bully. Ninepence? Right. But we can't supply paper to wrap 'em at that price.'

'I'm not botherin' about paper,' she said, coming towards the desk fumbling in her purse. She put ninepence before them. 'An' 'ow much more 'ave I to pay before I've cleared my rates? I'm about damn well . . .' She stopped in confusion, and looked at the parson. ''Ave I about straightened up?'

'Five shillings more, Mrs. Twine,' Cameron said. 'You've done well. Two more weeks.'

''Appen so.' She could not be flattered. 'An' I'll 'ave to begin on next in about a month.' She stuffed the clothes in her shopping-bag and went. Others came, timid men and women, bold men and women, children, unafraid, not knowing why they brought the money, some clean and neat, others shabby, with odd shoes and crudely cut-down clothes. Arthur watched the whole pageant, not able to think in straight lines at all, pulled outwards to the utter futility of these people's living—they had no reason at all to continue living, it seemed insane to him—pulled inwards to himself, and fearing. A sudden urge came to hurry away from the place, from the frightening waste of life. A sudden roar of laughter beat from the recreation-room waved downwards, rose again to a holding roar, died gradually. The fear in him died with it; he saw himself one with the parson and Cameron. How foolish to keep the eyes on rags and dirt and emaciated bodies and burning eyes, and begin thinking. And yet a frustration pained him as he tried to reach with his mind to other points where one might begin and alter matters. The Church. He had always conceived the Church as made up of beings somewhat different from the ordinary man. He could not think of them as 'earning a living'. They existed, surely, to complete lives wanting something; they ought to rush to places like this and work all the day. They ought to go round seeing that no woman or child starved, not even if they had to starve themselves. Forrester here . . .

'Well, I think they've all been who are coming.' The parson had risen. He was offering his cigarette-case to Arthur. Arthur took one; Cameron declined, and pulled out his pipe. 'If you'll balance the account,

I'll get along home and sort out the books.' He turned away, then hesitated. 'Or shall I help, and then take you up for a cup of tea as well?'

'No, thanks. I've a lot to do here.'

'Right. Come on, Gardner.' They went down the steps and into the street, then up a slight slope for two hundred yards to the end of a drive, where they turned in. Trees and close-cut hills of lawn spread on either side. In the distance a large house opened many windows to the summer afternoon. Across the highway a church tower stood black against the glow of sky. 'This is my place. Rather too big for my liking.' He seemed rather ill at ease. The young man beside him was calm, without wonder or that loose and nervous interest usual in those who had come with him on occasions from the Centre for some material help, or to do some job about the house or garden. 'I feel rather ashamed of it sometimes when I've been down at the Centre, ashamed at the comfort I enjoy. I *feel* like giving everything away at times.' He laughed shortly. 'But that would do no good, really—no essential good.'

'If you have a family, that would certainly be essentially evil. What I call essential good is doing helpful things one is not obliged to do.'

They went into the house, and through to the library, where the parson pulled two easy chairs to the open french windows. He pushed a button in the wall, and a maid appeared.

'Bring tea here, would you? I suppose your mistress has already had hers.'

'Yes, sir.'

Forrester went to a wall of books and began taking

some from the shelves, dropping them on to a side-table.

'There's this lot of Dickens can go—and Scott. If you'll pack them against the wall over there they'll be ready to load up in the car. These thrillers can go, too.' He laughed suddenly. 'My brother writes thrillers, Gardner. And makes a decent go of it, too. Have you ever tried to write? Most people do, some time or other.'

'A good many desperate things have run across my mind since I've been out. But not writing.' He was silent for a moment, hardly daring to utter what was staggering him almost. The loveliness of this place; the quiet, sunny room, the lines of books all seemed to combine to lift him to richer levels than he had known before. Something besides his brain was working, some thrilling pain was driving him, making something live within him he had no idea was there. He felt the love he had for Nancy, for his mother, the hate and anger against his father, his impatience of the pit, the long-holding of his ambition—all these suddenly became abstractions, removed from any particular. He was reaching forward and working with them, pouring them into vessels of his own making. He came down from the heights suddenly, ashamed. 'No, not writing.' But he laughed apologetically as if the words were a lie, now.

'You should try it. I have, but the results are all in my desk.' He dusted his hands as the maid wheeled in the tea-wagon. 'We'll eat.' He blew out his cheeks. 'This weather. Oh, dear.' They began the meal, and after, sorted out more books. 'If there are any you'd like to take home, you can help yourself, you know. If you'll come here on Monday morning about eleven, we'll take these books down. Be all right?' Arthur nodded. 'We shall have heaps more from others in the town. You'll enjoy sorting and cataloguing them, I'm sure.'

'I shall.' There was a hesitant silence. 'I'll go now, I think.'

Forrester shook his hand, and he left, standing at the end of the drive for a moment undecided which way to go, over the ridge or the longer way round by the Leawood bottom. The church clock showed twenty-past five; he didn't want to get home too early. He turned left, and dropped down the steep Princes Street, then began walking along the level curving by the river that led through Broadoaks, Leawood, Pentland Hollow, Nessfield, where it leapt up suddenly to Pirley. A quarter of a mile out of Belford trees which had lined the quiet road fell suddenly away, clinging now only about the river a field to the left. Arthur was lifted up. He was eager for Monday; Forrester's room and the books; Cameron, with his shrewd, wise face and silent laugh. But something worked within him away from all these; the rich joy he had experienced when the parson had talked about writing. Since he was fifteen he had never lifted his eyes from text-books. He had seen a long, narrow path stretching miles before him, and he had to study every inch of the way, and report at the end to earn his degree. Somehow, at this moment, all that living in blinkers seemed narrow and dry. But he couldn't understand the richness making him conscious of this. He only knew some new happiness had come to him. He looked about him and breathed deeply; at the river and its fringe of trees;

up to the bare, sun-gleaming ridge he might have now been atop; forward along the dull sweep of the . . . He stopped suddenly, his head jerked forward. 'Why, that's Nancy in front. Walking slowly. And she looks fatter.' He leaned on the low stone wall, watched her with fascination, knowledge creeping over him. He wouldn't overtake her, he'd turn back if she turned back, and she might do if she lived in the town. But she was turning up the lane to Broadoaks. He walked on, merely watching her, thinking nothing, saw her turn in at the gate of a large new house. Then he hurried past the lane end, only fell into meandering again when the hamlet was hidden behind him.

'You're spending a lot of time at that Centre,' his mother said, when she had given him his supper. 'And going all that way. What's the matter with that here?'

'They do nothing but play games—and bicker at one another, from what I can see about it. They want a boss there who isn't one of 'em. There is at Belford, and they're doing good work.'

'Yes, but does any of the men who sit there all day think of getting work, and what it means to be out of work?'

'I can't say that they do. I mean, I haven't noticed they do. That's just it.' He became thoughtful. 'But there's no work for them.' This was a strong burst, it seemed to indicate that he agreed with his mother's suggestive question, yet strained to excuse himself. 'It's better they should be there than sitting at home staring at nothing.'

'They can't think a deal about the women and children at home.' She sat on the sofa. 'It'll do you no good. Why don't you study? You ought to be able to do that under *any* circumstances.'

'I can't study here, and that's that.' He knew she was referring to his step-father's disturbing attitude more than the accident of being unemployed. 'I thought I could, but I'm no super-man. If he'd give me a chance, I'd study twelve hours every day.' He gritted his teeth in angry frustration. 'But he's a fool, a weak-brained fool, especially now he's drinking more.'

'Well, you're running away from him, going to that place every hour God sends.' She went out quickly, knowing she had gone too far. If it were not for her he'd have left the house long since, she was certain of that. 'Going out again?' she asked, as he walked through the kitchen door. She was eager to come to him again, eager to know how he was to her.

'Yes. I shan't be long, though.' She hardly heard the words; the tone of his utterance was enough, as eager as hers, emphasized to show he was not away from her. 'Just going down to Cyril Stuart's to borrow a book.' He was back in half an hour. 'I'm going to bed. Want to be up early in the morning.' He took off his coat and shoes somewhat hurriedly. 'Dad's coming up the street about slewed. I'll go. Got a couple of novels here. I'm going to read a lot of novels.'

'Novels!' She was taken aback, even the faint fear which had shot into her eyes at the information about her husband cleared. 'Novels!' She looked at the books he had put on the table while he took off his coat. He picked them up, now, as the gate clicked.

'Yes, novels.' He laughed. 'And plays, too. And poetry. I'll have a rest from text-books. 'Night.'

'Good night.'

He closed the stair-foot door behind him, closed his bedroom door fast. He did both consciously, but not until he was in bed did the full significance of it sweep him. Cowardice, so that he would not hear any of the possible storming and sleering from his stepfather. But his mother would be withstanding it. It worried him for a while, and he strained to hear, but no sound came, and he soon was absorbed in a book. In the morning he was up early, and went out immediately after breakfast before the other men were up. On Sunday the same, but Monday morning, when they had to go to work, he stayed in bed until they had gone. He didn't like it at all; a sense of shame sickened him as he lay waiting for them to go. He tried to think he was doing it to keep the point of his stepfather's nastiness from near his mother, but could not justify the thought. He went from the house in anger, in weak anger, because his mother had let him go without speaking. She looked ill. But what could he do if he stayed?

The Reverend Forrester was at his typewriter when Arthur was shown in to him. He left it at once and greeted the young man, but Arthur's eyes were half-away from him, looking at the machine.

'Been jotting down a few ideas for next Sunday's sermons,' Forrester said. 'Come on, we'll get the books down.'

Arthur stood for a moment blinking thoughtfully at the low, portable typewriter, then followed. In twenty minutes they were unloading them again at the Centre.

'If you'll get some of the men to carry them up, I'll go and talk to Cameron.'

Arthur went into the recreation-room and looked

round. He was immensely relieved to see Joe Harris, and he walked across to him at once and asked him to get some men to help him.

'Don't you carry 'em. I'll tell two o' these to fetch 'em.'

'No. I'll help as well.' He shuddered slightly to think of Joe's 'boss' attitude at its practical point; he standing while others did his work. The books were brought up, Joe stood watching. 'We'd better leave them outside, eh, Joe?'

'Yes. T'place won't be finished for a week. I'll see if I can't 'urry 'em up.' Harris examined the small room well. 'Come on, we'll go an' see Cameron; 'e'll get some more men on it.'

They went into the office and Joe began immediately. The supervisor listened, and backed morally a little from Joe's strong suggestion that men should be put on the job at once and kept there until the library was ready?

'I'll see to it, Joe. It's only the middle of summer, yet, and we're not really wanting it badly until winter. That's why we started it early, so the men could do it when they felt like it.'

'What 'ave you started bringing books for, then, a'ready?'

'That's something you don't understand, Joe,' the parson said shortly. 'There's more to do at the books than the place they're to be kept in. They need going through and cataloguing.' Forrester was rather impatient of Harris as a type. They came here and worked hard, revelled in responsibility and authority, yet it seemed pretty obvious that they were conscious of their independence. Indeed, two such had worked here before, and immediately Cameron had cut across their too extreme individual strength, they had left with light cynicism, then attempted to injure the Centre from the outside. Still, Harris seemed more sensible than they; he did not seem to mind his enthusiasm being directed and curbed. 'We'll see to it, Joe.' A knock on the door. 'Come in.' A man opened the door and bent round it.

'Could you come a minute, Joe?' Harris switched to the man at once, interested. 'There's a check fast in t'billiard-marker.'

Joe bustled out, diving his hand in his pocket for his keys. Cameron smiled, then turned to Arthur.

'Mr. Forrester and I have just been discussing you, Gardner. We wondered whether you'd like to go for —well, we could almost say it was a holiday.' He was looking into the young man's eyes, which were raised to his suddenly and seemed to hold guardedness. 'There are two of the men from here—young men—going to a Demonstration Centre for three weeks. One is taking a course in shoe-making and mending, the other one in upholstery, and we hope they'll come back with enough knowledge and ability in the crafts to be capable of teaching them to groups in the coming winter. We hope to have a full-time woodwork instructor so no one need be sent to learn that.' He moved in his chair as if adjusting himself to a switch-over in thought. 'We wondered whether you would go, too, and have a roving commission there; it is allowed, I think. You could pick up a lot of ideas, both in the organization of a centre and its practical working. It is supposed to be *the* ideal Social Service Centre. These two men go this coming Saturday. If you say you'll go, too, I'll write to-night and arrange it—and we should be much indebted to you.'

Arthur looked round the room, thinking quickly. He saw his mother, his stepfather, the dole office, the Court of Referees.

'What about my keep? And signing? And what if the summons comes for me to attend the Referees?'

'You'll sign there and draw your benefit there. The Court of Referees is not so important as this Centre, if you only knew it. They'll wait. What do you say? You'll enjoy the change, I'm sure.'

'Yes. I'll go.' He seemed to make an effort to pull himself free from a holding back, then became wholly himself. 'I may be able to help this place by going. I hope so.' He smiled, then his thoughtfulness was sudden again. 'Do we have to pay our own train fare? Where is the place?'

'Oh, it's about thirty miles from here. I shall run you over in the car,' Forrester said simply. He offered him a cigarette, continuing to speak quickly as if to sweep away the seeming awkward atmosphere in which the young man was conscious of his lack of means. 'I went over in—see, May. It's a lovely place, away from everywhere. I should think you'd like it.'

Arthur stayed for a while, then went into the recreation-room for an hour, playing darts, rings, or anything else he was asked to join. It seemed like a duty for him to do all this. He was unemployed and a member of this place ; if he came, went into the office, and home again, the men might 'look sideways' at him. And he wanted to be natural with them and they with him, especially if he was going to work among them. But he left at half-past two, when most of the men had gone for dinner.

'What about a go at bagatelle wi' me?' a man, thin, with two or three days' growth of beard sticking on sunken cheeks, said quickly, when Arthur had finished playing a man who said he must hurry away to his dinner.

'Well. I was just going. Aren't you going for some dinner?'

'None to go to.' He looked about him when Arthur came back to the long, narrow board. 'Got a fag on yer?' he whispered. Arthur produced a packet of Woodbines and gave him one. He had one himself when he saw the man waiting for a light, and he lit them both. 'If you want to get off, never mind playin'. I've bin lookin' at some o' them books you brought, an' I can read a bit.'

Arthur laughed and went. Outside, he hesitated which way to take, then dropped down the steep main street and walked along the bottom. Inevitably he had thought of Nancy, and a sudden strength had pulled him towards where she might possibly be. He felt so lifted up that he hoped he would meet her. He would certainly stop and speak to her. Along the narrow Bridge Street, past the clattering skyscraper mill, he walked, thinking of her, of the office she had worked in at the other end of the town, of his walking away from her without a word when she had told him she would have to be married to some one else. He had changed since then, somehow. Then, he had been moving on a comfortable and certain line, and nothing nor nobody else was quite as essentially important at the moment. Still, she had 'done the dirty on him', though he was sure it was not calculated; she must have lost herself for a space. Everything was in proportion again, more in proportion than it would have been at such a distance, and he still on the dry, thin line of academic distinction. He hoped he'd got through Inter, of course. He hoped he could start college full-time in October; he would be then at least economically safe whatever the attitude of his step-father. But his existence had broadened this last month, the world had suddenly become for him full of human beings, of all moods and make-up between tragic and comic, and none which deserved to be turned away from as he turned from Nancy, pushing her into the outer darkness with a quick, instinctive justification. He would like to talk to her now. The road, quiet and curving past Broadoaks, was hot to his feet now that it had crept from the fluttering shade of the trees and lay baking in the late noon sun. He looked up the lane lifting through the hamlet, turned suddenly, and walked on the grass verge fronting the line of old houses and the new one farther along where Nancy had turned in. He trembled a little as he passed the house, though he looked boldly into the lower windows. Nancy was at the bedroom window, and he did not see her watching quietly while he passed, or know that she pressed close to the window to see him round the bend on to the road leading to Dale.

He was home at half-past five. His throat hurt him as he smelt the dish his mother fetched from the oven when he had sat at table.

'I should think you've had nothing since your breakfast.'

'No. I haven't.' He tackled the savoury stuff at once. 'You knew I wasn't being in for your dinner--time, didn't you?'

'Yes. Of course I did. But you're late for t'other dinner-time as well. If I hadn't been bakin', it'd have been cold.'

She went into the kitchen again and brought him a piece of rhubarb pie. He looked up at her twice, tapped his plate with the knife in kettle-drum fashion, laid it down and received the sweet.

'I'm going away on Saturday.' She swung round to him. 'Only for three weeks—to a big Social Service Centre.'

'What's it for?' Her brain was quick to be hard on anything which might drag him away from what she wanted to be his narrow line of content.

'Well. Three of us are going to learn something about carrying on a centre—cobbling and upholstering.' He laughed. 'That'll be funny. I can't see myself . . .'

'Yes—but is there a job at the end of all this Centre stuff?' Her voice was impatient. 'Has the parson ever thought of recommending you for a job or telling you where to try for work? What about the man who runs it? And the Council, as you call it? There must be some managers of factories and shops, and office men. Can't any of these find you a job?'

'Give me a chance. I don't know any of them yet.'

'They know you well enough to use you.' She quickened from the tiredness that was creeping in her tone. 'Well, what have you to take? I'll get all your things washed up to-morrow. And for heaven's sake get well in with somebody with influence. You'll never get a job without, and that's a fact.'

He looked at her as she paused, and knew these were rousings from a patient waiting for him to be with her again in comfort. He felt fearful for a moment, she looked so worn and dry, then he smiled with self-shame and nodded agreement with her.

# CHAPTER VII

ARTHUR walked the four miles to Belford on Saturday morning, his suitcase hanging heavily, first on one side then the other as he changed hands. It rubbed and knocked against the side of his knee, tiring him quickly. Packed into it were the things a printed slip suggested were necessary—towels, changes of linen, an old suit 'to work in', boots for possible garden work, and other items. He wished, now, for he was on the open fields between Overdale and Belford and the sun was burning from a clear sky, that he had sported the tenpence for a bus ride. Still, he hadn't even thought of it when he had set out; he had thought of nothing forward. What he had experienced was relief, not at getting away from an unpleasant environment, merely, but that he could be cut from his mother for a while, and so attune her in some degree to the big break which would be inevitable if his circumstances did not change quickly for the better. His step-father was becoming unbearable, Albert seemed to be in another world altogether. They had nothing in common at all, now. Sid never forsook him, yet the contact was not easy between them, not smooth and free and rubbing warmly, but it was as if they stood apart jerking strong rushes of conversation across a barrier. But Sid, like the other two men, lived positively; none of them were turned aside from their own path because of him. It was different with his mother; she was bound to him with living strength, and yet had to smother every born expression of it.

If he could be sure she would not turn from life with that cynical loss of interest when he had broken completely from her, he would go and move from workhouse to workhouse until he found a job. But if he couldn't find a job here, what was the good of going away? Unemployment was everywhere, and people here did know him and what he was capable of. But it was the home-life. If he could get a job, everything would be all right. His mother had been rather cynical over the Centre, thinking the business-men interested ought to find him work. Well, they might do. He was sure the parson and Cameron would help him in that way, even if it did mean the Centre losing what they called 'a good man'. Still, this three weeks would do him good, he thought; he could climb out of his narrow home existence and see where he stood.

He was half an hour behind time, and the car was waiting in the inn yard, the parson and the supervisor and two young men by it.

'Come on, my lad,' Forrester greeted. 'We ought to have been half-way there, now.'

'I've walked,' Arthur said, 'and I'm hot, very hot. This case's a lot heavier than when I started, too.' He laughed with the others. 'Still, I'm sorry to have kept you waiting.'

'Oh, that's all right.' Cameron squeezed his arm and laughed silently; Arthur felt easy at once. Cameron had a peculiar effect on him; he felt moulded about by the supervisor, as if the man was himself grown old and mature and greater than anything which could come against him. 'Do you know these two young men who are to be your companions?'

'Well, I've seen them in the recreation-room and talked to them, but I don't know their names.'

'Oh. Well, this is Alf Cower, he's going to learn boot-making and repairing.' Arthur shook hands with a thin, shabby youth sucking his face thin over a tightly packed Woodbine. 'And this is his cousin Stan, who's coming back able to upholster any chair or couch we happen to have given us.' Cameron laughed, and the parson smiled faintly.

'Yes. 'Appen so,' the youth said independently.

The parson was fidgeting, he opened the rear door of the car.

'Well, let's get off,' he said. 'I've an appointment this afternoon. In here. It'll hold you three comfortably. Your luggage'll be all right, won't it?' He snapped the door to behind Stan, who had climbed in carefully, holding his case away from the smooth-fitting clothes moulded about his stiff, well-fleshed figure, guarding with one hand the rose in his lapel. Stan seemed a bit of a fop, his wide, innocent face seemed perpetually melted in an empty smile, and when the least thing occurred he made it the point of some pointless remark, and laughed richly. Alf, who sat in the middle, laughed too, laughed at him, and reproved him in whispers when his sallies seemed unfit for the ears of the two men in front.

'Shurrup, yer silly sod,' and he dug his cousin in the ribs, and showed him with his eyes those in front. But Stan got bolder, bending between Cameron and Forrester and offering some joke at which the supervisor snatched a smile and the parson appeared not to have heard.

In an hour the industrial country was gone. For

miles and miles pasture and woodland stretched in
faint undulation; odd farm-houses sprung suddenly
from the loneliness and were gone again; tiny men and
women worked in far fields. On the road an occasional
man walked at the head of a horse pulling a load,
walked slow and heavy as one tramping the yielding,
ploughed field. Suddenly the car swung into a narrow
drive and roared between intertwining trees, stopped
at the entrance to a quadrangle where a few men stood
about a doorway.

'This is where you report,' Cameron said to the three
when they had alighted and dragged out their luggage.
'We may see you before we go back; we're just calling
on the warden.'

The three went into the building, and were at once
greeted with an artificial smile from a young lady, who
asked them where they were from and their names. She
looked down a list, and told them the number of their
bedroom. The two Cower cousins were together;
Arthur's room-mate was named Evans, from the
Rhondda Valley, and he had not yet arrived. Next,
they showed the yellow unemployment cards to a
young man, who told them they would draw their
benefit from him each Friday, and that if they wanted
to send any money home he could supply them with
registered envelopes and would take them to the post
office six miles away. The Cowers laughed gaily at
this.

'Out of fifteen bob!' Alf grimaced at the clerk. 'I'm
goin' to forget I've got a 'ome for three weeks. I've
never 'ad a right drink or smoke since I've been on
t'dole, an' I think I can get through fifteen bob a week
'ere.'

'Don't be too sure,' the man said, knowingly.

They took their things, and found the room allotted. A young man showed them round. He was the instructor in charge of the boot-making, a thin, tough-looking ex-soldier. He took them to the quadrangle, two sides of which had been horse-boxes and now converted into bedrooms, each holding two single beds and a small chest of drawers in between. Other men joined them, and they looked into the rooms on the other two sides of the square—rooms where the different crafts were demonstrated—woodwork, boot-making, rug-making, upholstery. Then they went into the main building, into the dining-hall, the two common-rooms, into the small library upstairs. A part of the building was for staff quarters, which was marked plainly as such. From every window miles and miles of pastoral land stretched interminably, seeming to force one to make a life of the room one was in, to turn away from the outside world altogether.

Most of the men had arrived by tea-time, and Arthur found his room-mate, Evans, a man of about fifty, carefully transferring his things from suitcase to drawers.

'Well, we're going to be together in here for three weeks, man, and we may as well be friends straight away.' He held out his hand and Arthur took it gladly. 'I was a miner in the Rhondda until three years ago. Done nothing since. Where are you from?'

'I come out of Derbyshire. I was a miner and have been out about six weeks.'

At tea, and in the common-room after, the men sat about in groups, at first holding fast to the party from their own district, but soon they broke and fused with others, until complete freedom brought them into busy exchange of social service experiences. But from this general cameraderie new cliques grew suddenly, youth drew to youth vividly, and age sat together in slow conversation and smoking. Two Scotsmen—one, McLean, a young man who was himself not unemployed but worked as tutor in a centre and had come here for ideas, the other wholly unemployed, whose name was Laurie—a youth from Yorkshire, tall and as healthy as an animal, whose permanent home while he was out of a job was in a Gryth Fyrd camp in the Midlands, and Gardner, all suddenly decided to go for a walk until seven-thirty, when a general meeting was to be held in the large common-room. Other small groups were about on the road at the end of the drive, a road that seemed lost and useless coming from one horizon and running away to the other. The Cowers were sitting on a fence talking to two other youths, Shott and Jonson, lying on the grass verge.

'Where the 'ell does tha reckon this place is, Gardner?' Stan Cower said, as the four came up. 'I think it's off the damned map a'together. We've just asked a chap where t'nearest boozer is. Two miles, 'e said.'

'You couldn't get there and back before the meeting at half-past seven,' McLean said. 'It's a quarter-past six, now.'

''Ell. Got to wait till to-morrer for a drink.' Tom Shott groaned. 'Why, this place's nowhere.'

'You've come here to work, not booze,' Laurie put in, with dry good-humour.

'Work.' Stan laughed, short and high-pitched. 'Work. They expect me to go back and stuff chairs wi' 'oss 'air.'

'He an' all,' Shott laughed. 'I'm in the up'oldstery.'

'Yes, an' thee'rt goin' to do, an' a',' George Jonson cut in sharply, though he laughed at Shott's grimace. 'W'at will him at Centre say? 'E paid thy mother's rent on'y last week.'

'Well, I offered 'im a couple o' rabbits an' a part-ridge to straighten 'im.'

'Does tha think he wants any o' thy poached stuff?' Jonson turned to the others. 'Does tha know what this bloke does? Goes poachin' every night. An' 'e asked 'em at t'dole to alter 'is time from mornin' to afternoon 'cos 'e couldn't get up soon enough.'

'An' they did do, an' all,' Tom said, and laughed joyously. 'Come on, let's go into t'prison.'

Shott went, and with him two other Scotsmen. Jonson stayed until Arthur and his friends moved, then he walked up with them.

'He doesn't look like a poacher,' Arthur said to Jonson. 'As clean and respectable as a Sunday School teacher.' He laughed. 'And good-looking, too. Seems quite a harmless dandy.'

''E's 'ad four years at a reformatory—an' been in prison since for pinchin'. 'E's a devil. But 'e doesn't smoke or drink. Don't know w'y 'e was botherin' about a boozer.'

'If there'd been a couple on the doorstep of this place, probably he wouldn't. He seems loose, somehow. Like a child, always wanting something he can't have.'

''E is like that. If 'e does 'ave a pint it'll send 'im crazy. 'E'll laugh at nowt and do the damnedest things.'

'The two Scotties seem to have taken to him,' Arthur said. 'They are farther north than you, aren't they?' He was turning to the two Clydesiders.

'Oh yes,' Laurie replied. 'They're out of the High-lands somewhere.'

The general meeting began promptly at seven-thirty in the large common-room. The warden, an ex-army officer, tall, thin and apparently strange to his new appointment, greeted the ring of men sitting round with self-conscious attention, and emphasised the fact that they were here to work hard and fit themselves for service in the centres which had sent them. Then the secretary outlined the work of the course.

'As well as learning a craft,' he said, 'you are here to run this national centre. You will chose a chairman, a vice-chairman, a secretary and all the committees needed—craft, sports, finance and the rest. Serving on committees will, of course, help you to run your own centre better. Here, you will see how to organise both the occupational and recreative sides of a centre. You will do it here, and take the knowledge and ability away with you. Indoor and outdoor sports are to be held, cricket matches with two or three outside teams. You'll be fully occupied the whole of the three weeks.' The secretary laughed and sat down.

'Looks like it,' Alf Cower muttered.

A chairman was chosen—a young man who appar-ently had been here most of the summer, and took the voluntary physical training class. Others, it appeared, had stayed on from other courses, too. Two of these nominated and seconded the chairman; one became vice-chairman himself. Most of them seemed 'tough'; rather smooth to those in authority. The various com-mittees were formed. It seemed that the secretary had had information concerning the abilities of some of the men, apparently from the centres which had sent them, because he suggested names, and these were promptly nominated to authority in the work under discussion. Arthur became librarian and attached to the sports committee; McLean, chairman of the entertainment group and a member of the executive; Laurie, who was treasurer of his Clydeside centre, was put on the finance committee.

'A chap who's been 'ere told me to keep off these committees. Says you 'aven't a minute for yourself, if you don't.' Alf Cower pushed back his chair without sound until he was half-hidden behind Laurie. 'I'll keep out of sight. Be damned to bein' stuck in 'ere on committees.'

But, even as he muttered to Laurie, his name was put forward to be accepted on the crafts committee.

'Go on,' murmured Laurie. 'Say you don't want to serve. Go on, you'll be on in a second.' But Cower sat still, muttering curses. 'Too late now.'

'It's a' committees,' he muttered.

The secretary rose at the end of the meeting.

'You will find all notices as to work and recreation on the board near the dining-room door. They are not yet posted; they will be there on Monday morning. But I can give you an idea of the organization of the course. Breakfast is at eight, after which rooms must be tidied and beds made. Crafts from nine till twelve and two till five, dinner coming between at one. Tea at six, and then at half-past seven the evening programme begins.' He laughed, and some laughed with him, either humorously because of the wireless touch, or cynically for other reasons. 'Two nights there will be a sing-song or concert; two nights a whist drive; one night, Thursday, will be the general meeting, when matters of administrative interest will be dealt with, and also reports by you of the condition and working of your particular centre.' Arthur started slightly. He couldn't say anything about Belford; he'd not been there long enough. One of the Cowers would have to do it. 'Of course, the various committees will meet each week, bringing matter for discussion to the general meeting.' He looked at the paper in his hand. 'A rota of names will be drawn up for washing up after the meals, and for the bed inspection. A knock-out competition in each of the games will be arranged, prizes to be given to the winners. And there are plenty of games—darts, draughts, dominoes, rings, table-tennis, putting—well, you'll find them all. We have arranged cricket matches, too, with three villages, so please get some practice on our not-too-good pitch, and we'll have a trial game to find out the best eleven. We may arrange, too, to take a party in the bus we have—it only holds twenty, though—to Litchton, to see and go through the cathedral; or to Burtfield, to go through a brewery.' Lively interest moved the whole ring of men, and laughter broke loose. 'That apparently wouldn't come amiss.' He waited for silence; the grim, pugnacious president P.T. man banged on the table. 'I think that's about all for the moment.' He bent to the warden and whispered, and when the chief had nodded, he sent the chairman out of the room, then began speaking again. 'There is one other item, an important one. You will know what crafts we have here to offer you, and all of you have been allotted to one. But since the forms were sent to the various centres another craft has come along.' A young lady entered the room at this moment carrying a bag the size of one holding a tennis outfit. The warden and secretary rose to greet her, then she sat with them at the table. The secretary continued. 'This other craft is something quite different from anything we have yet attempted, and I leave it to Miss Lovegrove to explain, and, I think, give examples of the art she will teach.' She smiled and nodded when he looked down at her. 'And if any of you wish to transfer to her class, you may do so when she has finished.'

He sat down, and the young lady, who had been undoing the bag she had brought, rose at once, and began bringing into view brilliantly coloured pipes of varying lengths. These she set up on the table as she began speaking.

'I won't take up more than a few minutes of your time. These pipes are made from bamboo, and no more than seven small tools are used in making them. If I can get a class together'—she laughed apologetically —'though it will mean, of course, robbing other crafts, I will explain to the members the construction and way of getting music out of these things. In the three weeks, I hope to see the class make a set of pipes— two soprano, one alto and one tenor. And, besides that, learn to play. Even those who know no note of music can learn to play. We might even get to playing chamber music—some simple trios and such-like. I can't tell you any more, really. I'll demonstrate, now, what the pipes sound like and what they are capable of.'

She took each of the four pipes in turn and played on them—a slow, rich-toned melody, then a quick, light sprite of a thing.

'Well, that is all I can do.' She laughed as the whole audience clapped soundingly, and did not attempt to

say more because of the noise, though it seemed that
she would have done.

'Well, we thank Miss Lovegrove; it was really lovely.
Those who would like to make and play these pipes—
and I must confess I am almost carried away into
joining the class—will they please give their names to
me, and I will have them transferred from the other
crafts?' He whispered to the warden. 'The meeting
is closed, now.'

McLean, Laurie, Tom Shott and Arthur began talking
almost excitedly among themselves; then they came
across to the table and Miss Lovegrove smiled gladly
at them. Stan Cower came, too, to the utter surprise
of his cousin.

'Thee'll get it w'en tha gets back to Belford. Tha's
come 'ere to learn up—up'olstery. W'at's to want wi'
them things; they're nowt, only wooden tin whistles.'

'I'm goin' in that class. W'o wants to shove 'oss-'air
into sofas? Not me.'

'Tha'rt thinkin' more about lookin' at t'tart w'o's
teachin' it.'

'She's about only thing worth starin' at as I've seen
'ere, yet.' Stan winked at his cousin, who laughed in
spite of himself. 'Be a'right in this pipe class, eh,
Gardner?' He laughed at Arthur, who had come up.

The course proceeded as the secretary had outlined
—meals, crafts, committee meetings, general meetings,
whist drives and cricket matches, round after round of
the competitions. The staff distributed itself about the
tables at meal-times, though it seemed this was done
consciously to emphasize the 'fellow-feeling' without
which social service would be a failure. The warden
came less often than his staff. Arthur and McLean

were at his table, away from him by the bodies of two craft-masters. This was his first course as warden of such a place and they heard him telling of Italy, where he had lately completed many years of military service. They heard him say that women in cottages baked once a year, baked the bread hard and stored it, soaking loaves as they were needed. They heard him say he had met D. H. Lawrence once, and Arthur pricked his ears, and was about to offer a remark, but he drew back, not knowing why, except that when he looked into the thin face he saw nothing to give confidence.

'What do you reckon of the warden?' he asked McLean, when the meal was done and they two walked alone towards a deep belt of trees bordering the grounds.

'He seems to be trying to do his job. If he is ex-army it'll be difficult. I can't tell whether his aloofness is genuine or assumed yet.'

'There seems an—an unknowable mystery about him to me,' Arthur replied, his brows puckering uncomfortably.

'That's always good for prestige.' McLean laughed. 'But it's bad for "service to others".' Still, perhaps we shall get to know him better. A week's not gone yet.'

That evening Tom Shott, the Cower cousins and the two men from the Highlands cut the whist drive and walked up to the inn two miles away. This was no crime; the two other Scotsmen and Arthur and a few others had gone there on the Sunday evening; the Cowers and their Scotch friends were there, too. The secretary had come in and treated them all. There had been singing and small betting over the skittle table. The secretary had returned home in his car; the rest walked, singing and airing opinions on the National Centre. To-night, Shott, the Cowers, McDougall and Ferguson went alone. They had been itching each evening since Sunday, and now, on Wednesday, they had thought it not dangerous to cut the whist drive, though they would have felt much easier if Arthur and his two 'pals' had come. But these refused, as other men had gone walking and the drive might possibly have fallen through. They walked down the long avenue of trees after the card-game was over, and met the five returning. They were all well-primed, though Alf Cower and the younger Scot, Ferguson, carried theirs well, tense and silent. McDougall and Tom Shott shouted and sang together. At times Shott took a bottle of beer from his pocket, and offered it to the three who had met them, and now turned to walk to the house. McDougall had one topic on his mind; he could talk, or rather shout, about nothing else, cursing and laughing at the same time. The same morning, he had been fetched from his craft by the bed inspection men, who had taken him to his room and stood while he tidied round and remade his bed. In his muddled state he seemed to imagine the warden responsible for the morning's 'insult'.

'I'm going to throw the bastard out of his bed and make him make it again. Bed inspection. Bed inspection. I'll inspect his bed. Ha, ha, ha.' He shrieked with laughter.

'Shut up, you fool. Coxon'll 'ear thee.' Alf Cower dug him in the ribs with his elbow.

'Who's Cocky Coxon? I'll inspect his blasted bed. Oh, but he's got a wife. Ha, ha, ha.'

Alf Cower led his cousin away to bed. Stan seemed inclined to join the two noisy ones.

'That'll do.' Laurie put a hand over his mouth, and the man was quiet until they reached the quadrangle. Then McDougall began again, and Tom Shott started singing. A craft instructor came across with a candle in his hand. McDougall blew out the candle at once, then waved about joyously. Shott brought out the beer with a flourish and giggled foolishly, offering it to the instructor.

'Get into your kip, you fools,' he said, and struck a match which McDougall promptly blew out. 'You damned fool, get to bed.'

'I say, Redburn.' McLean followed the instructor as he moved away and lit his candle. 'You'll say nothing about this, I hope. They're damned fools. We'll see them to bed.' As he spoke McDougall began shouting again, punning on the warden's surname and threatening to turn him out of bed. 'I'll see to him.'

'It's nothin' to do with me,' the instructor said, turning away. 'Why should I say anything?'

They got the two noisy ones in bed and quiet, and in the morning the Scotsman was foolishly contrite, cursing himself for a fool. Tom smiled blandly; he seemed to remember nothing and was not worrying, either. But in the afternoon McLean, who was absent at an executive meeting, came into the pipe class and took Shott with him. The youth came back in twenty minutes smiling blandly.

'About last night,' he whispered to Arthur and Laurie who were sitting in front. Miss Lovegrove was busy at the piano, tuning a student's pipe.

'What's going to happen?' Arthur asked.

'Dunno. Mac was there as well. They said nowt to us. Only t'boss asked questions.'

McLean came in later. Arthur and Laurie waited
for him to speak, though they showed faint curiosity
in their manner, and he whispered to them at the first
opportunity.

'We've left them to the warden,' he said, motioning
with his head towards Shott, who was industriously
smoothing the mouthpiece of his pipe. 'I should think
he'll have them in and dress them down. Tom, there,
was as innocent as a baby. The warden didn't know what
to make of him. Admitted everything quite blissfully.'

The class continued, the tutor coming round to each
as they sawed off a length of bamboo, shaped the top
for the mouth, fitted a cork, and made the 'window'.
Then she took them in turn to the piano, found the
pitch of the pipe and suggested how much needed
sawing-off to bring it to the key. Weird and teeth-
grating tones popped and curved about the room; it
was so much fun.

McDougall was waiting for Shott in the common-
room. He seemed glad that Arthur and the two
Scotsmen were with him. His weak smile strengthened
a little as they all came up.

'He wants us, Tom.'

'Eh?'

'The Head wants us.'

'Oh, ar? Come on, then.'

'Buck up, Scotty,' Arthur said. 'He'll not eat you.'

The two went away slowly; the others chatted for a
few minutes, then went to clean themselves for tea and
the evening.

'We've got to go in the morning,' McDougall told
them when he and Shott came to them. Tears hung
in his eyes.

'What?' McLean was incredulous: his voice almost scraped as he uttered the word. 'What? Going? In the morning?'

The rest who heard the tearful Scot were dumb.

'He just said we'd got to go as if he was a gramophone,' Tom Shott, put in, without interest. 'Still, we s'll get our train fare paid.'

'Coming three hundred miles for less than a week.' Mac seemed to be talking to himself. 'Shan't go, though. Shall get a job in Derby or somewhere.'

'What are you, Mac?' Arthur asked. The question was merely to cut across the other's wildness of mind.

'Joiner. I'll get a job better here than in the village where I was.'

'It's a damned scandal,' Laurie said. 'That Redburn must have squealed, an' he said he'd say nothin'. It's all to get in good books.'

'There's one or two more that I wouldna trust an' a',' Alf Cower said. 'Them two who were 'ere last course an' who've stopped on. Seem to be a bit "creepy", I reckon. Round t'secretary.'

'Well, they couldn't creep round the warden, that is a fact.' Arthur laughed without humour. 'But it's a rotten shame, these two having to go . . .'

'He may be ex-army, but his way certainly isn't "ex" if he's going to carry on as he's started with these two.' McLean showed on his face the faint repulsion he felt. 'Come on, tea.'

'Oh, we'll wait for these two,' Laurie said. 'Get a wash and brush-up—quick.'

'Well,' one man said to another as they went in to tea, 'they shouldn't 'ave brought beer on to t' place. They were askin' for trouble.'

12

As the news got round that the two were to be sent
home, the tone of the place quietened. Men never
mentioned the matter to each other, except when they
were well away from the place, walking in groups.
There was no official announcement made. The warden
came to meals and the general meetings with the same
inscrutable face, and talked of Italy to the secretary
and Redburn, who were on either hand. Shott and
McDougall left while the others were at crafts, their
beds were stripped and their names taken from the
rota and committee lists. 'It's a bad thing for the
course,' McLean said, and on the day every one left
for home, he confirmed the utterance. 'It was a bad
thing for the course.'

Arthur worked at his pipes along with the rest,
finished one and painted it a shining red and black.
Then he spent odd hours in the other crafts, saw men
making boots, stitching soles to uppers, saw them strip-
ping soles and heels to repair them, helped to plane and
saw in the woodwork class, arranged hair and other
materials with the upholsterers, began following the
pattern, with hook and long thin pieces of cloth, that
was marked on a square of coarse sacking which with
work and patience would sometime be a soft, thick
rug. The members of each group worked happily,
talking, joking; at times one would sing or hum. The
dole-queue seemed out of experience, the emptiness of
existence and the long lounge at the street corner
something incompatible with these busy beings, all
outside themselves. In the short intervals after meals,
they sat in the common-room, the older men smoking
slowly and comfortably chatting; the young ones
alive at games or talk, some hurried to the cricket-pitch

for a 'knock'. The outside world was not permitted to creep in; there was comfort and recreation after work, in the general meeting the *activity* of the National Centre was discussed; the *activity* of the Local Centres; suggestions for improvement and extension of *activities*. No discussion seemed to live which veered towards the reality of unemployment. A member from each centre reported the numbers on its books, and any story of success from small beginnings was loudly applauded and appreciated from the dais where authority sat. McLean said his centre was large, was, in fact, a bequest from a rich Scot, and university men came and gave lecture courses on a variety of subjects. But, he continued, no man was allowed the use of the recreative section of the centre unless he was taking a course, which was free. This was deprecated from the dais, but McLean held on until a sense of discomfort sat about the room, holding some men still and silent, shuffling others on their chairs. When McLean sat down, the applause was not so vibrant.

'What was the idea, objecting to the way you carry on your centre?' Laurie asked of McLean, when the meeting was over and they sat with Arthur in his bedroom.

'It's just the same with every man who's in authority in an organization.' McLean was cynical. 'Numbers, numbers, numbers. They don't care what sort of blokes come in so long as the numbers are big. Never bother about quality, the strength is in numbers, not the kind of men making the movement. Like Trade Unionism.'

'Like adult education,' Arthur put in.

Arthur's room-mate came in at this moment and

looked slyly from the corner of his eye at Alf Cower sitting on his bed.

'Don't rumple his bed, Alf,' Arthur laughed. 'Freddy's a careful soul. He'll never have the bed-inspectors after him.'

'He's got a right snore wi' 'im,' Cower said. 'I couldn't get to sleep last night for 'im.'

'I never heard him,' Stan said.

'He has. And there's a whistle in it. I was going to tell him. And he was groaning . . .'

'I know all about it, man,' Fred said, good-naturedly. 'My old woman digs me in the ribs most nights.' He smoothed his bed, and swept his gaze about the set of drawers where his brush and comb and other things lay neatly. 'If I disturb you in the night just touch me on the shoulder, and say, "Now, Freddy". I s'll give over.'

'I'll come an' say, "Ner, Freddy",' Alf Cower said ominously. 'I'm only ovver t' partition tha knows.'

'I was in the war,' the Welshman continued, not heeding him. 'Fightin' the Turks. Saw a Scotty that'd been skinned. One o' your chaps.' This was to Laurie and McLean. 'You don't forget them things, an' if I dream . . .'

'O.K., Freddy,' Arthur said. 'Do you want to turn in. I'll go with these chaps a bit.' He winked at the others and they all went into McLean's room until ten minutes to eleven, when the lights went down for a second and brightened again.

'There's the signal,' Laurie said. 'Come on, Arthur.'

The whole place quietened and was blotted into the summer night. Arthur was just dozing to sleep when his room-mate began a snoring which soon broke into groans. Then he ran smoothly again with a snore which ended in a curving whistle.

Alf Cower groaned from the other room. 'Hey-up, Gardner. Shove summat in his gob.' Arthur laughed softly. 'Oh, I s'll screet if 'e doesna shut up.'

'Now, Freddy. Now, Freddy.' Arthur touched the sleeper on the shoulder and he sat up at once.

'Sorry, chum. Was I at it?' Arthur laughed to ease him. 'It's when I get on my back.'

'Tha wants to tie a bobbin in t'middle o' thy back.'

'Take no notice of him, Freddy,' Arthur laughed. 'Get off to sleep again.'

. 'I will do that, though, to-morrow,' the man said sadly.

The nights passed, and the days. Arthur went up to the library each evening and sat for half an hour, but very few came to take out books. The men seemed too alive in the free time to sit and read, talking in groups or walking or playing. While he waited, he wrote a letter in reply to one he had received from his mother, then he sat staring through the window, over the two wide fields and the deep woods reaching, rising as it were, into the very sky. The secretary came suddenly into view, a gun under his arm and a dog at his side. They disappeared soon into the wood. The world slowed suddenly for the young man; surgings he could not analyse flowed through him. He knew they were hung on to the violences of his life-stream—his mother, step-father, Nancy, the examination, the pit. These were real, the stuff of them was waiting for him in the real world. This place wasn't real at all, it was the falsest thing imaginable. Men were here, and none of them were their real selves, hadn't chance to be. That little man who'd been a knock-about comedian. Trying to live again as vividly as in his youth. Pitiable. And in the outdoor sports, fancying themselves as runners and jumpers, confident; as if by taking thought they could add a cubit to their stature. At meals, attempting to behave as if they were 'genteel', the meal altogether was unnatural to them. Oh, it was all so false. And why were the men here at all? Some of them, and he himself was among them, most patently for a holiday; others to learn a craft so that on their return they might get a job in a centre—a paid job. One man had said so definitely. No great training is demanded, he had said. Just need to be pleasant and know how to organize a bit. An organizer had come up from London one day to 'have a look round'. He had spoken with Arthur and McLean, and whispered that the way to get into the show was to get on a committee. McLean had said afterwards that he could have been sick all over the man.

A youth came in for a book, and Arthur was alive again. The warden came and took two books. Arthur trembled with excitement for a moment; he might now know the man and not the warden. He would be glad to know there was warmth in the man; McLean would be glad to know it, too. But he went again after he had selected the books, offering merely a few formal remarks about the job of being librarian. No other member of the staff came in; they seemed to be hidden away completely in the breaks between the organized business of the Centre. He had seen some of them rushing away in cars, glad, it seemed, to get where life was.

There was none here, that was a fact. All make-believe.

Lots were drawn one evening for the two outings. Arthur, McLean and Alf Cower were in the Litchton list, Laurie and Stan among those to visit the brewery in Burfield. Cower and some others who were in the cathedral lot were patently disgusted with their luck, and sought about busily for some one to swop trips.

'Doesn't tha want to go wi' Gardner an' Mac?' Alf asked of Laurie, who smiled irritatingly as he came up. He knew what he was after. 'What about swoppin'?'

'No fear,' he answered promptly. 'I'm for a cheap skinful as well as you. Call somewhere else. What about Slater?'

''E's lickin' 'is chops now, thinkin' about it.'

'I say, Alf,' McLean said suddenly, through the shout of laughter at Laurie's suggestion. 'There's that Welsh fellow. What's his name, now? Him in the next room to me. I believe he's down for the brewery. I'm sure he is. Get hold of him, he's a local preacher or something like that.'

'I know whom you mean,' Laurie said. 'That shy bloke. D'you know, I couldn't make out what was the matter with him the first week. Went about with a horse-sad face and black rims round his eyes.'

'He wears hard collars and a blue serge suit, eh?' Arthur said. 'I know him, he told me he was a Methodist. He seems always embarrassed, even when he's shaving.'

'I reckon he's four or five sisters all older than he,' McLean put in.

'I was saying,' Laurie said, 'I wondered what was

the matter with him, and I saw him with the house-keeper. He was like a little girl, writhing about as shy as hell.' He laughed. 'The woman gave him something in a paper, and he came out looking ever so bright. I asked her if he was ill, and she had to laugh. He told her he'd never been to the lavatory for five days.'

'I shouldn't ask him to swop, Alf,' Arthur laughed. 'A good binge'll set him up.'

'Thee take thee time. I'm goin' to find 'im this minute, before somebody else nabs 'im.'

It was a Wednesday when the brewery trippers were excused the afternoon crafts and crammed into the bus. It seated twenty, really, but thirty-two squeezed in somehow, and Alf Cower was among them; he gave a particular wave of his hand to the Welsh Methodist man, who had willingly exchanged. They got back for tea at half-past six. The brewery had obviously been very liberal with samples.

'And he sent Tom and McDougall home,' Jonson said, who watched the unloading. 'Hm. He wants to see this lot.'

The cathedral trip was next day. The secretary had arranged for a guide to meet them and show them round the place. He waved his hand across the wide front, pointing out the kings, then led the party inside, and began his parrot-like explanations. Arthur and McLean and a few others, after low mutterings to-gether, broke away and came outside again and sat on the grass. The sun, hot and brilliant, blinded them for a space, then they settled down on the sweep of green, some lying, some sitting, all smoking after the forced abstinence in the cathedral. Charabancs unloaded trippers; others loaded them and drove away. The scene was one of regular change. The youths and men from the Centre watched the groups of young women moving glad and free in summer clothes.

'I've almost forgotten what a woman's like in that shanty we've come from,' one youth remarked. 'I s'll be glad when we go back home.'

'Women. Hm. What good's women?' another said. 'I went to Burfield last Sat'day. Took all my money, what with bus fare and a drink or two.'

'I wouldn't walk a mile and a half to the bus to get to that place. An' back again at night, too. Might have done if there'd been a woman at end of it.'

'Take thee time a minute, an' let me finish. I did pick up a moll an' stood her a drink, then took her a walk. No good, though. I reckon they put summat in your food to keep you off 'em. Like they do in 'ospitals, tha knows.'

'I shouldn't be surprised,' McLean said dryly. 'And I'm ready to leave it. When you see people like this, you want to get back to the real world again. A lot of men packed together. It never seemed so awful to me as it does now. Organized up to the eyes; organized trips. A lot of men. Where's the nearest pub? Come on, Gardner, let's get drunk.' He was looking towards the cathedral door. 'Heck! Here comes the sec. and the others.'

'Well, let's get off.' Arthur, too, was swept with a wild rebellion. 'They'll wait for us.' He was on his feet. 'But it doesn't matter if they don't. I'm fed up.'

But the secretary came and shepherded them into the bus, and they rode away.

'It's been a dry job,' a man said. 'A bit different from that yesterday. What about a drink?'

'If we pass a pub we'll stop,' the secretary said. 'But we must be home for tea.' Somebody began singing *Home, Sweet Home*. 'Ah, here we are.' The secretary seemed relieved.

The men leapt down and were alive again, throwing off the dry, complaining individuality as the beer loosened them, fusing again into fellowship, forgetting all that was behind—and before.

Crafts finished at dinner on the last Thursday, and then sports were held. Most of the men strained unnaturally, running, jumping; there were some pitiable efforts to be what they were before the long idleness of unemployment devitalized them. At night was the last general meeting, and the warden said his official good-bye.

'To-morrow is your last full day here.' His tone seemed different now, somehow, more kindly. 'I hope you will go back to your centres and teach them what craft you have learned here. If you do, the object of this course will have been fulfilled.' He said more in this strain, then bent to the secretary, who whispered something. 'Oh yes,' he continued, as he straightened again. 'We want you to leave the place as you found it, clean and tidy—the grounds, I mean.' He laughed shortly. 'There have been a lot of those little green packets dropped about, the—er——' He bent to the secretary again, rose quickly. 'Er, Woodbine packets: I had forgotten the name of the cigarette. Well, those and other litter need disposing of. We should like some wood bringing in from the plantation; the garden needs a little attention. Each of these tasks can be done by a party, and I think it would be right if the secretary divided the members of this course into groups—as many groups as there are jobs to do. The tidying round can be done to-morrow afternoon, for some of you might wish to use the craft rooms for the last time in the morning. Then, of course, there is the concert in the evening; I hope the entertainment committee has arranged a good programme for us. I have heard a lot of weird noises coming from the pipe classroom. Maybe Miss Lovegrove has something good in store for us.'

The meeting broke up and the men dispersed, some to sit about the common-rooms, some to walking in the grounds, a few hurried to the games to play off the finals of the competitions. Arthur was one. He had got through to the final of the table-tennis, and now began playing a tall youth who had stayed on from a previous course. Arthur managed to beat him, and the few watching were glad, somehow. One could feel the reason, but nobody gave it expression. The tall youth and the others who were 'old hands' had been all right, had shown them the ropes and done much to get them into the run of the place, but yet they were not of this course, somehow. They had been easy and comfortable when the new-comers glanced about them carefully, timidly almost, had seemed to take the life as ordinary life, and the freshers had never fused with them really. The old ones were in the lead in every-thing, and were closer to the officials. Some were staying on, even after this course. It didn't go down, somehow.

There was a long envelope in the rack for Arthur next morning. It was from home, and a slip of paper fell out as he opened the letter within. He glanced at it,

saw that it was his examination result. There was an
F opposite Logic. His stomach went sick for a moment,
then he became quite normal again, and read the letter
from his mother, which said shortly that he might as
well have the enclosed, then he would know exactly
where he stood before he came home. He stuffed it in
his pockets, and went at once into the grounds. He
could not think clearly for a minute or two; then he
shrugged his shoulders and went back into the building,
where the men were gathering about the dining-room
door awaiting breakfast. Over the meal he turned his
thoughts upon himself, and marvelled slightly. If he
had still been on the thin line of living—at his lonely
job in the pit, coming home and pinning himself to
books—this might have broken his world into atoms,
undoubtedly would have done. But he had grown,
broadened in these last six weeks. He saw quite plainly
where he was in the stream of existence. He understood himself as a system, knew that the adjustment of
the one into the other depended in no great degree to
things and forces outside himself. His weaknesses had
brought him down as far as superficialities were concerned; his strength kept him steady, even content, in
essence. Failing an examination was no mighty tragedy;
it merely blocked a line where the possibilities might be
no greater than some still left open. Self-martyrdom
for the sake of a parent tortured by the other was in
no sense heroic; it could be foolishness, had been
foolishness in his case. Still, he was made up of these
strengths and weaknesses. He was no different from
anyone else; they were composed like it in varying
balances. None of the men here were likely to groan
and sink into utter inanition under the painful pressing

of unemployment. They had pitted themselves against it, and were using their environment. Yet he knew men who were lost to life because of it, men who sat at home and stared and rubbed their thumbs nervously over their fingers as they brought a possible future into concrete imminence. Still, he had had periods of spiritual stagnation. Fear cut across his line of thought. It was all right thinking he had grown and strengthened. He had, but he was removed from the special circumstances of home. He might, in the face of these, fall back—fall back. And he had failed Inter. He felt himself weakening, seemed to be sitting at home, his mother, his step-father——

'I've got a pipe to paint, Gardner. You anything to do?' McLean was speaking at his side. Arthur started, then clenched his teeth. Pipes — upholstery — rug-making. Oh, all the lot of the stuff he had tried his hand at in this place! What was it worth, what was the use of it? It had been waste of time, waste of life. The whole three weeks had been just a black-out of the things vitally near him in the real world. And the lights were coming up again.

'Well, I've one to finish—the last hole to do before I paint it.' He said this with a sudden burst. 'Yes, I'll come. Better than lying about all morning doing nothing. I'll be along to the pipe-room when I've straightened my room.'

He went. Straighten his room. It was a farce—all of it was a farce, the whole show. Then when he had tidied and made his bed the two inspectors would come round, maybe fetch him from the craft-room and wait while he remade his bed or hung up a towel which might have dropped from a nail in his absence. He had gone the round twice, once with Laurie, the other time with a sour man from the potteries. Laurie was one of the most decent men Arthur had ever met. He even envied him his nature at times, good-humoured, shrewd, and with no surface emotion. In the pipe-room where tools were lent and borrowed, if one asked for the loan of his or the return of their own, he always turned the 'my file', 'your knife', into 'our'. At the inspection he tucked in corners of sheets and blankets, shut a drawer, picked up a towel.

'This's the devil who fetched me out last week,' he said, when they came to one room. 'Still, I had a smoke.'

The other man had come conscientiously to his job, and peered at the beds and the toilet paraphernalia with keen eyes.

'Might as well do the job as it should be done,' he said, as he stood in an untidy room. 'It's regulations. Whose room is this?' He had gone to the door and read the two names printed there. 'Mossbank and Collier. See, Mossbank's in the rug-making. Don't know where Collier is.'

'With me, in the pipes.'

'You fetch him, then. I'll get Mossbank.'

They went for the two—two merry youths. Arthur smiled as he came with Collier and waved him into the room. Mossbank was already there with Sanders.

'Damn you, Colly,' Mossbank said. 'It was thy turn to straighten round. Tha can do it to-morrow, now.'

'O.K. I was late this mornin'. Ne'er mind, Mossy. We'll 'ave these two out to-morrow; it is my turn.'

'How do you mean?' asked Sanders. 'Whether we're untidy or not.'

'If it's like Bucking'am Palace in your room, you'll come out.'

The two had put the room in order, and had gone. Arthur was called out the next morning, and he went good-humouredly, though he knew his room was quite tidy; he'd done it specially to test Collier's sense of humour. But Collier fetched him, poking his head round the door of the craft-room and calling his name. They went along, McLean and Laurie grinning after them. They grinned, too, when they stood in Arthur's room and Collier pointed to the point of a sheet sticking from the bed.

'You've pulled that out,' Arthur said, and laughed.

'Fancy saying a thing like that. Everybody fetched could say that. Rotten thing to say.' Collier leaned against the door, pulled out a packet and offered Arthur a cigarette. They smoked for a few minutes, then Arthur made a move as if to go. 'Nay, straighten your bed first.'

Arthur tucked in the sheet, and went. He had enjoyed the joke. He thought of this, now, as he tidied the room, thought of other schoolboy tricks the younger men had thrilled to put over. He thought, too, of the slow men who had sat about in the free hours, letting time go by, rousing to work steadily in the 'shops', the youths quick and eager at cricket and table-tennis, the older ones staring long at the draught-board, and shutting one eye to take careful aim at the dart circle. But this was done. Each, now, was away from the other; each hung on to places far away, reaching to the real spot in the real world. And none knew what another was going back to, but it was certainly to less comfort and poorer food. And he himself . . . Oh, he'd get off to McLean in the pipe-room. If he sat on the bed, here, he'd fall into the same old helpless dreaming.

'Oh, I thought you weren't coming,' McLean greeted. 'Last day in here.' Arthur sat down, and began boring a hole in his tenor pipe. 'Not been bad, here. I can say I've enjoyed it now it's behind me nearly. Awful at times, though.'

'Damned awful,' Arthur agreed, feeling glad to be able to express himself. Then he felt suddenly ashamed at the embracing sense he had felt himself put into the words. 'But they've not been bad to us, really. We came to work and learn, and I could certainly help a centre along, now.'

'What are you going to do when you get back? I'm O.K. I shall have something to give; they'll be pleased with me. Might get paid a bit more if I start a pipe-making course.'

'I shall try at our centre, but they're more for games.'

'You should do as we do. Not let them in unless they take a course at something. There's you with pipes—and you could have a literary society and a drama group. And Alf'd take some for boot-making and repairing. He's made a rug, too. Well, a bit of a one, like you and me. You and he could do that.'

'Now, look here, Mac. Working in a centre isn't living. If I did all you said, I should never look for a job, never study or do anything for myself. I'm selfish enough to want some money and——'

'And a wife and a home.'

'No fear,' Arthur jerked out. 'But I want a job.'

'Well, you know what that London bloke said. Get on a local committee, then a district committee, and start shouting. Lots of Social Service jobs going.'

'Give me this note on the piano.' Arthur blew his pipe, trying the last hole he had made. McLean went and held the note while the pipe sounded. 'That's just it, isn't it?'

'No; a bit flat, but don't take much out.' He waited until Arthur blew again. 'That's it. You'll just have time to smooth it and paint it. What colour will you do it?'

'Black. All black.'

'You said that as if you felt black.'

'Did I?' The young man laughed foolishly, then he swept into a strong seriousness. 'No, I'll do it red, glaring red.'

They painted the pipes, and left them standing upright to dry, then went and joined the others in the common-room.

'We've been lookin' for you,' Stan Cower said. 'We a' goin' up to t' Green Man for one or two. Come on.'

Fifteen walked the long, empty road to the inn, and spent a rowdy hour before dinner; the table skittles were never still, the landlord and a helper pulled continually at the handles at the bar counter. Arthur felt happy and brave as they walked back, and dared to repeat stories he had heard in the stables down the pit.

'I'd a good mind to kick up a blasted row at dinner-time,' Alf Cower said, 'and see if they'll send me 'ome.'

'Nay, let's have none of that the last day, damn it all,' McLean said. 'They'd only say that Belford Centre was a nest of hooligans. And you've got your

13

people at that end to consider—them who sent you here.
The organizer's all right, isn't he?'

'Best chap I know,' Alf said, with less strength.
'Kept 'undreds out o' clink—them who couldn't pay
their rates. 'Asn't 'e, Arthur?'

'I believe he has,' Gardner replied.

'An' t' parson as well,' put in Stan.

'Well, then, think of him.' McLean was curt. 'He
might get the poke if complaints reach anybody in
authority.'

'I was only 'avin' a bit o' fun,' Cower said, a little
shamed. He did not join the song springing up among
the party until a few lines had been sung, but then he
brightened suddenly and shouted in thick tones.

In the afternoon the men split into groups and
cleaned and tidied the grounds, put the garden in
order, fetched wood from the plantations bordering the
drive. At tea they were vivid and hungry, freer than
usual, shouting across the room, laughing loudly.
Immediately after, they went to change and get ready
for the concert; the pipers for a final rehearsal, couples
to go over short sketches and duets. At night each turn
was presented with much ado, and ended in irrational
applause. The secretary was chairman and announced
the items, adding what he thought appropriate remarks when it was done. The warden sat among the
men in the audience, and seemed to come out of
himself, laughing and clapping with due fervour. At
the close he spoke quietly, thanking the artists, then
hoping in a general way that centres would benefit
from the National Centre, which, of course, meant the
men themselves.

At intervals the next morning the bus took groups to

one of the two railway stations each six miles away. Men were scattered in all directions—Scotland and the northern counties of England, the east and west, into Wales and the south. Men took the addresses of others, in note-books, on scraps of paper, and vowed eagerly to write when they got home. Arthur exchanged his with McLean, seriously; others gave him theirs and took his, but he could feel no intentness to remember, as they adjured him, to write soon. He smiled and nodded and took their hands, but his reaction was quite neutral; he wished neither to forget nor remember them. The parson and the organizer came with the car, and took him and the Cowers away, down the long avenue of trees, over the lonely country-side where the clear summer air glowed golden, through the stinking brewery town and busy Saturday villages. His spirits had sunk as the car door closed; he felt helpless, carried swiftly through a lovely land and not able to enjoy it. He was pinned in a shadowy place, and at the mercy of a machine and a man who had no thought for him personally except to see that he did not die unnecessarily. It was like that in his life; he could do nothing to save himself. He felt doomed, somehow, though he was as strong physically, mentally and spiritually as any other being. But he was pinned and driven along in utter frustration, far, far off his track, and no side road opened for him to rejoice in a positive push for himself. Alf talked all the time, to him, to the two on the front seat. Stan played short slow tunes on his pipes, laughed after each mistake.

'Have you your bus fare?' the parson asked Arthur, when he stood with his case on the pavement before the Centre in Belford.

'Oh yes, thank you — oh yes,' was the hurried answer.

'Right. Well, we shall be seeing you next week, I hope.'

'Yes, I'm eager to hear what you have to say about the place and the things you've done.' The organizer smiled silently into his face.

'Right. I'll be over one day next week, then. 'Bye. 'Bye,' he nodded to the parson, then turned away, and went with a dry, empty mind to the bus.

# CHAPTER VIII

For a few days after Arthur had arrived back from the National Social Service Centre, the house was more alive than usual. Sidney asked questions continually; the mother joined vividly at times; and even Albert was interested, though sometimes his questioning was ironic and meant to disturb.

'I suppose you're goin' to put in full time now at Belford, and make tables and rugs for all poor folks in t'place? Besides, you'll 'ave to be t'pipe bandmaster. I can see you wavin' a stick in front o' that lot. What's first thing they'll learn—Fifth Symphony or t'Unfinished?' He would laugh uproariously after such a harangue, and glance at his father, who sat grinning on the sofa.

But in a week or so it was all forgotten, and the dead feeling crept over Arthur and his mother. Sid and Albert turned to other things; the father sank into the old ugly silences which drove him to a revivification at the Miners' Arms. Arthur tried a few times to meet his step-father in conversation, and although the man answered with some sort of good grace, he was short in his replies, and usually found something to take him away from the young man's presence. But the son never stayed up to see the man when he came from the public-house; he took a book and went to bed. He was conscious that there was cowardice in this move, though it justified him when he noted that his mother showed relief because he did it. She looked older, much older, and dry and worn. He feared violence to break about her, and so avoided it for his part.

'There's a letter for you, Arthur,' she said, one morning, a week after his return. 'From the Labour Exchange, by the look of it.'

'Oh. Perhaps it's a job.' He hurried in, not eagerly, for there was in his mind a shadow that it might be something to jerk him into fear and worry, and her into fear and worry too. 'We'll soon see.' He tore it open. 'No, I have to attend the Court of Referees in the morning. Sooton at eleven.'

'About your exam days?' She tried to stop back the last word. The 'exam' seemed to pain her voice, though the whole sentence had come spontaneously as the logical question was born in her mind. The exam result had not been mentioned by either, and even this matter almost irrelevant to it brought silence as the woman said the word. She hurried to put it behind another thought. 'Do you think you'll get them?'

'I hope so; it'll help. It's worth facing the Court for.'

'Who are the Court?'

'Haven't the faintest idea. Shall soon know, though.'

Arthur paid two and twopence for a return ticket on the bus to Sooton, and arrived there at half-past ten. He asked where the Court of Referees was held.

'I'm goin' there,' a shabby man told him. 'Not to t'Court, though. I'm goin' to sign.' They walked on to a large chapel. 'Tha goes in at that side door an' up some steps. There's plenty o' cards to tell thee t'road.'

The man went in at the arched doors, Arthur at the side door. Another young man was entering, and they went in together, up winding stairs on to a balcony where other men sat or stood about, talking and smoking. It seemed funny to Arthur to see men smoking and spitting, to hear 'damns' and 'bloodys' in such a place. Below, the body of the church had been cleared of seats, and queues of men straggled to desks, each with the name of a pit hanging above it. It was as Pirley, queues for part-timers, for whole-timers, for young persons. It was as Pirley, the line of 'regulars' could be picked out at a glance. Behind the clerks the dim choir and pulpit lay as if neglected.

'Do they use this chapel—you know, on Sundays?' Arthur asked the one he had come up with.

'Oh yes.' His tone was uninteresting, like one who preferred stronger, richer topics. 'They must be makin' a bit o' money out o' lendin' this to t'dole folks. Got thi expenses?' Arthur shook his head. 'Come on, we'll go an' get 'em, then.'

The young man seemed to know the ropes. He led the way to a small room on the balcony, and called through a pigeon-hole.

'I've come from Offerton. One an' two, my bus fare,' he told the big, horn-rimmed spectacles which peered through. ''Ere's my ticket, if tha wants to see it.'

The man glanced at the ticket, then produced a shilling and two pennies without sound, almost miraculously, it seemed. Then he jerked his head up invitingly to Arthur as the other was signing the receipt-form.

'I'm from Pirley. Two and two, my fare.'

The man paid out, did not ask to see the summons to the Court. He supposed no one would be so foolish as to come to such a place as this unless under some sort of compulsion. They joined the group again, began

smoking and talking. One was just leaving in answer
to a call from an official.

'Stick to that.' A man held him by the sleeve, and
bent earnestly towards his face. 'Remember, stick to
that an' tha'll be a' right.' The other pulled free, and
went through the door the official was holding open.
'If 'e sticks to what I've towd 'im, 'e'll be a' right. Get
nine out o' ten what they're after when they come 'ere.
Don't thee come from Pirley way?' he asked of Arthur,
darting his face forward, and opening his mouth and
letting the lower jaw hang. Arthur nodded. He
knew, now, that this man was Cocks, whom he had
heard of in connection with cases brought to Sooton.
He had been a trade union official at one of the pits,
and was now unemployed, and spent a good deal of
his time fighting for money he considered was being
withheld from other out-of-works, either through the
straight National Insurance benefit or the Means Test.
''Ar thought so. What are you 'ere for?'

'I sat for an exam and did not sign for a week. I'm
here to try and get paid for it.'

'Hm.' Cocks thought for a while, then shook his
head. 'No. I canna say owt on that. It seems just a
yes or no position to me. You'll be lucky if you get 'em.'
He jerked away as the room door opened, and the man
who had been advised to 'stick to it' came through.
'Well, 'ow an' we gone on?'

'Gorrit.'

'Good. Ar thought so. Come on, let's goo.'

Arthur's turn came at five minutes to twelve. He
wasn't the last; three others had come since he and the
youth joined the group.

'They're gettin' fed up in theer,' the man said who

came out to give Arthur his turn. 'Shouldn't give much for t'chances o' last un.'

Arthur smiled, and went past the official who held the door. He wasn't caring what the decision would be; hanging about on the balcony watching the monotonous lines below, hearing uninteresting talk about him, had dried him up, and he was ready for the open-air again and change. The men about him were still 'bloodying', still smoking, still spitting. Below, the lines of men shortened, lengthened, the heads bending over the desks for a moment, then detaching and walking back to the door. He forgot all this, now, as he sat in a chair and looked at the five men opposite, two representing 'the men', two 'the masters', as it was said. A trade union official and a Co-op worker, a colliery manager and a business man were these arms of the balances; between sat a solicitor. He was chairman. He was patently the Court of Referees if occasion arose for plain legal ruling. He puckered his brows, and peered through rimless pince-nez at the sheet before him, then wrinkled his forehead as he looked over the glasses at the 'next case'.

'Arthur Gardner.'

'Yes.' He had paused for a moment, wondering whether to say 'sir'. He decided not.

'You are claiming four days' benefit for four days you failed to attend the Labour Exchange and sign. Is that so.'

'Yes.'

'You were taking the Intermediate Arts Examination at Trentingham.' He was peering at the sheet before him all the time. 'Is that so?'

'Yes.'

'Hm.' He took off his glasses, and wiped his face with his hand. 'Well, Mr Gardner.' He paused. 'There seems to be but one thing to say. Were you, on those four days, available for work?'

'That point did not arise. No work was offered me.'

'Maybe not. But would you have gone to any job had one been offered you?'

'I can't say. But to support my case, I could say I would.'

'Hm. Yes. But, of course, you should have presented yourself at the Labour Exchange and signed that you were fit and available for work. You did not do that.'

'Of course not. But if my exam days had been Monday, Tuesday, Thursday and Saturday, I could have signed Wednesday and Friday and have drawn a full week's benefit. Would that have been right? We are excused every other day but those.'

'We will stick to what did, in fact, happen, Mr. Gardner. You were not available for work on the four days you claim benefit for, and I'm afraid it cannot be allowed. Do you agree, gentlemen?' He did not look at the others he addressed, merely waiting with head bent. 'Or have you anything to ask Mr. Gardner?' Two shook their heads, two mumbled 'No', and the chairman quickened. 'I'm afraid no other decision is possible, Mr. Gardner, than that of disallowing your claim.' The clerk who sat apart and had been writing most of the time, now rose quickly and opened the door.

'Thank you,' Arthur said to the chairman, and walked out. The clerk called another name, and a man followed him and the door was closed. 'The bloody fools,' Arthur muttered, as he tripped down the winding stairs into the street. He felt amused and cynical. 'Available for work'. Still, it would have been startling to have received on the morning he was going to Trentingham a letter telling him a job was waiting for him that day. Would he have given up the exam? He wouldn't at the time; he might have done now. Still, it wasn't worth thinking about, now.

'I've got nothing,' he told his mother, and she was not moved out of evenness: the fact was not important.

'I see they did not allow your claim, Mr. Gardner,' the supervisor said to him, a few days later.

'No. I wasn't available for work, they said.'

'Well, weren't you satisfied? You weren't available for work, were you? It was about the only question they could ask you.'

'Work. Does anybody ever get work from here?' He made a cynical sound down his nose, and the man at the desk looked sharply at him. 'It's absolutely deadening coming here day after day.'

'If a job came which we thought suitable for you, you'd be sent to it.' The man was curt. 'That's all.'

Arthur went, angrily. He went home and had his dinner, then walked to Belford. Notices had been posted inviting members of the Centre to join a class for pipe-making, but no names had been given in as yet, and Arthur carried on with the library organization.

'We'll try again near the back end,' the organizer said. 'Cower hasn't managed to get many converts to his boot-making, yet, either. Still dribblings into the shop as before, but no enthusiasm.'

'I shan't be able to come more than twice a week for

a while,' Arthur told him. 'I may begin studying again.'
He did not know why he told the man this; desperation
of the moment forced it from him. Every day here
would mean, somehow, that he was in prison with no
chance of changing his present mode of life and
circumstance.

'Right. Just come when you feel like it.' The
organizer understood, even though he did not show it to
the young man. He knew the hopelessness and the
frustration eating into him, knew that there was no
satisfaction for him to be working here. 'I should
begin studying again if I were you. And if I can help
you, say the word.'

Arthur did not go to the Centre for a fortnight; then
when he did, it was with no apologetic air. He was
beginning to hate the place, somehow, and it was
frightening to have to come and see the same men time
after time. It meant they were still out of work, still
out of work. He was the same, and here the knowledge
was pinned down on him. He was the same; his life
was going uselessly, like theirs. He'd tell the organizer
that he couldn't come any more, he would. But he
left again without saying this; it would have meant
cutting himself off from another contact, nay, from the
only real contact, pleasant one, that he had. There was
too much silence at home, too much loneliness roaming
about the fields and the town.

'A card for you from the Labour,' his mother said,
when he came down one Saturday morning. 'You
have to go there, this morning. Perhaps they've a job
for you.'

'A card?' He read it, faintly disturbed. 'Why
couldn't they tell me yesterday when I signed?'

'Perhaps whatever they want you for happened after you signed.' She glanced at him quickly. 'You've done nothing to be scared about, have you? You've not been too pleasant with anybody just lately.'

'I'm not scared at anything they can want me for,' he said, with bold cynicism. 'I don't care whether they cut my dole to nothing. I'm fed up.'

'Fed up! It hasn't taken much to feed you up.' Her voice lost strength. 'Why don't you study again? And you said you were going to read a lot of novels——'

'I can do nothing—nothing. If I could get on again at the pit—oh, or anywhere—I'd never touch another stroke of studying. It does you no good. I'd play football, billiards, go to the pictures three or four times a week. Those who lived like that when they were at work seem to be happy even when they're out of work.'

'You wouldn't—you know you wouldn't.'

'Well, I s'll clear out and go on tramp if something doesn't turn up soon. It wouldn't be so bad if those you lived with acted decently. It's as bad as if you'd done a crime to be out of work. It seems so bl—dashed crazy to me.'

'The lads are all right with you, aren't they? And I am. Hm. If you knew how many sleepless nights I——'

She broke off, and turned away to hide her weakness.

'If it wasn't for you I'd have been gone long since. Still, it might be a job.' His tone was cheerful, though he was cursing inwardly at himself for having permitted her to suffer by his outburst. 'I hope so, for the Lord's sake.'

The head clerk attended to Arthur. He looked at the reference and number on the postcard, then went through a sheaf of papers on his desk.

'Latham, the furniture people in King Street, asked me to send round two men at three o'clock this afternoon. There's a job for them. I'm sending you and another. You'll have it?'

'What's the job?'

'They didn't say. They wanted two men, that was all.'

'Sandwichmen?'

'Probably. Though they didn't say.'

Arthur thought wildly for a moment, anger swept him, then he felt like laughing boisterously. He controlled himself suddenly.

'Three o'clock, you said?' The man nodded, showing no state of mind in his face. 'Right, I'll be there.'

'If the job is just for to-day,' the man said, 'you'll come in and sign on Monday, and tell the clerk you were working on Saturday. You won't draw benefit for to-day, of course.'

'Right.'

He went home, walked across the fields blindly until some one came up from behind and walked with him. It was Joe Saunders, an out-of-work from Condor.

'Ner, Arthur.'

'Ner, Joe.' They walked on together, talking of what Joe wanted to talk about. In Peathill, before Saunders branched off through fields to Condor, Arthur made his effort. 'I say, Joe. How do you go on if they offer you a job at the dole, and you didn't take it?'

'Well. Sometimes they suspend you for about six

weeks. But you can go to t'Court o' Referees an' fight
it, if you like.'

Court of Referees. He left the man, and walked on,
cynically amused for a while at the thought. Then he
fell serious. He knew his mother would ask him why
he had been called to the Exchange.

'Well, what did they want you for?' she did ask, after
he had been in a while and his step-father had gone
out.

'Oh, nothing. No job, if that is what you're waiting
for me to say. I should have told you straight away,
whoever had been in. No, just a renewal of my
claim.' He had renewed his claim the previous day,
giving him another hundred and twenty-six days'
benefit. 'Another six months and I'm on the Means
Test.'

'Six months. You'll not be out of work another six
months, surely.'

'I don't know. One day's like another. I've as much
chance of getting a job to-morrow as in six months—
or in six years, for that matter. Can't do anything, a
job'll just have to hit me. And it may never hit me.
Might have the offer of two jobs at once; might never
have an offer nor an opportunity.'

'You're talking silly.'

'I'm not talking silly, either. Just luck whether one
gets a job or not.'

'Oh, well.' She heaved a great sigh. 'I shan't be
here in six months if you haven't got a job.'

'You're talking silly.'

'Hm.' And she went into the kitchen.

At half-past two he left for Pirley, stuffing a cap in his
pocket when his mother was out. He wore one when

snow or rain fell, not otherwise, and to-day was sunny.

'Shan't be in for tea,' he told her. 'Might go to a cricket match, might go a long walk. Anyway, shan't be in till supper.'

Latham's furniture store was at the top of King Street. Four large plate windows shouted SALE with huge red lettering. A shabby man of about thirty-five was standing near the doorway. Arthur was striding in at the doorway. All the way up King Street a sickness had been pulling at his stomach. He had cursed silently at the nervousness which strained to make him linger and put off entering or even reaching the store, until he had burst forward and assumed a confidence he was far from feeling.

'Hey, chum,' the man called nervously, and with some desperation. Arthur stopped suddenly, and turned to the man. 'I—have you been sent 'ere from t'dole?'

'Yes. Why? Have you?'

'Yes.' The man's eyes showed utter relief. 'I've seen you there.' Arthur was strong now. The man was strong. Nervousness dropped from both in a moment. 'Is it san'wichin'?'

'I don't know. I bet it is.' Arthur looked at him, seemed to be the man's friend in a moment. The other showed a reaching forward, too. 'Done any before?'

'No. 'Ave you?'

'No,' Arthur said, and they were both glad. 'Come on, then, let's go in. Do you want?'

'I'm not botherin', ner you've come. I 'ad thought o' committin' suicide.' He laughed apologetically. 'Come on, then.'

They went in, and a man came to them at once.

'Yes?' he asked. 'What——?'

'We're from the Labour,' Arthur said, at once.

'Oh yes.' He stepped aside and looked behind a screen. 'You're the two sandwichmen we asked for.' He did not look again into their faces. 'The boards are here.' They moved to behind the screen, where four posters glared with the same red letters as the window. 'You'll go round the main streets until nine o'clock, when the store closes. You can come in a bit before that, we want to get off prompt.' He watched them hoist the boards about them, helped them as they wriggled slightly to make the shoulder-bands sit comfortably. 'O.K.?' The other man mumbled. 'Oh,' the storeman said, as Arthur fetched the cap from his pocket and pulled it well on. 'Don't both go the same way round.' He looked at the SALE! SALE! SALE! critically, at the LATHAM'S! LATHAM'S! LATHAM'S! then said, 'Right. Get off, now.'

Arthur went first through the door into the street.

'Up or down?' he jerked to his companion.

'I'm not botherin'. Down.'

He moved away with a nervous laugh. Arthur was swept suddenly with a great bewilderment, a fearful bewilderment. He kept his gaze far ahead as he moved round the corner on to Market Street. The late summer afternoon, sunny and still, seemed to swim about him, the lines of stalls to his right were vague blurs, people moving across his vision were shapeless patches of colour. He passed the other man down Church Street, and grinned shortly, without humour. But soon he adjusted himself, and the world moved into focus. When the man came round the next time, Arthur kept his eyes on him until he had passed, and knew what he

14

himself looked like. What a fool he had been to tackle
the job, what a fool! He'd chuck it, ask the man if he
would chuck it with him. The man was approaching
him again. No, he wouldn't, the worst was really
over. Youths and young women in tennis attire moved
cleanly through the shining afternoon, not conscious of
themselves, talking without reserve, continuing con-
verse, and glancing easily into each other's faces, even
while they separated for a moment to avoid a couple of
dogs attempting copulation. Arthur passed on cursing
in thought, though he didn't know why.

'W'at about some grub?' the other man asked, at
six o'clock. 'Pubs are open, now. We can go round
t'back an' 'a'e a drink if we 'a'e nowt else.'

'I'm ready for some. We'll go to the back of the
Crown and leave our boards there. This time round.'

They had half an hour's rest, ate two pennyworth of
chips and drunk a pint of beer.

'By God, it makes your shou'ders sore,' the man said.

'It does. What about chuckin' it?' Arthur asked,
with no strength. 'They'd pay us for three hours,
wouldn't they?'

'They might do. Ar dunna know, though. We've
done slackest three hours; there'll be more folks about
from now till nine. No. They'd not pay us. We'd
better stick it. Ar am, any road.'

'O.K. Let's get off again.'

'We'll swop roads round, now, eh?'

'I'm agreeable,' Arthur said, hoisting his boards.
'Come on.'

Pirley streets were crowded, now, people flocking
into the first house of the pictures, women shopping
and men with them, or alone beginning a round of the

pubs. Arthur passed down King Street, along the bottom where the crimson flush of the Empire lights, just turned on, stained weakly the dulling daylight. A long queue was filing slowly into the 'ninepennies', the more select 'shillings' had a wider entrance door—in wet weather was shelter here for many patrons. Inn windows glowed faintly with lights, their doors gaped open. Crowds were in the street, now; young folks more vivid than on workdays, better dressed than when they sat at home, slower after a day's work in the pit or the factory, and not so free in spirit with another early morning and tiring work before them. Saturday night was the peak point of their week's living; the males full of the sport they had lately left, eager and loose towards the girls walking or standing about the town and not unwilling to be invited to the pictures or to an appointment later, abandoned as to the time-factor, conscious that no alarm clock or a parent's impatient voice would break into next morning's early hours. A group of youths and girls stood bending with laughter on the pavement across from the church. Arthur lifted his cap slightly from over his eyes, and looked up at the clock in the tower.

'Why, that's Arthur Gardner wi' them boards on,' he heard a youth say quickly. 'It is.' A girl denied it scoffingly. 'It is, I tell yer.'

'We'll see when he comes round next time,' she said.

The group turned to themselves again, and Arthur passed on. The youth who had recognized him came from Wingrove; he hadn't seen the girl's face. She must live there, too, or she wouldn't have known him. He'd a good mind to hop it, he hardly dared go round again.

But it didn't matter who saw him, he was as good as anybody in Pirley, and a damn sight better than most. A foolish boldness rushed through him, and he looked about slowly; from the market stalls his glance moved across the wide road to the people mingling and passing Boots '. He almost stopped in his slow stride, his stomach came suddenly into his throat, or seemed to do. Nancy's eyes were wide open and gazing straight into his. And his mother's head turned to see what had moved her, but he dropped his head before he met her eyes. O God! He moved on, quicker; he couldn't help trying to hurry. Nancy had been leaning casually on the door of a car which was obviously hers, talking to his mother, who stood, it seemed pathetically, with her shopping-bag pulling down at her right arm. Had she seen him? If she hadn't, would Nancy tell her? No, she wouldn't, he knew that. The young woman suddenly became important to him. He marvelled that the importance seemed greater than that thrusting him towards his mother. She had looked lovely, at ease, yet gently sad about her mouth and eyes until the fixed surprise grasped her features; the leaf-green dress smooth about her shone like her shining hair and cut softly into the living glow of the flesh of her arms and neck. She had ripened and was full in bloom. He was reaching out to her. She must have had a . . . How ridiculous! It was only three or four months ago. She must be carrying it. That's what made her seem full and ripe. He hardened slightly, moved along with empty eyes until a car swerved to avoid him, startling him into the gutter again. The other man grinned as he passed him up King Street, but Arthur did not see him. He was just rousing into careless cynicism and heeding no one. What did it matter who saw him, now?

'You're right, it is him,' the girl opposite the church said. Arthur heard her and looked into her face, and she averted her gaze.

'Towd yer, didn't I?' the youth replied. 'By gum, 'e's come to summat, 'asn't 'e?'

''Ow do you mean, "come to summat"?' another girl said. 'That job's no worse than any other. But it's a shame. Everybody said 'e'd be a schoolmaster wi' all 'is studyin'.'

The lights in shop windows and from the front of the inns and picture-houses were strengthening, pushing across the street and keeping the blue darkness at roof height. It smoothed the faces of people, lifted youth to greater freedom and boldness and to an eagerness to fuse with the other sex. Arthur saw a youth and a girl detach themselves from a group and pass by the side of the market stalls into the darkness and silence of the street leading to the loneliness about the hospital. They had laughed in breaking from their friends, but now they walked in silence and away from each other. It was the beginning. Arthur had begun like that himself with Nancy. He used to play football on Saturday afternoons, come home and have tea, then change into clean linen and week-end clothes. He had felt fine, then, new and free and eager for the lights and business of Pirley on Saturday night. And he had 'got off' with Nancy, fallen away from his friends, glued himself to a line of study and become too serious-minded. And look what 'he had come to'. Still, what had he come to? He was alive and healthy in the normal sort of way, and to earn money carrying these boards round was no worse than any other way. But then, he'd been pushed off the real track of his living, there could be no mistake about that. He could have worked on another level, a higher level, he could say, without being snobbish. Still, he was here, and it was no good thinking things. But it was so easy to live when one was safe on a line, safe and comfortable without danger of being chucked into a dole queue. That man at Trentingham in the Training Department, he'd never forget him. Made him angry for a while, though people might laugh at him for feeling that way. The man, he was a man, one of the oldest taking the Teacher's Certificate, and he was talking to others who like himself had to go that afternoon into a school in the city for practical work.

'I've got to go to Mountain Street,' he had said, after others had given out the school they were deputed to. 'That lousy place. And play "ring-o'-roses" with the blasted kids.'

His friends had laughed uproariously, but he himself was disgusted, and had gone angrily for his coat. Arthur looked at him and hated him as he flung away. Wished he'd had his chance of full time at college and a safe job for life afterwards. But now, as he stood for a moment while the Hippodrome crowd pouring from the first house cleared a little, he laughed cynically. His anger, then, was merely his enviousness, people might say. Well, perhaps it was.

The crowd cleared, near passers-by careful not to knock against his boards. Some were laughing over the Micky Mouse; some talking seriously, almost with emotion, of the star in the big picture. Others reached towards other things, forgetting the past at once.

'What the 'ell are thee doin' wi' them on?' He turned quickly, and Albert stood by him. Sidney was staring as if dazed.

'They sent me from t'dole,' Arthur said. He felt worse at this moment than at any during the time he had walked round, not even excepting that of meeting Nancy's eyes and seeing his mother. He had, now, to relate inward things to external, had to adjust himself to a world examining him.

'Well, of a' the fools. Ar'd 'ave seen 'em in 'ell before Ar'd a tackled a job like that, dole or no dole.'

'I've nearly finished, now. Nine o'clock.' He felt he had said nothing. It came out of him partially as an excuse, partially to appease Albert, but it did not come from his brain at all.

'Finished! I should never'd begun. Ber!' Albert was disgusted.

'Going to the pictures, Sid?' Arthur asked quickly. People were staring, might possibly think a sandwich-man was begging or insulting decent citizens. The youth nodded brightly. 'I'll get off.' He walked on without another word, and the two brothers went across the road to the Hippodrome.

'This's last time round,' the other man said, when they met under the rose-glow of the Empire. 'Twenty to nine.'

'O.K.,' Arthur said shortly. 'I'm ready.'

The shopman was at the door when Arthur turned down King Street.

'I'm waiting for you,' he said. 'Where's the other chap?'

'He'll be here any minute.' They went in, and the

man helped Arthur off with his boards. He laughed. 'Have we got you any custom? The letters,' he nodded towards the boards, 'are big enough to hit anybody.'

'Well, we s'll have to wait and see. Here's your money. Six shillings. Sign this receipt.' Arthur was signing when the other came in and bumped down his boards. 'Hello. Come here and get your money.'

'Six bob. Six bob. Thanks. A bob an hour. Not bad.' He looked at Arthur. 'Come on, let's go an' 'ave a drink, eh?'

'No. All right. Good night.'

'Good night,' the man said, and was busy at once preparing to close the store, forgetting them.

They had two drinks at the bar of the inn opposite the Empire. A thin man played the piano atrociously; women called across the long room to him, and he smiled as he turned to them, playing much worse with his attention taken.

'I'm going,' Arthur said, setting down his glass.

'O.K.' The other rapped on the bar. 'I'm stoppin' 'ere a bit.' He winked and nodded towards the women. Arthur smiled.

'Right. 'Night.'

He walked home slowly, wondering whether his mother did see him. It worried him faintly; the worry strengthened, hurrying his feet. He must know if she had, and how she had taken it. She was alone when he walked in at five minutes to ten, sitting alone with a book on her lap.

'Reading, mum? What is it?'

'One of the Hardy books you brought the other night.'

'Oh.' He was not so eager. 'Which?'

'Oh, I was just looking through—see, what is it?' She looked at the cover. '*Jude the Obscure*.'

'Not a very pleasant one.' He pulled off his raincoat. His cap stuck an inch or two from the pocket, but he did not see it as he went to the dark stair-hole and hung up the coat.

'Where's your cap?' He started, remembering.

'Cap!'

'I saw you in Pirley.'

'I wondered whether you did. Nothing to be ashamed of, is it?'

'No.' There was a curve in the utterance of the syllable. The tone said there was no disgrace attached to it, yet . . .

'Did—Nancy point me out to you?'

'She didn't.' The woman was calm. 'She tried to keep me from seeing you. When I did see you, she got into her car and went home crying.' She rose. 'Do you want any supper?'

'I don't.' He was savage in his answering. 'I'll go to bed.' But he sat on the sofa with eyes turned to the centre of the home-pegged rug, a red diamond on a field of black. His old clothes were in that rug, his brothers', step-father's. He remembered his mother sitting last winter filling the expanse of coarse sacking with small pieces of cloth, one piece at a time, patiently, with an eye on the pattern. And at times she had looked up at him fastened to his books; she had made no remark, sat silently working for hours not to disturb him. He glanced at her as she moved from this room to the kitchen. She was preparing supper for the man and youths who would be in soon, the man any moment now, for the pub would have 'turned out'. A wave of strength flowed through him. 'I've been thinking, mum.' She put down the cheese and looked up with interest, his tone was inviting. 'I'll write to Trentingham and see if there are any classes going. Might make a pound a night—for twenty-four nights, one a week. Or twelve—or a short course of six lectures. It'd all help.

'I should. Tell them you're out of work. They ought to do something for you. What could you lecture on?'

'Oh—well, literature generally, or drama or the novel. I could mug anything up. I would do.' He was eager.

His step-father came in and threw his cap on the sofa near Arthur, his hand rested on the table to steady himself, the dark hair over his forehead was ruffled and streaks of it stuck to his damp brow, his mouth was moving with a kind of heavy amusement.

'Hm. We've got a san'wichman in t'family, I can 'ear.' He laughed shortly. 'Made me look a blasted fool in t'taproom, though.' His mouth pushed out, ugly, dangerous.

'Do you want any supper?' his wife put in. 'Coming in in that state. I don't know what's come to you, lately.'

'What state? I can see you two talk about me when I'm at t'pub.' He flashed into anger. 'That bastard'll never 'ave enough money to get drunk on. San'wichman. 'E'll damn well clear out o' 'ere if 'e comes them games. Makin' *me* look a fool.'

Arthur rose quickly, his mouth pulled small. He saw his mother step forward with startled eyes and open lips drawing in a sharp breath of fear. With an effort he blinked his gaze from holding the man, and went upstairs, not looking at either again. Immediately after breakfast next morning, and before any of the men were down, he wrote the letter, took the package of food his mother had prepared, and set off to catch the 'hikers' train' at Leawood; it ran every Sunday from Derby into the Peak. Arthur posted his letter in Pirley, and walked down to Leawood. He boarded the train, and left it again at Bakewell, then walked through Stoney Middleton to Eyam, and back through Monsal Dale, where the valley was crowded with young people from Sheffield who shouted and sang, played cricket and football with improvised bats and balls, pieces of wood from a tree and paper tied round with string. He left them quickly, and sat in a Bakewell inn until train-time. Nancy and he used to come out here. They never ended the day like this; they used to walk until the last minute or two, and get to the station as the train was due. Still, what was the good of thinking of those things, now? Another jar of beer and forget them. He'd have to go steady, though. The train journey had cost him one and three, and this ninepenn'orth of beer. Didn't know why he had come out here. He could have walked about Leawood and Tansley Moors and it wouldn't have cost him anything. Still, the sooner his money was gone the sooner he'd clear out of Wingrove and that deadening house. Oh, he was always so damned brave when he was away from it—and his mother. He left the inn angrily, and was moody all the journey back. His spirits rose again walking home. If he got a course of lectures he'd be all right for a while. But what was the use of being all right for a while? He might get a job, or he might get into the adult educa-

tion movement for good. He knew some who were
making a hundred and fifty a year at it.

A reply from Trentingham came in a few days.

'DEAR GARDNER' (it said), 'I am glad to hear from
you again, though sorry to know you are not continuing your studies. With reference to your inquiry,
I am afraid all classes and tutors for them have been
arranged for the winter. If, however, we are asked
for a short course in literature by some village, I will
keep you in mind. All the best. Yours.'

So that was that. He showed the letter to his mother,
and marked no reaction. He wished, now, that he had
not burst out with his intention, there would have been
no need to notch her mind with this new disappointment. She always seemed slower, more silent after
such, as if she had reached upwards only to fall lower
than the first state. Her suffering was in that she hid
all emotion. And so the weeks went on as before. He
went occasionally to Belford, suddenly took it into his
head to study, and spent hours in the front room, became
impatient of that, and lay about reading novels. The
weather kept him in more, now. He sat reading and
staring emptily while the three days of Pirley Fair
passed, and children cried excitedly as they hurried up
the Wingrove street in the mid-October afternoons,
and came home slow and penniless in the evening to
leave the street to rowdy drunks at midnight who had
given themselves to the abandonment of fair-time;
while the frightened dogs howled against the shatterings
of bonfire night; while his mother mixed and cooked
the Christmas puddings and stored them away, then

turned to making mince-pies and cakes, careful with
the icing, smoothing it neatly. Christmas in the adult
household was even quieter than ordinary times. The
three Shirley men were out all the days except for meals,
and most of the nights except the one previous to their
returning to the pit. Even Mrs. Shirley spent an evening next door, though she did not prepare to go until
Arthur, who had sat in all day, put on a scarf and overcoat and went out himself. He was glad when it was
all over. It had been merely an emphasis to his out-of-
work condition. But on the first of January came a
letter from Trentingham, and he permitted himself
some eagerness, though he managed to hold himself
from calling to his mother until he had opened it. He
did call, however, as soon as he had read it.

'Mum.' She came at once because of the tone. 'I've
got a class. Only a short course of six lectures, but it's a
start.' He paused, but she did not speak; she watched
his alive face. 'I can do this easily enough. Six lectures
on drama. See? One on pre-Shakespearian, one—or
two, perhaps—on Shakespeare, then Restoration and
the Romantic Comedy in one, then two on the moderns.
I'm not too sure about the moderns, but I can get it
up by the time I want it.'

'Well, that's good. Where have you to go?'

'Oh, it's Fritchburn. You know, that little village
about half-way between Pirley and Leawood? You
know, you turn up that hill for Steep; it's about the
top of that hill.'

'It's a long way, isn't it? I mean in the winter
weather.'

'Oh, there are buses running past the bottom of the
hill, twenty minutes away from the village.' He looked

at the paper again. 'First lecture, third Tuesday in January. Manage——'

'What about the dole?'

'Well, I shan't sign that day, that's all. It'll keep me in benefit a week longer. And the six pound'll eke my other out until about then.'

'I don't know why you put your twenty-five shillings on the table in front of your dad every Friday. It only keeps him against you.'

'I shall put it there until I've none to put.' His tone had gone hard, he was away from everybody.

'And what then?'

'I've some left yet, and that's all that matters.'

The first lecture was something of a trial to him, though he had walked about Condor Common for hours rehearsing it, timing it. Eighteen people attended, a dozen who seemed really serious in attention, the rest were the superficially curious sort. He talked for an hour until half-past eight: the next half-hour was given to discussion, but that was very feeble, and it amounted to nothing more than another lecture. Three young people who had attended walked down the mile-long road with him to the highway, cutting through the Lea Valley. They lived somewhere in the bottom, at Newlands, Leawood or Rillway. The two girls were obviously teachers in an elementary school, the youth appeared to be some sort of clerk.

'Are you at Trentingham University?' A girl asked this with warm interest, and looked into his face as they passed under a lamp.

'No.' He backed morally.

'Do you teach?' It was the youth this time.

Arthur laughed ironically. He was really glad the

question came. He had more intelligence than the three of them put together: they were nothing more than varnished mill-hands, the grain of them was no finer, not so fine as many he knew. He was glad to answer.

'Oh no. I'm an unemployed miner,' he said.

They were a few yards from the Pirley-Leawood road, where Arthur would catch a bus. Only the unordered falling of feet sounded for the rest of the way; no word escaped, there was just a slight quickening of pace.

'I get my 'bus here,' Arthur said, pausing at the joint of the T-road. 'Good night.'

'Good night,' they said, politely enough, but he knew he had lost them as members of his class. He was a fool, right. He ought to have buttered them, told them he belonged to the college, and thrown his cultural weight about. Like David Neil said he did, talked as they wanted him to talk; that was the way to keep a class. Only numbers mattered; do anything to keep your numbers.

The lamp across the way, placed specially to light this T-junction, shone on an oblong paper stuck to a board near by. Arthur saw his name in large capitals, and he walked across and read the notice of the lecture he had just given. There was nothing about the subsequent five. Must be getting fresh ones out for each, he thought.

When he got down from the 'bus the next Tuesday, he glanced at the small hoarding. His name, and the subject of that evening's lecture, were in the same bold type. He climbed to Fritchburn, not thinking of the lecture. Last week a faint sickness did pull at his stomach until he reached the small school and had said his first sentence, which he had rehearsed many times in the bus and up the hill. Now, his thoughts were casual, his mind took impressions as they came.

The three with whom he had walked down last week were missing. Most of the others were there; he counted thirteen just before he began. He was standing at the teacher's desk reminding the audience that this and the next lecture were to be on Shakespeare, when Nancy walked into the room and took a seat among the people at the back. Nothing disastrous happened in his mind, he did not permit it to swerve from the stream of his immediate thought or be blotted from it, but it lost some strength, and he gripped the desk to help him hold his discourse to the level he had begun on. She had an enfolding fur coat about her, hiding the lines of her body, but her face was as lovely as ever, her eyes and mouth lived as she looked towards him for one moment.

'Good—very good,' the village parson said, at the close of the discussion. 'But not quite as successful as last week. You seemed to have to strain more to get across to us, your audience.'

Nancy was passing to the door as the old man said this. Arthur smiled at him, he looked wise and generous.

'Yes, that's true,' he replied in a low voice. Two desires were straining within him; one to break from the old man and follow the young woman, another to stay inside the room long enough for her to have time to get away. But the matter was decided for him. The rest of the people had gone, some with a smile and nod for him, others with a pleasant 'Good night', a few without taking leave at all. The parson suddenly put on his hat.

'Well, I must get off. Friends will be waiting outside to walk home with me. I go the opposite way to you. Good night.'

'Good night,' Arthur said. He gathered his papers and followed, bidding 'good night' to the caretaker, who had just come in to lock up and put out the lights.

'Can I give you a lift?' Nancy was leaning from the door of the Hillman. He jerked his head quickly at the invitation.

'No, thank you.' His refusal came almost instinctively, then his brain functioned to give the reason, or a reason. 'I get the bus at the bottom.'

'I can give you a lift to there.'

'It's all right, thanks.' He could not push a 'no' at her again, somehow.

'I want to talk to you, Arthur.'

If she had left his name off the end, he would have got in; he felt he would, but that seemed to smack him in the face.

'I don't think our talking would lead anywhere. It couldn't.'

'We might get to be friends again.' In the dimness of the reflected light of the headlamps she saw his face harden, and she spoke again quickly. 'I'd like to know about these lectures and where you've got to in the world.'

'You saw me in Pirley, didn't you?'

'Yes.' She was reluctant to utter the affirmation. 'But——'

'Well, that's where I've got to.'

He strode away at once, not angry, but the corners

15

of his mouth were turned down slightly. Nancy released
the brakes, and the car drew alongside him, travelling
with him, but he kept his eyes ahead.

'Good night, Arthur.'

'Good night.'

The car shot forward, and he heard the car go into
second and whir down the steep hill. The glow of her
lights was soon lost in the darkness. She would not
come again to the lectures, he felt sure. He was glad,
and then again, he was sorry. Oh . . . A sudden
looseness played about him. Well, he was a fool.
Why hadn't he got into the car and played on the love
she seemed to have for him. He could have got her to
drive out somewhere lonely, and . . . Oh, he was a
fool. Still, she wouldn't come again.

She did not come again. He was rather disappointed
that she hadn't as he climbed the hill to Fitchburn for
the last lecture. She might have brought a breath of
warmth into the moulding coldness of his sensing that
the class was a failure. From the Trentingham point
of view, that was, for he was satisfied that the small
core of six persons who had attended every lecture had
been interested, and had benefited culturally, as was
the intention of the organizers. But that wasn't good
enough; twelve, or thereabouts, should have 'qualified',
that is, put in four attendances out of the six. They
hadn't, though. Three had attended three times, but
even if they came to-night, it would mean that only
nine had 'qualified', and that wasn't good enough to
get the grant. Some had come one night, some two.
Dances and whist drives and a rainy evening had kept
them away. To-night's weather was not inviting, either;
snow had been falling all afternoon, and six inches of it

lay about the roads and fields, trees were heavy with it, the sky was hanging black and heavy, still pouring it down. In the bus which had brougltt him down, the conductor was saying that the service would be suspended if the snow continued, for soon Nessfield Hill would be in an impossible state for the buses to climb. The wind was getting up, now, driving the snow into Arthur's back as he plodded and slipped towards Fritchburn; large wet flakes they were, which stung as they caught his cheek and the back of his ears. It was no good hoping for a good attendance to-night. He himself would have preferred the fireside on an evening like this.

He hurried as best he could up the hill, thought suddenly of how he used his coat as sails coming home from the pit some days when the wind was behind him. He wouldn't do that here, on the highroad, people might think him crazy. Instead, he thrust his hands deep into his overcoat pockets, and bent forward to shield his neck and climb the hill more comfortably. The room was empty when he walked in, though the time was twenty-five past seven. He opened the register and looked at it, saw the initials of the assistant organizer from Trentingham who had visited him the third lecture night to find out how he was progressing. Twelve had been present that night, eight the next week, seven last Tuesday. Oh, it was hopeless! Still, he was not discouraged essentially; he had felt rich and comfortable delivering each talk, forgetting the superficial fact of numbers listening. If he didn't get any classes next winter—well, he didn't, that was all. He could have got the qualifying number if he had liked. But perhaps it wasn't so easy as in that tutorial class he knew which stretched over four years. There the students and the tutor had reached the familiar level where each called the other by the Christian name. During the last year, and towards the end of the course, when some one was away who could possibly qualify, the tutor had said with amusement, whether genuine or to cover the motive it was not possible to discern, 'You, Mr. Brown, will be Mr. Jones to-night', and Mr. Jones was the one away whose presence was so vitally necessary to help get the Government grant. Well, he couldn't do that. For one thing, he wasn't bold enough; for another, he didn't know the people well enough. Still, he wouldn't have done it in any case; very few tutors would, he was sure. But qualifying was really the main thing with classes, Trentingham measured a tutor by it. If his class did not qualify he wasn't a success, and classes would not be given to him. Nothing more certain than that. Well, he had failed. But he was breaking fresh ground; there never had been a class in this village before, and the task was a difficult one. He had known one man work for three years at one-year courses, and get together an interested group of twenty or more. Then those who gave out classes had delegated another to take a tutorial, a much better paid course.

Three people came in at half-past seven. One walked to him at the desk.

'Good evening, Mr. Gardner. What a terrible night!' Arthur smiled, and agreed. 'The vicar asked me to apologize to you for his absence, but he says he really dare not risk the weather at his time of life.'

'Mrs. Munday sent a note to me and asked me to say the same for her,' another man said.

'Thank you,' Arthur replied. 'It really wasn't fit for any of you to come. I don't suppose any more will come.' He glanced at the clock. 'Twenty to eight.' He watched the three take off their coats and come to the fire with hands held out. 'Will you sit round the fire to-night?' They laughed agreeable affirmatives, and drew chairs to the blazing coal fire. 'If you would prefer to talk informally on drama and not listen to a lecture, I would be glad to agree.'

'Oh no. Oh no, Mr. Gardner,' a young man said quickly. 'I'm wanting to hear something about modern drama. Give us what you've prepared, then we'll talk.'

The others agreed, and Arthur carried on as he had done before. The discussion after was vivid, and absorbed the whole mind and attention of the four. They started when the door opened and the caretaker came in.

'Oh. I beg your pardon. I thought you'd gone.' He was retiring again.

'My. It's a quarter to ten,' one said.

'Eh? What?' Another jumped up, and made for where his coat hung. 'I've never missed havin' a pint last thing at night for years. I'm no drinker but I like one last thing. Makes you sleep. Well . . .' He came to Arthur and took his hand. 'I'm glad to have heard you. Hope I shall again. If you come to talk in Fritchburn again, count on me.' He went. 'Good night.'

'I shall have to go too,' Arthur said, gathering together the register and his notes. 'My bus goes at ten-past. I shall just do it. Well . . .' He turned to shake hands with the two men who were getting into their coats. 'Thank you for coming. Good——'

'There is no bus now, sir,' the caretaker put in.

'No bus?' Arthur swung to him. 'No bus.'

'No. My wife's sister's been down to get one to Pirley, but she's had to come back and stay the night. They stopped runnin' an hour since.'

'Oh dear,' one of the men said. 'That's bad for you, Mr. Gardner.' Arthur looked at him as he hesitated. 'Well, if you like, we'll put you up for to-night. My wife would make you comfortable, I'm sure, though——'

'Thanks very much, Mr. Slack. But I must get home. I shall manage. Is it snowing now?' He turned to the caretaker.

'Comin' down thick. A foot thick it is. An' the winds blowin' like—like hanover. A' awful night.'

'Oh well, I've faced all weathers lately. I s'll get home before midnight with a bit of luck.'

'You can't go,' Mr. Slack said. He had opened the door and a whirl of snow rushed in. 'Not in this.'

'Thanks, but I must. I'll get off, now. Good night."

'Good night,' the three said flatly, then muttered among themselves, and went to the fire to finish dressing.

Outside, he ducked his head at once, and bored into the wind and the horizontal snow-lines rushing against him. He almost lost his breath for a moment as the soft crashes of snow pelted his mouth and nostrils. His mouth, now, he buried in the scarf about his neck and chin, and guided himself along by keeping the walls and house-fronts, which jutted up to the pavement edge, in the corner of his right eye. He battled for twenty or thirty yards, and was gradually adjusting himself to the conditions.

'Arthur!'

His chin jerked from the shelter of the scarf, and the wind whipped keenly across it. He stopped suddenly. A car stood by him, cutting dully into the snowlight of the night. Nancy was holding up her face from the lowered window.

'Get in, Arthur. Come on, I'm freezing.' She held open the door. 'You can go in the back if you like, but it's warmer here.' He climbed in beside her, felt his side mould into hers. 'A rotten night for your last talk. Not many there, I suppose?'

'No.' He kept his eyes on the screen-wiper, watched it sweep the pattered snow to the top of the glass and leave it there, a thick, dark line. He tried to fasten his mind to it, but the knowledge of her beside him, the soft touching of her, dragged his thoughts into raggedness.

'I should have liked to have heard all of them. But you didn't want me to come. Did you?' He did not answer. They were running slowly on the level until suddenly the road dipped sharply. 'This is a nasty hill at the best of times.' She sat forward, peering through the screen, her hands gripped the wheel with the tightening of her mind. The back of the car swung suddenly, she turned with the skid, capably, easily. She seemed to be oblivious of him, but she burst out suddenly, jerking her words with the uneven rhythm of her driving. 'You don't know me, do you? That's what's bothering you. You won't talk until you know all about me.' Her voice was half-breaking, half-fierce. 'I had my baby at Christmas. Eight weeks ago. Before its time, and it was dead.' The hill curved, and she was intent on the driving, but she jerked thoughts all

the while. 'That's all. I'm normal again, now. I was
a fool that I didn't say it was yours. Though it wasn't.'

He had started. She said the last three words to push
him comfortable again. 'There. Whew. A nasty five
minutes.' They were at the T-road, now. Arthur saw
the headlights shooting full on the small hoarding
ahead. His name and all the other matter was blotted
out, smoothed white by the glancing snow. 'Two
miles straight, now, then that awful Nessfield Hill.'

'You can drop me at the bottom. It isn't safe to take
the car up. Besides, you'd have to come down again.'

'Oh no. I'm going back through Overdale.'

'It's as hilly that way.'

'They're not so steep, though.'

He watched the wiper for a while, through Pentland
Hollow and until they were nearing Nessfield. The car
pulled round the bend and under the bridge near
where the stile led to the young woman's homestead.
Faint bewilderment rushed through him, then he called
up a fierceness to steady it.

'Why did you come to-night?' His tone softened with
each deliberate syllable.

'Why *did* I come? I knew it was your lecture night,
and I knew the buses had stopped running. I phoned
down to the Trent office in Belford to see.' They were
running over the lonely quarter-of-a-mile stretch between the stile and Nessfield village. 'We know this
part of the road pretty well, don't we?' He did not
answer. 'You'd never have got home in this lot.'

'I should. It takes a lot to beat me.'

'All right. That's how you always were. How's
your mother? She didn't seem very well when I saw
her in Pirley.'

'She's no better. Does your—do they know where you were coming?'

'I'm at my mother's here.' She jerked her head to the right. 'I have been there since tea, but I came away early and phoned from the box in Pirley to see whether the buses were still running this way. Then I came straight to Fritchburn.' They ran through Nessfield and on to the lonely bit of road before the hill. A man was fighting his way along the pavement, obviously to Pirley, for there was no house between here and the town. As the lights glowed about him trellised with the snow-lines, both Arthur and Nancy felt an intimacy with him, that to pass him by was wrong.

'Look at that poor bloke,' Arthur said. 'You've as much right to give him a lift as me.'

'I *thought* that,' she replied, as the lights cut away from him. 'But I *felt* differently. He's nothing to me.' Silence for a few moments. 'Now for the hill.' She bent forward again, watching the road as the car front lifted to the hill.

'I'm a fool, Nancy.' She gripped the wheel, waiting. 'I'm not worth the bother.' His tone was melting. 'But it's this damned out-of-work business.' He flared out strongly, still individual, though. 'No, it isn't all that. If I'd a real father and a decent home-life, I could have taken my Inter again in November.'

'I looked in the July and the November exam list for your name.' The car trembled slowly, so slowly, up the gradient. She watched the road ahead intently. 'Was I the reason you failed?' He did not reply. 'Come on, Swallow.' She bent forward still farther, as if helping the car she addressed. 'Come on. Another fifty yards.' Her voice curved coaxingly; her very ease, or apparent ease, ripped through his mind with painful violence.

'Do you still love me, Nancy?' The question came suddenly, from nowhere, as it were. She showed no sign that she had heard it, but kept her eyes fixed to her driving; they remained open for longer than usual, as if mighty happenings in her mind were taking all her powers. When she did permit her eyelids to fall, they pressed out the tears that had been swimming there, pressed until they fell and broke on her cheeks. She opened them again, and continued staring ahead, adjusting herself to speak calmly. The car was roaring over the brow, steam whipping away from the bonnet.

'Why do you think I came to-night?' Her voice was even. She changed gear as the car ran straight. She was glad of the physical movement; it emptied her mind for a moment, relieving the shooting criss-cross of thoughts his question rushed to life.

'Stop.' His voice was low, without life. She drew to the kerb, and the car stood throbbing dully. She waited, her hands resting on the wheel; waited, trembling with rich emotion in which there was no pleasure, no delight, merely the vital response to some right due to her being. 'Nancy.' She turned slowly to him, her lips open, no eagerness in her eyes, merely the waiting. Strength flowed into his eyes and mouth, and he gathered her to him, meeting her lips with his and holding, holding. The wind rushed about the dark room of the car, and the snowflakes dashed vainly to establish themselves on the track of the screen-wiper. Before, Pirley lights threaded the night with long beads of light; behind was the dark bowl of the Lea Valley. To him she was soft and warm and fragrant. He was hungry for her, and

the hunger was pure, and it was not appeased even
though he held her close and fast. But when they were
apart once more, both rested satisfied.

'I'm glad for that, Arthur.' No thought of the past
or future was with her.

'I seemed to have come down to what I ought to
have been when——'

'And I have come up to meet you, if you are going to
talk like that,' she cut in. 'We'll get on, now.' Joy
showed through her, now, as she bent forward to the
brake lever. The car purred towards the town. 'I'm
satisfied, now, somehow, Arthur.'

'I'm satisfied, Nancy.'

Through Pirley, white and deserted, down the
Hillocks and along to Peathill, they rested in their
contentment, the mere soft touching of shoulders and
hips was enough to hold them fused in selfless pleasure.
As they approached the opening of the Wingrove road,
Arthur put his hand on her glove, and pressed gently.

'I'll walk from here. Only ten minutes. Draw down
there, and you can go back that way into Pirley.'

She ran the car a few yards past the end of the
Wingrove road, and stopped. There was silence for a
moment, the beating wind and snow was lifting over
the houses behind and shrieking into the sky. Only
soft, undriven flakes showered silently.

'I'd better go before . . .' His hand was on the door.
'No.' He took her to himself again slowly, and she held
to him without any eager pressing. 'I've asked you
nothing about yourself, Nancy,' he said, releasing her
lips. 'I don't want to know. It would do no good to
know. I'm satisfied with to-night. I love you, and
because I know you love me, I'm satisfied.'

'I do love you, and I'm satisfied now. But aren't you happy at home?'

'I shall stay as long as my mother lives, whatever happens,' he replied shortly. 'When she goes—and it won't be long if things don't alter—well, I s'll go. And be glad to get out.' They sat for a moment or two without speaking. 'Still, I s'll remember to-night, Nancy. It'll carry me a long way.' He kissed her again, and she clung, now; she was not so strong as she thought. He disengaged her arms, gently, and stepped back through the door. Their eyes were fastened to each other's, each recognized what the breaking of the gaze meant.

'When—if you do leave home, Arthur, will you let me know?'

'I shan't promise that, Nancy.' He knew no reason for saying that. Instinctively he *felt* that when such a time came, he would be away from every one and everything, bottled within himself. 'No, I won't promise that.' He broke gaze, and immediately knew that to stay longer would ruin the richness of the relation. 'Good-bye, Nancy.' He pressed her hand and turned away, moving heavily through the yielding snow to the Wingrove corner, where the wind blustered and the whirling flakes pelted him stingingly. He heard the dull thud as the car-door slammed to, looked back to see the dark shape melting into the darkness of Steam Mill Hill. He could not hear the broken sobbing nor see the lovely face crumple into weeping.

'Snow's not delayed you any,' his mother said, looking up in surprise when he walked in.

'Buses had stopped running, but I got a lift in a car as far as Pirley.'

'You've finished, then.'

'Yes, only to wait for my money, now.' He took off his overcoat and scarf as one without a care. 'Only three there, to-night, but I feel satisfied, somehow. Any supper?'

She stared at him, then brightened herself and made his supper.

# CHAPTER IX

On the first of March Mr. Shirley came home from
work at half-past twelve with his hand bandaged, and,
with his wife's help, washed himself and went to the
doctor.

'Three weeks' job,' he said, when he came back.
'Broke one of my fingers. Come on, I can eat a bit o'
dinner, now.'

And so it was for three weeks. 'Fetch me this',
'Get me that', cut across the woman's usual theme of
domestic labour. The man was irritable and helpless;
when Arthur was in, he became almost unbearable. If
the son helped his mother wash up, or took out the rug
and shook it, mutterings of 'Only fit for skivvyin''
came from the man. If Arthur sat about while his
mother was busy, the man would say to her, 'Can't
he help a bit? Dunno how he sleeps at night, lyin'
about all day.'

After a week, Arthur went out each morning at nine,
and sometimes did not come in again until tea, when his
brothers were home. He walked when the weather
permitted, which was not often; spent most of the morning in the Co-op reading-room when snow or rain fell.
Some mornings and some afternoons he sat in the
billiard hall in Pirley, and watched the occasional
games. There was a 'best' table among the dozen in
the room, and most of the games were played on it.
The wall seats were usually crowded, though not many
came to play. Mostly, the youths and young men there

were unemployed. A pit half a mile out of Pirley had lately closed down, and these were they whom the other pits of the company had not absorbed—the 'left-overs'—and there was not much hope for them. They were cynical and appreciative over the games two of their number were playing; discussed, almost quarrelled at times about, the respective skill of the leading exponents of the game—Lindrum, Smith, Davis, Newman. They talk football, of players and the matches won and lost the previous Saturday, those for decision at the week-end. But the conversation was more alive when the matches were talked of in relation to the 'pools'; then there were cuttings-in with 'three sure draws', 'four away certs', 'seven homes'. Inevitably on Mondays came the inquest on their efforts in forecasting, swearing volubly over 'hard lines', or 'some fool kicking through his own goal', or 'missing a penalty', mistakes which had 'lost me five quid'. They talked of the English cricket team touring Australia, and Arthur talked with them; he listened to the dirty stories, and laughed with them. They never talked of work, nor of the 'dole', unless over some special circumstance connected with it. Theirs was a world in which everything had been cut except talking. So they talked endlessly.

The atmosphere was not so alive in the reading-room. There were older and slower and more-worn men, who dozed over newspapers, and, towards the end of the month when flat-racing started, came with bits of paper and a stub of pencil, and put on their glasses, looking down the racing columns of each daily and copying some horse's name. Occasionally the librarian came in to tidy papers left in disorder, and immediately hands closed over the pencils, and scraps of paper and pages rustled over. Arthur smiled as he watched them, some winked at him, and he winked back in support. The week that the Lincoln and the Grand National were run, the room became crowded, men stood waiting to snap up a newspaper laid down, two or three near moved quickly to any chair a long-sitter left. Excited mutterings buzzed continually, broken at times by long-toned disagreement or quick agreement over a neighbour's choice. One said loudly, 'I'm goin' to stick to my fancy', and went at once, leaving a companion to turn again to the sheet, and stare and pull his mouth awry as he moved his mind among the 'probable starters'.

Arthur looked through the newspapers, and read the stuff other than the news. He read *Punch*, *Great Thoughts*, the *Millgate Monthly*, the *British Weekly*, but, most of all, he lingered over *John o' London*. And even the reading matter in that held him less than the advertisements offering success to any who would take a course in 'Short Story Writing or Journalism'. Sometimes, as he read through them, a strong reaching-forward made him vivid and alive; at other times a low-toned richness moved him. He invariably left *John o' London* until the last, and, immediately he had done with it, got up and went out, usually to walk over the fields dissatisfied and ill at ease. He knew what was the matter with him, and he was almost ashamed, he felt presumptuous. When the thought bit persistently into him that it was possible he might soothe that uneasiness and driving pain with attempts at writing something, a faint sense of shame flowed through him. . . .

Not always did he walk home with this in his mind,

other matters often pressed closer. Sometimes he had a companion and was glad to talk, though those who knew him never attempted to bounce frivolously the conversation. It was usually on a strong and sensible line, even though the topics might range from football to the winter misery of some families on the Means Test. One man talked to him of this, and Arthur said very little, though the urge was strong within him to ask how he would be dealt with under the system. But he knew without asking; the real desire pushing him was to hope the man would comfort him by saying it was just possible some benefit would be allowed him after an investigation had been made into his circumstances. He did not ask, because he knew the hope was false. He had seen what had happened to single men who lived at home and whose fathers were working. They merely went to the Exchange on Wednesday afternoon to have their Health Insurance cards franked; they never attended on Friday when the money was paid out. When he had left the man at Peathill, he walked on mechanically, seeing nothing. Lines of thought moved outwards and forwards; at the end of one was his mother; another, his stepfather; at the end of a vivid and persisting one was himself, with a bundle over his shoulder, walking in strange parts of England.

He came out of the billiard saloon one morning at half-past eleven, and a dry, blasting wind caught and moulded him with deadening cold. Until he was away from the channelled streets he was conscious of every inch of skin about his body, and beneath was pain, the undefinable ache of exposure to cold. But on the fields he hurried and beat his arms about his chest until his blood ran quicker and warmer. Still he hurried up

16

the fields towards Peathill, the wind dashing water
from his eyes; hurried past the man bent thinly against
the rushing cold; hurried towards the woman pushing
awkwardly through the stile on to the highway. The
cold seemed to have beaten her into slowness, into
heaviness. At the end of her straight-down left arm
hung a basket, pulling her body awry; the other arm
was curved about a parcel she hugged to her side.
He'd help her if she was going into Wingrove. Why, it
was his mother. Heavens!

'What're you doin' comin' to Pirley a mornin' like
this?' His utterance was loose and swift, indignant,
baffled. He was taking the basket and the parcel as he
spoke. 'Couldn't I have brought what you wanted?'
He began hurrying again, as if setting the pace needed
for keeping comfortable, but she could not respond.
'Are you cold?'

'I am.' Her agreement was strong, quick, meant to
give the impression that she felt mere superficial discomfort. But he looked into her face and saw the eyes
dulled and the mouth tight. 'Aren't you?'

'I'll bet you're frozen through,' he replied, suggesting
by his tone that he knew hers had been false, that the
brightness had been put on for his benefit. She did not
answer. 'What have you been for? Something I could
have brought, I should think.' He was accusing,
suggesting she need not have come out in this weather,
but she had not wanted to bother him. Or, maybe, did
not like asking him to 'shop' while her husband was
about.

'No. I didn't know about it until after you'd gone.'
She was taking short strides along the slippery pavement, walking gingerly, using no energy. 'I don't

know why people don't put a bit of salt in front of their houses. You could get on.' They turned the corner on to the Wingrove road. For twenty or thirty yards a row of houses sheltered them from the wind, then they broke into the open again and began to battle, bending their heads to the right for comfort to ear and neck. 'Oo. If it snows, now, it'll stop.'

'What did you say you'd been for?'

'Your dad's starting work to-morrow and he wanted some new moleskins. They'd none to fit him at our Co-op, so I had to go to Pirley.'

'Couldn't he have waited a day until they got some?'

'Well, Sid needed some pit-boots, so I thought I might as well fetch 'em all at once. Besides, I've done some shopping as well. I'll have the parcel if you're cold. You can't knock about much to keep warm when you're carrying things, and your hands are fast.'

The wind faced them again as they turned on to the village street, blasting, piercing. Neither spoke, but bored through as quickly as the woman could manage. The warmth of the house and the relief from striving bewildered them for a moment, and they stood unable to begin taking off their coats. Arthur stood, almost foolishly, with the 'shopping' still held to him.

'Get any?' Mr. Shirley asked casually.

'Yes,' his wife answered dully. 'They're there.' She let her head fall slowly, indicating the parcel her son was putting on the table.

'A man's been about 'is insurance. Wants to know if 'e can 'ave it o' Friday. Fifty shillin's,' he said.'

The woman and the young man looked startled, then

she went into the front room to take off her coat as her son spoke.

'Right. I'll draw it to-morrow.' Arthur's voice was quite calm. 'See, though. You have to give notice if you want to draw above two pounds.' His mother was coming back. 'See. The Co-op committee sits on Thursday, doesn't it?' She nodded. 'I'll give notice to-morrow, that's Wednesday, an' I can draw it on Friday.' That ended the matter for him, and no one spoke, but he seemed to feel that the man had got some kind of kick from telling him the news, especially as it had startled him for a moment.

Mrs. Shirley went into the kitchen and sat before the fire. She sat still, numbed too much even to hold out her hands to the warmth. Her son saw her begin to tremble, she swayed suddenly forwards, and, with a cry, he caught her. Her head jerked downwards and hung on her breast as he arrested her body.

'Eh! Dad! Come here, quick! Get some brandy. Mum's fainted.' The man hurried in, turned back to the cupboard for brandy, hurried in again, and poured some down his wife's throat as Arthur held back her head. 'I'll carry her upstairs.'

'I'll carry 'er upstairs,' the man rapped out. 'You get a 'ot-water bottle.'

'Sending her to Pirley a morning like this. And you know she hasn't been well lately.' His words were swift and hot.

'An' who's damned fault is that.' He lifted the woman from the chair. 'Come out o' t'road. If you'd get some work, she'd 'ave nowt to bother about. Idle rat.'

Arthur was helpless before the circumstance, the

man bitter against him, stating one side of a truth—
safe to state it because he was holding the woman
gently, surely, in strong arms. For one flashing
moment the young man wished his mother dead, so
that he could pour himself physically, and in streaming
hot speech, on the man. But he weakened, and pushed
the kettle crushingly on the fire, then fetched out the
rubber water-bottle. Mr. Shirley stayed until his wife
came to, then left the bedroom to get the hot milk
she asked for. Arthur ran up at once.

'Do you want ,the doctor, mum?' He looked into
her face eagerly, saw the dull eyes, the quivering
mouth. She shook her head, swallowed hard, attempted
to summon strength into her features.

'I shall be all right if I stay in bed to-day.'

'You won't. You must have a good rest. I'll do the
house-work.' The woman smiled faintly. 'I can
manage.' She closed her eyes, her mouth trembled
again.

'What about your insurance?'

'Don't bother about that. I s'll draw it to-morrow.'

'How much will it leave you?'

'About a pound.'

'Take your dad's book and draw it from that.'

'No.' Footsteps sounded on the stairs. He helped
her sit up as the man came into the room with steaming
milk. 'I'll go and peel some potatoes and make Albert
and Sid some chips.'

'Do an egg each for them, as well. You must get the
same for your dinner.' She took the cup from her
husband. 'Shall you have egg and chips, dad?'

'Can do.'

Arthur and his step-father sat at the table in silence

over dinner. The stairfoot door was open, each mouth stopped working suddenly and together when any sound came from that direction. The two brothers came from the pit, slurring heavy boots on the 'end'. Albert was whistling feebly. Both peeled off their clothes and banged their tin bottles in the sink, then sat at the table. Arthur handed them plates of egg and chips.

'Where's mum?' Sidney asked suddenly.

'In bed,' Arthur answered at once. 'She's not very well.'

Sidney left the table at once and clumped upstairs in his pit-boots. Albert sat for a moment or two, then he followed. Arthur clenched his teeth and waited.

''Ave you 'ad the doctor to 'er?' Sidney asked, when he came down. Arthur shook his head. The youth went into the middle room where his father was. 'I'm goin' to wash me an' fetch the doctor. Don't you think we ought to do? What's a matter wi' 'er?'

'I thought of 'avin' 'im in to-morrow if she's no better,' the man said. 'She's all right. Wind an' t'cold must 'ave exhausted 'er comin' from Pirley this mornin'. She'll be all right when she's rested an' 'ad some 'ot drinks.'

But she was no better in the morning, and Mr. Shirley did not go to work. He fetched Mrs. King from across the street.

'Could you do a bit for us while t'missis's bad?' he asked. 'I'll go an' ask doctor to call. It seems to be gettin' on to 'er chest.'

Arthur went to sign on Wednesday and Friday, and came straight home, though there was nothing to do. Mrs. King, under orders from his step-father, cleaned and tidied the house, prepared the meals and attended to his mother. The doctor had said she must stay in bed until he told her she could get up. Arthur sat with her at times, but the strain on both was too intense. He knew it was through him she was lying there, what the man had said as he carried her upstairs was true. She knew he thought this and attempted no artificial manner with him, preferring to lie silent. He would leave suddenly and go downstairs, sitting staring at nothing when Mrs. King was in her own home, moving from one room to another out of her way when she was here. His two brothers said little to him, or to each other for that matter, when they came home from work. The wireless was silent; the father did not go to the public-house, but sent one of the youths for a pint of beer each night. Mrs. Shirley improved, and came down for two hours on Sunday, lay in bed again most of Monday, then told her husband she could manage all but the washing. Mrs. King finished on the Tuesday and the house was as before, the wireless lived, the man was gone for long hours at night. But Arthur watched her and was not satisfied; he saw the effort thrusting her into slow activities, the drooping at odd moments when she let go of herself. He hurried from signing, and made her sit while he busied himself clumsily with the house-work. He shopped, choosing meat to his mother's directions, cooking it, cooking fish, and then, when the men came from the pit, going out while she served the meals.

But he did not hurry home on the following Wednesday; he walked slowly, blindly almost, along the Pirley fields, not minding where he trod, though the mud in places reached to his shoe-tops. He kept in the middle of the yard-wide field path, bounded on one side with a hedge, the other with strong fencing. Women tiptoed past him, squeezed along the side of the hedge, men picked a way carefully, but he just pushed his feet through the mud, ploughing along. There had been a cut across his life this morning.

'This is your last week of benefit, Mister Gardner,' the fat, bald clerk had said. 'If you wish to make application for transitional benefit will you fill in this form and bring it back on Friday.?' The whole speech flowed mechanically from him.

Arthur had looked at it foolishly.

'Can't I fill it in, now?' he asked. He had looked at it, and had become suddenly afraid of what it meant. If he took the thing home he'd never fill it up; he'd think about it too much, think himself into hopelessness. No, he'd hand it in again at once; he couldn't lose anything, they couldn't take anything from him. . . . But couldn't they? He was answering this question to himself as he walked over the fields. He wished that he hadn't filled in the form—still, he couldn't get anything if he didn't, and, well, it would have been hopeless at home.

'I shan't have any more money from the Exchange after this week,' he told his mother as soon as he got home. 'Had my number of days.' She did not say anything, but sat quietly with her hands on her lap, her mouth was closed, but there was no strength in it; her eyelids drooped and lifted slowly, drooped and lifted, a heavy pulsing moved in her neck. He looked at her, wistful and weak, and a dangerous strength flashed him into activity. Why not kill her and set himself and her at peace? But he guided the emotion into a more rational channel. 'I'll go round every pit these next two days. I'll get a job if—if——' He hesitated momentarily and she came in to relieve him, not meeting him in the attempt to sooth them both— she neglected his outburst, knowing, as he knew, that it was mere words—but keeping to the ground-level of the situation.

'It means you won't have to sign, then?'

'No. Well, I should go on Wednesday to get my insurance card franked. Still . . .'

'What about the Means Test? Won't they allow you anything under that?'

'I don't know. I've signed a form asking them to do.'

'You pay your board and keep yourself. I don't see why they shouldn't. A man comes to see you, doesn't he?' Arthur made an affirmative noise. 'What does he ask?'

'Oh. He'll inquire into my circumstances, and then the P.A.C. will "—well, decide whether to allow me anything or not.'

'Well. I hope your dad's at work when he comes.'

She had quieted him and was satisfied. They had dinner in a one-sided manner. Arthur did all the talking and eating; she sipped hot milk, and answered questions or agreed with tired monosyllables.

'You'd better go to bed,' he said as soon as the meal was done. 'I'll wash up and put their stuff on.'

'I think I shall have to do,' she said tremblingly. 'I don't feel very well, just now.'

He went behind her upstairs, not helping her; neither wanted to think it had come to that.

'Where's mum?' the other sons asked when they came home, and went upstairs at once almost before Arthur could tell them.

'Where's your mother?' the father asked of Albert, when he came in and the sons were at the table.

'She's in bed again,' Sidney burst out, it seemed as if it was to save himself from crying. 'I don't know what's up wi' 'er. She looks awful.'

'Well. She can stop in bed for a bit. 'Ave you done till Monday?' They said they had. 'That's a' right, then. We can manage wi'out Mrs. King—we can do t'work between us.' His words, his attitude made plain that the 'we' did not include Arthur. 'She must 'ave doctor in t'mornin' again. Be there at nine for 'im, Sid.'

The next day was real agony for Arthur. His step-father kept him from the theme of household work they pursued; he sent Albert or Sid upstairs with hot drinks, pointed out duties for them to do, talked to them as they worked. Arthur went out into the garden; he felt, somehow, the end of everything had come.

'Why don't you let Arthur 'elp?' Sidney complained to his father. 'Let 'im see to mum, 'e'd like that.'

''E's not seein' to 'er. I can do that.'

'It's not 'is fault 'e's out o' work,' Albert said, with some appeal in his voice. ''E'd work if 'e could.'

'It's 'is fault 'e's out. It's 'is fault your mother's up there.' The man's tone was bitter. ''Im an' 'is books. Thinkin' they'd get 'im in some thousand-pound job. 'E got sack, didn't 'e, for muckin' about wi' 'is learnin' instead o' mindin' 'is work? An' where 'as it landed 'im? An' where is it landin' your mum? Eh? Where is it landin' your mum?' He was angry with the last question; it was anger telling that circumstances were such as could have been avoided, there was sympathy for the woman in his voice.

Neither of the youths mentioned Arthur again, and when tea was over they went out and stayed out until ten o'clock. The father seemed ill at ease about half-past nine, listening for footsteps on the 'end', glancing continually at the clock. Arthur sat reading. He knew the man wanted some beer, and wondered how he could frame a suggestion that he should fetch him some. Arthur went upstairs for twenty minutes, came down at ten-to-ten with the definite intention of offering to fetch his stepfather some beer. He knew it was no good attempting to solve the situation the other way, saying he would take care of his mother while the man himself went to the public-house.

'I'll fetch your beer to-night, if you like, dad.' His tone was even, he tried to make it 'friendly'.

'Who wants any beer?' Mr. Shirley pulled himself into easiness in a moment, sat down and made himself interested in the evening paper. No other word was spoken until Sidney came in. 'You're a nice un, stoppin' out all this time an' your mother lyin' up there.' The man's tone was nasty. 'Couldn't find time to sit wi' 'er a bit. Besides, there was plenty o' things you could 'ave done.'

Sidney's eyes filled with pain, he was condemned within himself. Albert, who came in a few minutes later, backed morally at the same accusation.

'Mum wanted to lie quiet, she told me,' the young man said. 'I'd 'ave stopped wi' 'er all night, if you'd 'ave said so.'

Both sons ate some bread and cheese hastily, then

went upstairs and sat with the mother for a while, only speaking when she led them in speech. They did not come down again, and Arthur and the father soon followed to bed.

'Letter for you, Arth,' Sidney said next morning. 'I was at t'gate an' t'postman pulled a face when he gave it me. "I'm not very welcome when I bring these things", he said.' Arthur chilled as he took it, and turned away to break open the window envelope though which his name and address showed plainly as he pressed the transparent strip close to the folded sheet within.

'Where's it from?'

'Means Test man's comin' this morning.'

'Who?' Arthur jerked round suddenly, startled from the abstraction out of which he had answered his brother. His stepfather looked down at the loose paper in his hand as Arthur faced him. 'Means Test man comin' 'ere? W'at's that for? W'at's 'e comin' 'ere for?'

'He's coming to see me, if you want to know.' Arthur was telling him calmly, consciously choosing words and tone to avoid giving opportunity for loud nastiness to come from the man. 'I've run out of benefit, and the Means Test man has to come before I can have any more. You know that, don't you?'

'I don't know as 'e's comin' through t'door, if 'e does come. 'Im comin' 'ere, why . . .'

'That's silly, dad,' Sidney broke in. ''E goes to everybody w'o's been out a long time. It's 'is job. An' Arth'll get nothing if 'e doesn't answer 'is questions.'

'Well. So long as 'e minds 'is business an' nobody

else's, 'e can come. But if 'e gets pokin' 'is nose into anybody else's, 'e'll go out neck an' crop.' The man turned away. 'An' I've 'eard of 'im doin'. 'E mustn't start it 'ere, though.'

Arthur sat on the sofa for a while after Sid had left him and occasionally he glanced, it seemed unconsciously, towards the stairfoot door. Physically he showed that his intention was being pulled this way and that, his fingers pulled at the flesh on his cheeks, rubbed across his forehead, pushed at his nose. Suddenly he went upstairs and stood at the foot of his mother's bed, his back to the window. She looked at him without interest for a while, supposing he had come to 'keep her company' and talk when she felt like it. But her eyes narrowed, and she tried to examine the shadowy features; from his poise, she could tell he was being silent and still in a detached sort of way. Her mind worked, groping for some point she could relate to his mood. Suddenly she found it.

'It's Friday. You should sign this morning, shouldn't you?' Her voice was more alive than of late.

'I have to stay in until the Means Test man's been.'

There was a void for wholly a minute.

'I think I shall get up a bit, this morning.' Strength was in her voice, almost a brightness. 'Get the middle room warm and I'll be down in about an hour.'

'Don't talk silly. The doctor . . .'

'He said I could get up on Saturday, didn't he? It's Friday, to-day. One day . . .'

'You mustn't. The man'll want to see my insurance policy and my National Deposit book. Where do you keep them?'

'I'll find 'em.'

'He might be here before you come down—if you are coming down. I shouldn't.'

'Why not. If I feel like it . . .'

'Dad might start kicking up a row when the man's here, and it'd only upset you.'

'It would upset me more to lie here and hear it.'

She closed her eyes and did not answer when he spoke again, so he went down. Why had he told her? Oh, he'd had that out with himself on the sofa. He'd gone up to tell her, because she'd have come down if she'd have heard a row. And the sudden shock might have, yes, even killed her. It had been better to tell her.

She came down at eleven and sat in the corner under the little side window. Mr. Shirley was in the garden, moving about the path bordering his bulb-bed. Ugly gaps broke the white crocus ring, the daffodils were not so large and rich as in other years. He puckered his brows and pulled his mouth small. A motor bike rattled up the hill and stopped at the gate. He turned and looked towards the street; a man was taking a book from his inside pocket; he peered at it, glanced from it to the house, then set his bike at rest and came to the gate. Mr. Shirley walked into the house.

'What you doin' up.' He showed surprise when he saw his wife; other matters seemed to have been wiped from his mind. 'He said you 'ad to stop in bed till to-morrer.'

'I felt like getting up a bit . . .' She paused shortly as a rattle sounded at the door. Her husband looked at her quickly, looked at Arthur sitting on the table and a significant light shone in his eyes. He said nothing but went to the sofa and took up the news-

paper. Arthur was down from the table now and
moving towards the middle door; he hurried a little
when the knocking sounded again. The woman was
listening with head bent; the man listened, too,
all but his legs was hidden behind the newspaper.

'Does Arthur Gardner live here?'

'I'm Arthur Gardner.'

'I'm the Means Test investigator.'

'Come in, will you?'

'Thank you.'

A thin man of about forty followed Arthur into the
room; he was bundled about so with motoring clothes
that the thin, small head perched on top looked
comical. But the expression on his face was quiet, in
his eyes a far-away look seemed to suggest that he did
not want to notice anything. 'Good morning,' he
said without holding the gaze of either the woman in
the corner or the man on the sofa. His voice was
quiet, too, almost apologizing for his visit. The woman
returned his greeting and watched him lay his cap and
gloves on the table and pull round the leather satchel
from his back to where his hands could deal with it.

'Could I have a chair?' He was standing rather
aimlessly.

'I'm sorry,' Arthur said and reached one.

'Thank you.' He took a foolscap-sized book from
the satchel, swung the case again to his back, and sat
down. 'Your crocuses are nice, and your daffodils.
Soon have summer here, now.'

'Yes,' the young man said. 'You'll be glad the
winter's over, I'll bet.'

'I shall.' He had unscrewed the cap of a fountain
pen and pushed it on the other end. 'Now, Mr.

Gardner, if you'll give me the particulars I want——'
He rested the pen near the top of the sheet. 'Your
name?'

'Arthur Gardner.'

'Full address?'

'Church Street, Wingrove, Condor.'

'Occupation?'

'Miner.' The man behind the newspaper might
have had a slight cold, for just then he sniffed.

'Married.'

'No.'

'See.' The man was moving his hand down the
sheet flicking dashes. 'No rent—rates,' he ended a
long mumbling. 'Any life insurance policies?' He
was questioning again. 'If so, how much do you pay?'

'How much do I pay, mum?'

Four shillings a month.'

'Shilling a week.' The man mumbled it. 'Could I
see the policy, please?'

'I brought it down. Where did you put it, Arthur?'

'It's here.' He fetched the paper from behind a tin
on the mantelshelf. The man looked at it and handed
it back.

'I must see your bank book, if you have one.' Arthur
gave him that and he made an entry on the sheet, a
one-figure entry. 'Do you pay into any sick club?'

'Two shillings a month in the National Deposit.'

'Are you earning anything? Any Trade Union pay?
Army pension? Compensation? Sick or club pay, or
relief of any kind?'

'No. I've nothing coming in at all. Nothing.'

The man moved his pen to another section of the
ruled form. Mrs. Shirley rose from the chair and

turned to look through the little window. Arthur was standing beside the man; his gaze moved to the questions the pen was at. He stiffened and swept a glance to his mother. She stood with one eye closed—a habit of hers—watching something in the garden or on the street.

'Could I have the names of the other members of the household?' The question opened the woman's eye, rustled slightly the newspaper.

'Albert Shirley, senior. Harriet Shirley. Albert Shirley, junior. Sidney Shirley.'

'What relation are they to you?' The man looked into his face, the difference in surnames puzzled him.

'My mother has married twice. I'm her son. They are my stepbrothers.' He stumbled the words, curving around the straight truth he could have uttered, straining to avoid mentioning the man.

'Mother, step-father and step-brothers. Is that it?'

'Yes,' Arthur agreed quickly, relieved.

The man was writing. Arthur looked at the questions to follow, and his heart almost stood still.

'Where do your step-father and step-brothers work?'

'Check number.' 'Pays to home.' 'Wages.' Arthur was reading the questions, shuddering into bewilderment; his legs seemed thin lines of pain, the back of his neck hurt him, and a heavy weight hung to each eyeball. He got no sense from the man's question and murmured, 'Pardon.'

'I said, "Where do they work?"'

'Oh—sorry. Shenton Colliery, all three of them.'

Mrs. Shirley sat down again; her arms rested on the chair arms, her hands gripped the wood, she was pulling strength into herself. Arthur glanced at her, saw a greyness in her face, closed eyes. He tore his gaze from her and swept it to the sofa, but saw only the legs of his stepfather hanging below the stretched sheets of newspaper. The man had not moved during the questioning; the two pages had occupied him the whole of the time. The Means Test man had done writing and he glanced at the newspaper before he asked the next question. He was a mild sort of a man, not quite strong enough for the job; the invisibility and silence of whatever was behind the newspaper upset him. Still, he'd his job to do, his money to earn, his wife and children to keep. He was gaining courage in the way a weak man does. This was just a 'case' in hundreds. But the man might have shown himself, he did not even say good morning, had not spoken once. Oh, he must get on.

'Could I have their check numbers and the wages they earn?'

The dry dashing of paper sounded. Mr. Shirley was on his feet.

'Put that bloody pen up an' gerrout.' The investigator jerked his head sideways. 'Tha can look. Come on, get off that chair.' The man did not move; he could not quite grasp the circumstance. On occasions he had had people who refused to answer some of the questions, or disclose particulars of income, but they usually did it merely with words and a tone which said plainly that if benefit could come to them only through uncovering the nakedness of their living, they'd do without it. He had talked to them and in some cases, many cases, had got the information—when they knew every one else had to give it, and no one could possibly get benefit without answering the question, they came round, most of them offered it eagerly. But this man looked dangerous, as if he was leaping straight through all sense to avenge blindly some insult; the head thrust out boldly, the eyes small, the corners of the mouth turned down in weak anger and sleering. 'Come on. Can't tha bloody well 'ear?'

'But . . .' He bent backwards slightly; the other's face was so near, it was out of focus. 'But . . .'

'But—hell. While tha stuck to 'is business tha was all right. If tha's done wi' 'is business get thee gone.'

'I'm afraid it will damn every chance of Mr. Gardner getting anything if this form is not complete.' The investigator was standing up now, on the opposite side of the chair to Mr. Shirley. 'I'm telling you this for his benefit, and, of course, for yours as well.'

''Ow do you mean, "mine"?'

'He'll still need keeping, won't he, if he's allowed nothing?'

'Leave it as it is, please.' Arthur stood by the man, between him and his stepfather; he was alert for any physical move from the latter; his voice attempted to satisfy them both at once, to reassure the Means Test man that he would come to no harm, to make plain to his step-father that he recognized his authority and would bow to it. 'Let it go as it is.'

The man looked at him, saw the seriousness in his eyes.

'You'd better sign your name here, then.' He handed Arthur the pen and pointed with his finger to a line at the foot of the form. 'If you don't, the thing can't go before the Committee.'

Arthur signed and the man slid the block of forms

into the satchel, fastened it and swung it round to his back. Then he picked up his cap and gloves and went to the door, Arthur following him.

'Morning,' he called, but none answered until Arthur left him at the door, then he gave him back the adieu.

Arthur let the door knob stay in his hand for a moment or two after he had closed the door on the man; he was relieved to be from the other room. His mother looked awful; he had glanced at her a few times during the interview and had marked surging and draining of strength in her; her face lifted to him when she knew he was looking at her, the loose mouth and half-closed eyes at other times. And the man, ugly and spiteful, thrusting himself big between Arthur and life, appeasing nothing within himself, even though he saw his nastiness bear the intended pain in others. A sudden impulse almost forced him to open the door and go into the garden for respite, but he pulled his thoughts clear of it. His mother would be waiting in there; she had left her bed just to help him morally in the face of his father. It would be treachery to run away and she there. Besides, she needed watching; she seemed, in moments of detachment, like someone dead. A sound came from the room, a short, dry sound. He hurried through the middle door.

'Keep your damned paws off that.' He forgot his mother; he was a hot point focussed on his step-father's hand, which had taken his bank-book from the table and was turning over the pages.

Mr. Shirley allowed the book to close, then he tossed it back to the table. A short, sharp sound came down his nose.

'Fat lot there to bother about, I must say.' He took up the newspaper—a weak, defensive gesture. 'Thirty bob. Why . . .'

'It's thirty bob on the right side of havin' to humble to you, any road.' He picked up the book, the policy, and the friendly society things, fumbling them in his anger. 'Talk about pokin' noses into anybody's business, you've some room to talk.'

'Tha should get some work, an' 'ave money come in honest. Still, pit'd never 'ave done for thee. Too big ideas.'

'Pit had to do for you, accordin' to what I can hear. Kicked out of a good job, an' had to have the pit.'

'Why, you bloody young swine.' The man was on his feet, the paper dashed behind him. 'Tha can get out o' 'ere.' He moved forward and Arthur put up his fists, dropping the books on the table.

'Don't fight.' The woman was sobbing weakly; the two words, imploring, rode out on a stronger burst; it meant straining for her to be heard, her weeping was scarcely audible, merely like jerked breath.

The two men fell away from each other and swung to her. The husband pushed the son roughly aside as he was bending to her.

'You shouldn't 'ave got up,' Mr. Shirley said, with kindly reproval. 'You know you weren't fit. It was only becos o' 'im.' The corners of his mouth dropped down. 'Don't think I don't know.' He lifted her gently to her feet. 'Come on, back to bed. You've undone a' Doctor Ross's work. 'E'll know. An' 'e'll grumble.'

Arthur looked into her face as she passed him, heavy against her husband's arm as it encircled her back, but she did not see him, her eyes were almost closed, her lower jaw hung a little and was to one side.

'Let me help you,' he said to the man. 'She can't walk.' There was pain in his voice, and the husband was startled. He looked into her face, then immediately picked her from the floor, carrying her.

'Oppen that stair-foot door.'

Arthur obeyed and the man took her up to bed. When he came down again, the young man went towards the stairs at once.

'Keep down.' The man's tone was definite. 'She wants no bother.' He began to clear the table; the other two sons came in as he was spreading the cloth for dinner. Sidney walked to the wireless and switched it on—it wasn't important to Sidney what was coming over. An orchestra was in a forte. 'Shut that damned wireless off.' The father's voice was a restrained scream, thin, high. The noise snapped off. 'Come in blunderin' and thinkin' o' nobody but yersen.'

'What's up?' The youth was guilty and scared. His eyes opened in fright. 'Mum again.' He made for the stair-foot.

'Keep down. She's better wi'out so much bother. Let 'er lie still.' The youth turned, sat in a chair for a minute or two, then roused himself and helped with the dinner. 'You can make your mum a drink of Ovaltine an' take it 'er,' his father told him when the meal was almost ready.

Arthur watched his brother preparing the drink, marked the careful measuring and mixing, the bright face-light when it was ready and he was carrying it to the stairs. 'Wish I was Sid.' He started at the thought which rushed into him; the words seemed to be said

inside him, so real and earnest had been the sub-
conscious yearning for the simple world of which his
brother was the centre. He heard Sidney mounting
slowly; the steps forced him to count. Six. Seven.
Eight. The youth did not intend any spilling. Arthur
left his chair suddenly and followed his brother.

'Mum. What's up, mum? Don't you want it?'
Sidney's voice, thin and quavering with concern, met
him as he reached the landing. 'Oh . . .'

'I'm here, Sid.' Arthur hurried in; his brother
stood by the bed, helpless it seemed before circumstances which were not fitting around his preparations
and intention. 'What . . . ?' His speaking failed as
he looked at his mother. Her eyes were half-closed,
like one drugged; her mouth sagged, ugly in its looseness. 'She's dying.' Arthur was off his balance for a
moment. 'I'm sure she's dying.' He clutched his
brother's arm and the liquid jerked from the cup and
pattered on the carpet in quick drops. 'We s'll have
to have t'doctor. Shout dad.' He bent to the bed
quickly. 'Mum. Mum.' His voice was soft. 'God,'
he breathed heavily as she did not respond. 'God.'
He was afraid.

Mr. Shirley hurried in, pushed past Arthur and
looked at his wife. Because of the shakiness of the two
about him, he was direct; it seemed that he fell natur-
ally into a mood which was in antagonism to his stepson; there seemed always a battle going on between
them, even when both were silent and occupied. Now,
Mr. Shirley felt some vague conquest over the young
man in that he was composed in face of the other's
unsteadiness  It did not, of course, shadow any of the
concern he knew as he bent to his wife.

'Mum.' He took her hand. 'Mum.' He straightened. 'You'd better fetch the doctor, Sid. Tell 'im your mum's bad.'

The youth hurried down, wild-eyed, sobbing dryly. Arthur went down, too. His head, neck, chest ached, the pain of not-weeping. Albert came in from the garden; he had gone out until the dinner was ready.

'Where's Sid rushin' off to?'

'Mum's ever so bad, Albert,' Arthur told him. 'I'm sure she's dying. Sid's gone for the doctor.'

Albert went upstairs at once, came down and went across the road for Mrs. King. When she went to the bedside, Mr. Shirley came down and the three men had dinner. Sid had been on his bike to Condor and was back in twenty minutes.

''E can't come before three,' he panted. 'But 'e'll be 'ere then.' He had rushed back with this message as fast as he had rushed to the doctor—everything was important to Sid when he was helping his mother. He was the 'baby' and she had kept him in that relation, as there had been no other child for the baby-mantle to fall on.

'Get some dinner,' his father said. 'An' we'll wash up.'

Tones were even and words few, now. The sons were eager to help, eager to be busy so they need not talk. Mrs. King left at two, saying she would come when the doctor arrived. Mr. Shirley went on to the yard with her, not wishing to discuss the mother while the sons were present. Arthur and Sidney went upstairs at once and found their mother different; she was out of the coma which had hidden them from her, though she gazed at them for some moments without blinking, as if meaning to be sure her mind was working properly. Her eyes held Arthur, held Sidney, then wandered away.

'Albert.' The two syllables were slow, hardly audible.

Arthur went to the top of the stairs and called for his step-brother. He came and sat with them, and when his mother had let her eyes rest on him, she turned away satisfied. Sidney was restless; he left his chair suddenly and bent over his mother and laid his cheek against hers; he was in agony until he had known her that way. The other two clenched their hands as they watched him; they were craving for the soothing contact Sid was enjoying, yet knew they would deny themselves of it; mentally it was repugnant to them to 'go through the same actions in turn'.

The contact seemed to awake the woman more. She blinked quickly as Sidney stepped back.

'My baby,' she murmured, and smiled at the ceiling. Her head turned to the others. 'Winchester,' she said suddenly. 'Yes, remember Winchester.' Her eyes moved from Arthur to her husband, who came in; she looked at him thoughtfully for a few moments, turned back to the son, then again to the man. Then she closed her eyes and lay still. All bent forward, not breathing, to hear if she breathed.

'She's asleep,' Albert said. 'Let's leave 'er.'

'Oh! By gum! I've got to sign. I'd forgotten.' Arthur hurried into his scarf and overcoat as soon as he got downstairs. 'Shan't be longer than I can help, Sid.' He was about to hurry out. 'Is there anything I can bring from Pirley?' he asked of Mr. Shirley.

'Tha should know better than me. Look in t'pantry

an' see.' The man dismissed him and the subject by leaving the room.

'I don't think I'll bother,' he was saying, as the man passed out. He transferred the conversation to Sidney. 'We can get what we want from one o' the shops here, can't we?' His brother gave an affirmative grunt. 'Shan't be long,' he ended.

'Don't know why he didn't learn to ride a bike,' Albert said nervously. ''E'd 'ave bin back in no time.'

''E allus goes about thinkin'. 'Ardly looks where 'e's goin' w'en 'e's walkin'. If 'e tried to ride a bike 'e'd either stop peddlin' an' fa' off, else 'e'd run into summat. 'E'd not be safe on one wi' 'is blinkin' an' thinkin'.'

Both felt as if some strength had been withdrawn from them when Arthur had gone; their mother's condition terrified them; the father's calmness kept them awed and silent; each felt some kind of weak anger against their step-brother because he could not at this moment ride a bicycle and get back quickly to them. They sat in the house, heads on one side, waiting for sounds from upstairs, yet dreading to hear them. Albert startled his brother by leaving his chair suddenly and going into the garden. Mr. Shirley had come in and tiptoed upstairs. He had said somebody must be in the house, and now that he had come in, Albert felt he could go out conscientiously. Sidney followed at once, and they walked about until their father came out again; they went in again, then, and sat. One would not have gone in without the other.

Arthur was hurrying to Pirley. When he got to the Exchange a queue was at the 'regulars' table and he

had to join it. He writhed at the slow moving up,
picked his fingers, tapped on the floor with his feet,
forced himself to read the warning notices plastered
about the walls—notices of prosecutions for misrepre-
sentation of circumstances, of false evidence to get
benefit. He knew he was a fool doing all this to hasten
his turn. If he had told the men in front that he had
to get back home because some one was ill—he need
have gone into no particulars—the men would have
told him to pass to the table at once. He had seen
such happen many a time. And he daren't speak.

'Bit late, aren't you?' the clerk suggested with faint
irony when Arthur reached the table.

'Had the Means Test man, Joe,' he replied, and the
round, shining-faced man went to another box for his
book without another word.

He signed, and went into the other room for his
money; he watched the manager take his check, call
out 'RB 5486', wait until the clerk at his side repeated
the term and said 'Fifteen shillings', then he initialed
the check, tossed it into a box and counted six half-
crowns from a stack and slid them under the wire
fence.

'Thank you,' Arthur said, sweeping them into his
hand. His last pay day. Fifteen bob. In the Co-op.
another thirty, and six quid to come from Trentingham.
He'd last another month or six weeks. Might get a
job within that time. He'd have a damn good try.
It was hopeless at the pits, of course, hopeless. The
summer would soon be here and short time for the
miners; they'd set nobody on in summer. He'd learn
to ride Sid's bike and go to Derby and have a look
round. And if he got a job he could buy a bike of his

own. He'd have to get something soon, there was no doubt about it.

He was half-way up the Pirley-Peathill fields, his head bent to the ground, blinking and thinking. The afternoon was crisp and calm, splendid with sunlight, but he was not aware of it. He was not aware of anything external until some one loomed vaguely in his path, had stopped and was making peculiar, snatching noises. He swerved slightly and looked up to apologize. It was Sidney, his face pulled with fear and grief.

'Mum's dead,' he said at once. It gushed from him; it was all he wanted to say, all that he had come to meet Arthur for. He seemed relieved immediately, and waited without purpose for his step-brother's will.

'Dead,' Arthur repeated, and said no more for a long time as they walked home. 'Who was there when she went?' 'How did she go? Quietly? Or suffered?' He wanted to ask all these questions of Sid; they rushed up from the weak feeling in his stomach. But he held them. There was no point in knowing the answers. There was no point in soothing the youth at his side, whose breath was jerky and loud. The big fact was in being, and irrevocable, windy playings about its surface was foolishness; his mother was dead; for her part she was silent, for his part, too, he would be silent; it was the end for both of them, the relation was broken, she was away from him, he would be away from her, there was no other sensible adjustment. 'How long since?' he asked suddenly, when they were near the gate. He felt he had been cruel to the youth, keeping him pent within himself when he might be needing the comfort and strength of fusing with another.

'About an hour after you'd gone. She—we thought she was asleep. Then she murmured and I ran up——'

'Is Missis King here?' He cut in to spare himself the details Sidney was rushing into, gaining speed in his utterance, breaking and melting nervously.

'Yes, she's 'ere. I fetched 'er as soon as——'

'Where's dad?' This question brought them along the 'end', on to the yard. He was keeping Sidney at bay until they should come into the house among the others and away from direct conversation.

''E went to t'doctor's when I came to meet you. 'E'll not be back yet.'

They were in the kitchen now. Mrs. King was moving about in the middle room; she seemed to be doing nothing really.

'Hello, Missis King,' Arthur greeted as she looked up at his coming.

'Well, Arthur, lad,' she gave back, and there was sympathy for him and a big sigh for the circumstance in her tone.

'Can I go up?'

She nodded, her mouth quivering at once, not able to speak; the knowledge that a child was asking to see its dead mother was overwhelming to her. Arthur clenched his teeth in face of her emotion and went upstairs strongly, though, out of the woman's sight, he weakened and hesitated for a moment before going through the open door and breaking into the peculiar silence of his mother's room. But he thrust himself in and stood beside her, silent and not consciously thinking; hanging as it were, and letting thoughts, remem-

brances and judgments wash over him. It was his
fault. Her hair used to be chestnut colour, purely
chestnut, and not so long ago. These patches of white
were hateful marks. It was as much his step-father's
fault, the awkward fool. And these sentimental clowns
say people look lovely and peaceful in death. She was
ugly, the slits of her nearly closed eyes glistened horribly,
her mouth was pulled into a fixed show of one beaten
at last. It was her own fault, too. Her face used to
be alive and eager, eager for all her sons, eager for
her husband and home. She loved to surprise them
all with nice things; playful she was at those times.
It was all over for ever; she had finished. A mighty
sense of tragedy rushed suddenly through him. It
need not have been over. People killed people in other
ways than by physical violence, in ways more cruel
than war. Forty-eight. Forty-eight. God! Grey! Old!
His step-father's voice sounded downstairs and he
switched into conscious relation with his world. She
was lying there, still and away from him. He hardened.
There would be no sentimental bridge until he should
be away from her. He was away from her now; their
relation had ended when she had looked vaguely at
him and muttered 'Winchester'. He left her suddenly.

Mrs. King was throwing a white cloth over the table
surface and Sidney was waiting to place cups and
saucers on it. Albert came from the pantry with the
butter, which he put in the hearth to soften. Mr.
Shirley sat on the sofa and he looked at Arthur as he
came into the room. He spoke at once, seeming to
have saved the remark until his stepson should be
within hearing.

'I shall sleep with you to-night, Albert.'

Sidney lifted his eyes from the table where he was laying the cups orderly. The sense bewildered him slightly.

'Where do I go, then?'

'With me.' Arthur spoke quickly for the youth's sake, then went at once into the garden, where a dry wind blew coldly through the twilight. The doctor came while he was mooning about and left again when he stood on the yard. Mr. Shirley came to the door with the bald-headed young doctor.

'I don't think she tried to get better, really, Mr. Shirley. The worry must have been too much for her, as you say. It's a pity, but—well.' He gave Arthur a peculiar glance. 'Send round for the certificate, Mr. Shirley, in surgery hours, will you?'

He went, and Mr. Shirley drew back into the house. Arthur went in, too. He must have been telling the doctor that his mother had died through worrying over him. The thought did not move him; he sat at the table and poured himself a cup of tea, he ate the bread and butter and jam set out. Mr. Shirley was consciously attempting to go through the meal as if circumstances were normal; Albert stared down at the table, eating mechanically; Sidney was nervous and fumbling; he glanced about him as one half-fearful, half-ashamed that his manner should be observed. At night he watched Arthur closely and went up the stairs with him to bed. In the night he whimpered a few times, and Arthur put his hand to him and the youth rested again in silence. At seven in the morning Sidney followed Arthur out of bed at once; they found Albert and his father already down and preparing breakfast.

'See. We should sign this morning, shouldn't we?'
Mr. Shirley asked over the meal.

'We s'll lose three days if we don't.' Albert was
plainly suggesting that it was important they should
go to Pirley, or any other place for that matter, so
long as they moved about and had not to sit thinking
or looking at each other.

The conversation point seemed to remind Arthur of
some omission. He felt in the hip pocket of his trousers
and brought out six half-crowns; he laid them on the
table almost under his step-father's nose.

'I s'll give you the other ten shillings this afternoon.'

The man seemed shattered for a moment; he looked
at the money, blinking himself into realization of what
it meant; then his eyes stayed open in detachment,
his jaws ceased moving. The two sons watched him
from the corner of their eye, holding their breath.
They wanted no row while . . .

'You'd better keep it an' do a bit o' shoppin' in
Pirley some time to-day.' The man spoke evenly and
resumed eating. Arthur did not answer. The sons
were obviously relieved; to them the father's tone had
seemed conciliating, almost kindly. They looked up
again when he continued speaking. 'We'd all better
ca' in t'Co-op. an' get some black this mornin'. It'd
be as well to 'ave ready-made suits. They'll last
through t'dirty weather till summer. They'll soon fit
us out in t'Pirley shop.'

'We might not get away from t'dole as an hour or
two,' Albert said. 'You know what a crowd it is when
all t'pits are signin'.'

'Well, you'd better get 'em, whatever time it is.'

The three sons walked to Pirley together; the father had gone half an hour before. Mrs. King came in just before they left; she glanced at them with heavy motherliness as they stood faintly forlorn and seeming to be waiting for initiative from one another.

'We might not be back very early,' Albert said as Arthur made a move towards the door. 'We're goin' for some black. Did me dad tell you?'

'Alright, duck. You'll 'ave a good meal waitin' for you, whatever time you come back. You mun eat, whatever you do.'

'I shall be back at twelve, Mrs. King,' Arthur said. 'Have me something ready, then, will you?'

'Right. Yes.'

They walked through Peathill facing a dry, cold wind; not until the hedge bordering the pathway through the Pirley pit fields was sheltering them did any one speak.

'I suppose we s'll bury 'er on Tuesday,' Albert said. 'Wonder whether dad'll let us go to work on Monday, Sid?'

'I dunno.' Sidney hurried to slide the talk from him. 'What do you think, Arthur?'

'Nay. Doesn't concern me.' He was silent for a moment, then a look of ugly determination set his face. 'I shan't be here either Monday or Tuesday.' Both youths stopped and he continued walking. They caught him again at once.

'Eh?'

'I'm clearin' out this afternoon.'

'Eh?' Both let the easy syllable fall out without knowing they had spoken; their whole beings were just suspended; themselves the complete expression of the murmured 'Eh?'; waiting and asking for repetition and confirmation.

'I say I'm clearin' out.'

'Clearin' out?' Sidney was still suspended. 'Clearin' out?'

'Don't talk so crazy,' Albert cried, with strength. 'What would folks say?'

'Folks? Who are "folks"?'

'You can't, Arth.' Sidney was alive again and bursting into thin, nervous speech. 'You couldn't. Mum——'

'I've got no mum, nor you, so that's enough.' Arthur was quick to cut him from sentiment.

'What you goin' to do, then?' Albert was calm again, though a faint disgust was in his voice.

'That wouldn't interest you.' The answer came cynically, then Arthur left him for Sidney. 'Say, Sid. There'll be six quid come for me in a week or two. Put it in the bank with yours an' I'll have it when I come back, if ever I do.' The two brothers walking beside him were quite passive now; they had been knocked back into a state of mind which might be termed 'wooden'; they strained to create thoughts and ideas on the situation; they rested, waiting for thoughts to strike haphazardly, but their heads remained without life; listening to Arthur's stream of talk was the only thing they were capable of. 'Will you?' he jerked out as the youth moved beside him and did not seem to have taken in the request.

'Eh? Oh, save the money for you? Oh yes.'

'And there's my insurance. If you care to pay the rest of that between you, you can have it.'

'I'll pay it,' Sidney muttered, more to take the item

from Arthur's mind than anything else. 'It'll do instead
of me takin' one out. We'll divide it when you come
back.'

The conversation ceased and each seemed relieved
as the fringe of the town neared. Sidney and Albert
turned along Bayton Street, the way to the Exchange;
Arthur kept straight on.

'What time shall you be home?' he asked the two.

'Between half-past twelve an' one, I think,' Albert
said.

'I might be gone by then. Still, I shall come this
road. Anyway, I'll see you before I go.'

He moved away strongly; Sidney was melting,
drooping. They continued along Bayton Street after
watching him a moment.

'I want to withdraw from the Society,' Arthur told
the Co-op. clerk who looked at him through the
pigeon-hole, then picked up the pass-book he laid
down.

'Oh yes. Er. Could you state the reason for your
withdrawal? We like to know why members leave.'
Arthur did not reply for a moment; he was wondering
how to frame the reason. But the young man put the
words into his mouth. 'Are you leaving the district?
Or——'

'Yes. I am leaving the district. That is the reason.'

The clerk went away satisfied; Arthur breathed
easily again and stood calm after his quick agreement
with the man's suggestion. In five minutes he was on
the street again with the thirty shillings in his pocket
and no Co-op. pass-book. He went to the Boot and
Shoe Department and bought a strong pair of boots;
they cost him eighteen and sixpence, and he looked at

the change from the pound-note with a cynical eye.
Eighteen pence. That was what he was worth now;
the other ten shillings was for the rest of his week's
board and must go to his step-father. Eighteen pence.
A pint of beer and twenty Players. Yes, he'd have a
pint of beer. He went into the Cock Hotel opposite
the Empire and stood against the bar; there were ten
or a dozen men in the long, narrow room, most of
them miners who had been to sign. None of them
knew Arthur, and he came out in twenty minutes
without having spoken a word except to the slow
woman behind the bar when he asked for his jar to
be filled again and for her to bring him twenty cigarettes. In the bright, cold street again he shivered and
turned to leave the town; a woman who lived just
below him on the Wingrove main street saw him come
from the hotel, and she seemed to be staggered. He
saw her, too, but turned from her gaze calmly and
walked towards the fields.

Mrs. King ladled some soup for him as soon as he
got in at ten minutes past twelve, then gave him some
turnip and potato mashed together, and some meat.

'I'm clearing out, Mrs. King, as soon as I've had
my dinner,' he said suddenly while she waited for him
to have done with the plate of tart and custard she
had asked him to help himself from.

'Oh yes. You won't be in for tea, you mean.'

'I'm not coming back at all.'

'Eh?' He did not repeat anything; he knew she
had heard. 'Before—why, what about your—your
mother?'

'I can't help her if I stay. I don't want to see her
hawked about and put in the ground; I can see nothing

solemn in that. We'd finished with one another the moment she stopped breathing. I'm going. There's nothing for me to stay for, now.' The woman was staring at him with frightened eyes.

'You're not badly, Arthur, are you? In your 'ead. Does it 'urt you?' She was crying almost.

'I know what I'm saying, Mrs. King, if that's what you're wanting to know.' He left the table and she gathered the plate he had used, staring at him while she reached it. 'I s'll be going in a few minutes, now. Oh! Give him this when he comes.' He put a ten-shilling note on the table. 'It's the rest of my board for this week.' She took it, more to humour him, it seemed.

'I must go an' see to our Frank's dinner,' she said, after glancing at the clock. "E 'as to go out sellin' this afternoon a bit.'

'Right. I shan't lock the door if I go before you come in again.'

'No,' she said, and went.

Arthur sat down again and began to think. The woman thought him crazy; she had been glad to get away. Bah! He got to his feet impatiently, sat down again, and changed into the boots he had bought, then put on his overcoat and scarf. He was conscious as he moved about that he was trying to make his interest in his actions smother that which was driving him upstairs. He knew he'd have to go upstairs; yet he wanted everything to be done by then, so he could go straight out of the house and be gone from the pull he knew would remain with him. It was all right for him to tell folks that he had done with her. Oh! What the hell was he mooning about for? There was nothing else. He went upstairs suddenly. Hm. They had folded her hands across her breast and tried to put her mouth easy; the grey-brown hair was smoothed since yesterday. He felt wild with anger suddenly, as if he could do murder, as if murder would relieve him, he felt. Then the impulse came to go down into the garden and fetch some snowdrops, the late snowdrops under the hedge at the bottom of the garden. Still, they'd say, 'He left some snowdrops in her hand before he went. Shows he must have thought something of her.' The old women's lips would tremble at the telling, Mrs. King would revel in the recounting. Bedamned to them. He ought to be standing before her in his undergrad. gown, now, and her alive and telling him laughingly that he was swanking. She ought to be dandling his and Nancy's child. Oh! He jerked himself into emptiness of mind and looked into her face steadfastly for a few moments, then turned and went from her presence.

In two minutes he was out of the house and the door pulled to behind him. He walked on the end, through the gate, and turned up towards Peathill. A few steps and he was level by the window where she lay. He stopped, looked up. Something mighty was pulling him back up the stairs; his whole being, with his throat as centre, was one rich, melting, working system; for one brief space his brain and thought-line were drowned deep in a sea of selfless yearning, of love and sympathy and a great sorrow that things had not been otherwise. He moved suddenly, marked the blinds drawn next door and across the road, heard the loud wireless in King's pounding rhythmically. No good if he went back and up the stairs, she'd be just the same—dead in the centre of the world. No, they were nothing to each other, now; he was free, he had gone down with her to death and he himself was stripped almost of life, but he could begin again and build himself another way. This road to Peathill lay before him and it was leading to life again, away from the strangling ties and bonds that had bound him for so long. He dragged another thought quickly into his mind each time a kind of joy at being free rose from his subconsciousness and thrust its truth on his brain; he pulled the vision of her lying in ugly stillness to his mind. He made it sober him, though all the time he knew he was being false.

He entered the narrow pit field-path; footprints and the thin tracks of bicycles were frozen fast into the bound earth. Men and youths were coming home from signing; one was cursing to another that he had been kept so late and would miss the kick-off at Derby unless he had some luck with buses. Some spoke to Arthur, others nodded, none passed without some sort of salute; it was the way of villagers and miners; some came from Condor and did not know him, but all the same they could not pass another so close as the narrow path brought them without acknowledging the existence. Half-way down the first field a youth riding on one pedal of his cycle slurred to his side. Riding was not allowed on the footpath and this method of half-riding was generally used to cover short distances when no policeman was about. Arthur turned to him; it was Frank King from across the road, the son of the woman who was 'doing for his mother'.

'Hello, Frank.'

'Ner, Arthur. 'Ear tha'rt runnin' awee.' Arthur

was not surprised at this from him; he was a wide-eyed, plain-minded youth.

'Yes,' Arthur said. 'Have a fag.' The youth took a cigarette from the proffered packet. 'Doing a bit this afternoon, eh?' He looked at the small attaché-case strapped behind the bicycle. Frank sold studs and pins and small things like that, riding to the isolated hamlets and villages outside the industrial region where one could take a story of being unemployed and use it with some success in helping to sell articles at extortionate prices. He worked so for three days a week and signed on the other three; he presumably was selling the stuff for some one who stamped his insurance cards and thus kept him in benefit, making certain of never having to submit himself to a Means Test.

'I've one or two calls in Pirley, then I'm goin' into t'Lea Valley—tha knows, Leawood, Nessfield, Pentland 'Oller an' Broadoaks. Some money to be made in these outlyin' parts, Arthur. Tha should 'ave tried it instead o' runnin' awee.'

'Broadoaks!' Arthur had started at the name and could not help repeating it. 'Do you call at all the houses in Broadoaks?'

'There's none above a dozen. I think I do. Why?'

'That house, that first house on the left going up. The new one.'

'Yes, I do. I do, by gum! She's a decent . . . Why!' Sudden remembrance came to him. 'Why, she knows you, doesn't she? She asked me one day w'ere I come from, and w'en I towd 'er she asked me about your family. Yes, she did. Is she some relation?'

'No. She knows us, though.' Arthur hesitated a

second, then continued resolutely: 'Tell her about my mother, Frank. And that I'm going away.'

'O.K.' He put a foot on the pedal. 'There's your Sid and Albert comin'. An' thy dad. I'll ger off.' He rode away on one side of his bike, leaning over to keep balance. Arthur forgot him at once; the three approaching were on top of him almost and his mind became a confusion of thought-snappings, faint fear kept strength from any intention. He wouldn't be long with them, was the only certain idea he had. His step-father might not stop at all; he could not know that he was going away, unless, of course, the lads had told him. But there was a definite intent on the man's face as he came near, a step ahead of his sons. His eyes were holding Arthur's eyes, his mouth was firm.

'W'eer the 'ell does tha reckon tha'rt gooin'?'

'How do you mean "goin'"?'

'Tha knows w'at I mean. Runnin' away.' He looked up and down the field-path, it was dotted with people coming towards them. His words rushed out, he wanted to settle the matter before any one was within hearing. 'Tha can come on back wi' us. An' if tha wants to leave 'ome tha can go as soon as thy mother's buried. W'at will folks think an' say?' Arthur was looking away from him, over the fields towards Greenwich. 'W'y, tha'rt crazy. Fat lot tha cared about thy mother.' He blinked quickly as Arthur brought his eyes to meet his, and backed morally. If he had said 'cares' instead of 'cared' Arthur would have let him ramble on.

'That'll be about enough. I want to talk to these two.' The man knew in a flash from the tone that the relation between him and his stepson was now a plain one; he was wise enough to see that they touched at no point nor was any third system common to them. Mr. Shirley walked away muttering; the poise of the young man he turned from might have suggested that he did not mind a fight in public. He was not risking that. Arthur held out his hand to Albert as soon as the man had gone. 'I'm going, then. I s'll write and let you know how I am. Good-bye, Albert.' He took Sidney's hand. 'Now, Sid, buck up.' Sidney was weeping without sound; his mouth was quite out of control, twitching and turning down alternately. Arthur suddenly saw his mother through the youth, and the strength, holding him easy and almost cheerful, flowed from him. His own mouth trembled. 'Look sharp and get married and I'll come and live with you.' He smiled into the boyish face and gripped the slender hand. ''Bye, Sid.' He turned away quickly and left them standing. He walked on, to the wooden bridge over the railway, steeling himself against the desire to turn and see them, but here he did stop and look back. They were at the stile on the Peathill street, waiting for him to be lost beyond the bridge, and their hands shot up at once when he faced about to them. He waved and they strained to reach higher, it seemed, then he broke from them and hurried round the bend.

Pirley streets were quiet; a few men hurried along towards the market-place to join the small crowd of football fans who waited for the Derby bus. On the market square itself the stall-holders gossiped among themselves and ate food they had brought. A woman walked along the alley set with greengrocery and, at

the far end, fish. Arthur heard the voices stream to her
as she passed each stall. 'Now, lady . . . Nice oranges,
lady. Herrings, kippers, bloaters, cod. Pick where
you like . . .' They settled to their food and gossip as
she passed to another alley. Voices curved there for
her benefit. At the top the pot man was unloading his
wares, the cross-eyed man who spat from the corner
of a closed mouth. He had joked with Nancy and him
one Saturday. . . . He was dreaming until he had passed
the post office, until the cold wind cut into him as he
turned the corner on to Nessfield Hill. Nessfield. It
was no good thinking anything about this place, he
might as well go through with a strong mind. He was
in the centre of the road at the bottom of the hill
when a bicyle bell drove him to the side. A voice
hailed him rushing past. Frank King.

''Owdy, Arthur.' Arthur did not answer the shout;
the other would not have heard.

In the wide empty world beyond Pentland Hollow
the greening trees by the river-side hummed wind-
driven, and the cold-splashing water glinted at times
as a stone threw a flash into the light. In Newlands
children waited for a Pirley bus; they were talking
eagerly of the matinee ahead of them. Arthur glanced
up the hill leading to Steep and Fritchburn, then
across the road at the discoloured rag of paper hanging
from the small square of wood where a week or two
ago his name had stretched clean and neat. A sound
came down his nose and he walked on through Leawood, and the Derwent was beside him now, bigger
after taking in the Lea waters. A tramp had come
from the Matlock road into the village and was now
two hundred yards ahead as Arthur gained the open

road. The young man trembled a little as he looked at the man, who appeared to have three overcoats about him; his hands were thrust into his pockets and he was bent to the head wind. A small bundle was fastened somehow to his back. Arthur overtook him and expected to see a pained face turn to him when he saluted the tramp, for the man seemed in agony with every step he took, hobbling along on the outside edges of his boots.

'Cold, isn't it?' Arthur greeted as he came alongside.

'Eh? Cowd. No.' The tone was bright, the face easy and strong after he had looked Arthur up and down and found that he had nothing to fear or hope for. 'Cowd. Wait till it snows, which'll be in an hour or two. Then it'll be cowd. I'm 'opin' to be out o' it.'

'Where are you makin' for?'

'Derby. Do it by dark. You on t'road?'

'Yes. Can I come with you. This is my first day.'

'Knowed that. Could see that. Got a smoke?'

They were half-way along the mile and a half curve to Broadoaks when a car pulled up near them and Nancy looked out. The tramp continued as if he had seen nothing. Arthur stopped.

'I was sure you'd dash out to find me, Nancy.' He laughed shortly. 'Silly. I wanted you to know about me—and things, but——'

'Where are you going?' She glanced fearfully at the hobbling figure along the road as she stood beside him on the road.

'With him. To-night I shall sleep in Derby workhouse.' He saw her shudder. 'As good as anywhere else, isn't it?'

'Can't you stay about here somewhere. Don't do that. Don't go to those places. I'll lend you some money each week until you're settled. I'll try to get you a job.'

'I knew you'd say all that, Nancy. I knew you'd say it and I've thought of an answer.' She looked at his mouth and saw cynical strength. 'You're wanting to save me from suffering—you think walking from workhouse to workhouse and hobnobbing with tramps is suffering—you want to save me from that because you love me. Why don't you come with me and share it all if you love me. But I wouldn't ask you to do that. I wouldn't have you. No fear.'

'And I've got to sit in a theatre to-night while you . . .' She was speaking half to herself, conscious of a mighty comparison.

'Don't worry about me, Nancy.' He was kinder now. 'I shan't let it kill me. You go to your theatre. Derby, is it?' He could have bitten out his tongue at the slip. She paled and her hand pulled at the button on her coat until it snapped off. But she answered quietly, taking his remark as if it had no past context.

'Nottingham.'

'I'm sorry, Nancy.' He paused. 'The youth told you about mum.' She nodded, her mouth trembling. 'I'll get off.' He took her hand. 'You can take it from me that you'll be the only living woman I shall think about.' He pressed her hand and released it. 'But you'd never get beyond my brain again, Nancy. No woman'll ever get past my brain again.'

He looked into her eyes for a moment. All she had

intended flowed from her, and instead of putting her arms about him, holding him for the last time, kissing him, she bowed her head and let him turn away.

'Good-bye,' he said, but she did not answer, and he went. She watched him for a while, watched the distance between him and the hobbling man grow less. But before Arthur caught him she drove away in her car, drove towards Leawood, away from him, away from home.

'Thowt you'd a brought yer pal an' t'car an' lifted us into Derby.' The tramp's voice was one-toned; Arthur could not decide how the remark was intended.

'Oh, she was going the other way,' he gave back, safely.

They walked on, into Belford. Arthur's companion nudged him as they passed the gates of the workhouse.

'Nivver stop 'ere. Try to miss this bloody place. Mester's a slogger—a slave-driver. I'd sooner crawl to Derby any time than stop 'ere. Nivver stop 'ere.'

Arthur laughed. He had met the workhouse master in connection with social service work and had found him most human. Obviously the fault was in the tramp.

They walked on towards Derby, through Milford, Duffield, Allestree, Darley. These places were just 'the road' to the tramp; to Arthur they were battle-fields where he had fought with pals for the sake of Wingrove's position in the football and cricket leagues, where girls had tried to 'click' with him after the matches, where he had learned how beer tasted. The lamps by the roadside grew in brilliance and power until they became kingdoms of light on their own. The wind's voice was rising as if sounding the alarm for the world to hurry to shelter from the millions of white flakes riding behind. Already in Nottingham the air was busy with them; people passing from cars into the theatre bent heads sideways to the cold driving. Already in Wingrove the ledges of bedroom windows were white and smooth. Now, as Arthur and his hobbling companion turned in at the gateway of the Derby Institution, the white snow-lines reached forward and marked them.